# THE AUTHOR

Charles Cox was born in Dodge County, Georgia and is a retired United Methodist Minister with more than fifty years of ministry in the pastorate and in industry. His roots are as deep in South Georgia as those of the pine trees in the family business that enabled him to earn two degrees from Emory University. He is married to Carol, his high school sweetheart, whom he met in Cochran, Georgia. They have two children and four granddaughters.

# APPRECIATION

Chi Chi and Janis,
Proofreaders who care.


# INSPIRATION

Mary,
Always the teacher.

# The Ravenwood Trade

A Novel of
Faith Lost and Faith Found

## Charles E. Cox

# *The*

# *Ravenwood*

# *Trade*

### A Novel of
### Faith Lost and Faith Found

## Charles E. Cox

### First Edition

### Copyright © 2013
### All Rights Reserved

Cover: TITLE: Battle of Chattanooga--Gen. Thomas' charge near
Orchard Knob, Nov. 24' 1863--parts A.O.T. Potomac, Tenne. & Cumbd. engaged
{{PD-USGov-DHS-CGAUX}} – for public domain images
from the US Coast Guard Auxiliary.

PUBLISHED BY
BRENTWOOD PUBLISHERS GROUP
4000 BEALLWOOD AVENUE
COLUMBUS, GEORGIA 31904

# DEDICATION

*To my wife, Carol.*
*Our daughter, Cindy,*
*her husband, Spencer,*
*their children, Sara and Lizzie.*
*Our son, Charlie, his wife, Claire,*
*their children, Helen and Taylor.*
*Always there with love.*

# 1

Confederate Chaplain Patrick Ravenwood was in hell, and hell was Clonnerville Prison, one of several temporary prisoner-of-war camps set up by Union forces to house Confederate soldiers captured during the battle of Atlanta. The camp consisted of three former cotton warehouses, which now reeked of sweat, filth, human waste, and hopelessness. An eight-foot high fence encircled the compound with crude guard towers, strategically located, giving the guards a clear view of the grounds around the buildings. Ten feet in from the fence and forty feet out from the warehouses was the deadline, defined by a line of short posts spaced ten feet apart. To approach the deadline was an invitation to be shot by guards, who were not particular in their interpretation of its location.

Each warehouse contained approximately two hundred fifty prisoners, more than twice the estimated capacity of each building. The worst conditions existed in Warehouse B, where fifty wounded Confederate prisoners were housed in addition to approximately two hundred able captives. The wounded were crowded into the northeast corner of the building, which gave them some protection from the heat of the afternoon sun. No other concessions were made for them, no matter how critical their wounds.

Chaplain Ravenwood and privates Jud Cofer and Deke Bracewell were captured in the battle of Peachtree Creek on July 20, 1864, when their company was pinched off from the rest of their regiment in a flanking maneuver by Union forces. General John B. Hood's Confederate Army of Tennessee had attacked the Union Army of the Cumberland, which was under the command of General George H. Thomas. Despite some early advances by Confederate forces, the Union army held its ground and eventually forced Hood to withdraw. The battle, one of several in Sherman's Atlanta campaign, was a bloody defeat for the Confederates. Hood's Rebel forces suffered an estimated 4,800 casualties. The Union Army of the Cumberland had approximately 1,700 casualties.

The chaplain and the two privates survived the battle unscathed, but all the other men in their company were either wounded or killed. Cofer and Bracewell were captured when they surrendered after running out of ammunition. Ravenwood was captured as he sat in the mud behind them holding a dying Rebel soldier in his arms.

After their capture, they and one hundred other prisoners were transported in railroad cattle cars to Clonnerville, Georgia, where the prison was located. Those who were able were marched from the railroad to the prison compound. Captives who were unable to walk were transported in two-horse wagons. Bringing up the rear was a wagon that contained the bodies of six prisoners who died en route. Only a few of the townspeople paused and watched as the prisoners slowly made their way down the main street of Clonnerville. One of those who watched was a bedraggled Confederate veteran, on crutches because of a missing leg. As the prisoners passed in front of him, he came to attention and saluted his captured comrades. He never moved until he had honored every one of them, even the dead in the last wagon.

After a very perfunctory registration, the prisoners were given sleeping pallets and assigned to their respective warehouses. Ravenwood, Cofer, and Bracewell had the misfortune to be assigned to warehouse B. It was there that they first met Union Sergeant Buck Hagan. If Clonnerville Prison was hell, then Sergeant Buck Hagan was the devil himself and proud of it.

Standing with feet apart and hands on his hips, Hagan glowered at them for a full minute before he spoke. "Awright, you Rebs, listen to me, and you listen good. You done heard all them camp rules. Well, you 'bout as well forget ever one of 'em, because you gonna hear my rules, and them's the only ones that count. You ain't just Union prisoners. You're my prisoners, and you're in my building. Now, I got only two rules, so pay attention. I ain't gonna say 'em twice."

He stalked back and forth in front of his bedraggled charges, looking at each prisoner with contempt. Finally he spoke again. "My first rule is, you will do what I say. Anybody who even thinks he can do different will wish he was dead. The second rule is, any prisoner who attempts to escape or even so much as steps on the deadline will be shot. Nobody has ever escaped from Warehouse B and lived to tell about it."

When Hagan finished, the guards escorted the three new prisoners through the compound gate and into their assigned building. Once inside they were left standing with no further instructions. As their eyes grew accustomed to the darkness, they were astonished at the squalid condition of the prisoners, especially that of the wounded. Never had they seen such deplorable conditions. It was as though they had been set adrift in a sea of misery.

"My God!" said Pat.

Neither Jud nor Deke said anything. They were both overwhelmed by the suffering mass of humanity that lay before them.

# 2

Although chaplains were considered noncombatants, Cofer and Bracewell had come to know Pat as a man who would pull his load in a combat situation without ever firing a shot. They first met him when volunteers were recruited from the little town of Pine Creek and surrounding communities for the 27th Georgia Infantry Regiment, of the Confederate Army of Tennessee. Cofer and Bracewell were inducted as infantrymen and assigned to Company C. Pat was inducted as a chaplain and assigned to the same company.

The three of them had served together from the day of their enlistment and had gone through several major campaigns. They had endured the horror of battle, the discomfort of inclement weather, and long marches. Now they faced their greatest challenge of the war, that of surviving in Clonnerville Prison.

Sensing that survival was their primary concern, Pat insisted that they care for the wounded even though they had no supplies, no bandages, and no medication. This was a daunting task, fraught with hopelessness, but Pat realized that if they sat idly by and did nothing, they too would become casualties of war, so the three of them began walking among the wounded, searching for some way to aid those who could not care for themselves. His plan was simple. Survive by serving.

Pat decided to help the wounded by writing letters to their families for them. He believed those letters would help keep their spirits up and give the prisoners a sense of being in touch. It would also be meaningful to their families. He requested pencils and paper from Sergeant Hagan, but it was several days before Hagan grudgingly complied with his request.

Early one morning, after receiving his meager supply of grungy paper and stubby pencils, Pat was seated on the clay floor beside one of the prisoners writing a letter to the young man's family. When he finished, he returned to his own pallet and sat for a while longer watching the daggers of sunlight carve their way through cracks in the boarded windows. He relaxed a little and allowed his mind to wander back to his early years on the family farm.

He could almost hear his father's voice, "Morning comes mighty early on a farm."

"It comes early at Clonnerville Prison too," he thought, "and the days are mighty long, just like the nights."

He was stirred from his reverie when Jud Cofer handed him a cup of the slop Sergeant Hagan called breakfast. "Morning, Chaplain, just thought I'd let you know that 'No-Name' died last night. Leastwise, he was dead when I checked on him this morning. There's talk that Hagan kicked him something fierce when he was brought in because he wouldn't stop calling for his ma. Some of the other prisoners said the boy was out of his mind. He didn't even know what he was doing."

Pat was careful not to let his slight irritation show. "Jud, just because we never knew his name is no reason to treat him with little regard. He was somebody's son, and it's likely they will never know what happened to him. As for Hagan, you mark my words, he'll get what's coming to him some day."

"I apologize, Chaplain. It won't happen again. I'll see what I can do about gittin' him buried."

"Thank you." Pat said as Jud turned away. Then he added, "Jud, you're a good man."

Jud and Deke approached the deadline on the west side of

11

the warehouse and called to Hagan who was playing cards with guards Rat Perkins and Jake Lawton near the prison fence. Irritated at being disturbed, Hagan groused. "What the hell do you stinking Rebs want?"

"One of our soldiers died last night. We need to bury him." Jud replied.

Exasperated, Hagan, who was losing money in the card game, flung his cards down. "Can't you Rebs get it through your thick skulls that you ain't soldiers no more? You're prisoners, my prisoners. As far as I'm concerned, if a Reb dies, it's good riddance."

"Perkins," he growled, "this game is over. You and Lawton go git a shovel for these two so they can bury that soldier, as they called him. Stay with them and watch them close. If one of them so much as even looks like he wants to run, shoot both of them."

Hagan turned back to Jud, "You've got one hour to dig a hole and plant'im."

The service was conducted in the prison cemetery, located on a hillside outside the prison compound. Pat had to conduct the service from memory because his Book of Services and his Bible were lost when he was captured. When the brief service was over, Jud took his shovel and pounded a rough board into the soft ground at the head of the grave. On the board he had scratched, "KNOWN ONLY TO GOD."

As Pat, Jud, and Deke were herded back toward the prison compound, they encountered Colonel Douglas Randolph, the prison commandant. He was accompanied by two guards and Lieutenant Pringle, his aide, who was carrying a small package under his arm. The colonel, a former U. S. Marshal, was called into military service as a captain in the early days of the war.

He proved to be an excellent field officer in combat situations. In no time, he given command of a regiment with the rank of colonel. However, the loss of an arm, and a severe leg wound as a result of Rebel artillery left him demoralized and physically unable to command a combat unit. He had been a good officer at one time, but due to his wounds, he had been shunted aside and relegated to the thankless task of commanding a prisoner-of-war camp where there was little food for the prisoners and where many of the guards were cast-offs from regular line units.

Lieutenant Pringle was no cast-off. He had come from a good family and was a clean-cut young man. Although he was an officer, he was lacking in combat experience. As much as the Union army needed men in combat, it was unlikely that Pringle would ever be assigned to a combat unit. Thanks to the influence of an uncle, who was a Union senator, Pringle had become Colonel Randolph's aide with neither the Colonel nor the Lieutenant having any say-so in the matter.

"Good morning, Chaplain. I see you've had another funeral," said the Colonel.

Yes, sir, that's the fourth one this week from our building. We didn't even know his name, though I understand he was from somewhere down toward Savannah."

"War is hell, isn't it, Chaplain?"

"So I've heard, Colonel," replied Pat.

"By the way, Chaplain," said the Colonel, "I've heard about your writing letters to the families of the wounded, so I managed to scrape up some writing paper for you from my own supplies. I also got a Bible for you from the Methodist Church over in Clonnerville."

Showing more than a little exasperation, the Colonel turned to his aide, "Pringle, what are you waiting for? Give the man the paper and his Bible."

"Yes, sir," the flustered Pringle replied as he handed the paper and Bible to Chaplain Ravenwood.

"Thank you very much, Colonel. I will put both to good

use."

"You're quite welcome, Chaplain. Writing the families of these men who can't write is a good thing, and I commend you for it. I trust your own mail has been coming through in our weekly mail deliveries."

He was about to speak again when Pat interrupted him, "The prisoners in our building get very little mail, Sir. Some weeks, they get nothing. I suppose it's what you might expect under the circumstances of this war we're in. As for my own mail, I haven't heard from my wife for awhile. Actually, it has been about two months since her last letter."

"I suppose you have been writing her."

"Yes, sir, I write to her at least once every week."

"Any children?"

"Yes, sir, I have a son."

"You are very fortunate, Chaplain. I had a son. He was killed in the Battle of Chancellorsville. Our Union forces suffered over 17,000 casualties. He was one of them. Lee's army whipped us, but they had 13,000 casualties themselves. Just think, one battle resulted in more than 30,000 casualties. My son was dead three weeks before I even knew about it. Of course, I was having my own problem then, thanks to one of your Rebel artillery shells, yet I lived. Why couldn't it have been me that died instead of him?"

The Colonel continued, "I hope I don't offend you, Chaplain, but where is your God in all this? If he's around, then I'm afraid I've lost sight of him."

"I'm sorry for your loss, Colonel, but as you have already said, 'War is hell,' and I am afraid many more sons will die before this hell is over."

Pat immediately regretted his insensitive response to the colonel's grief.

For a moment, the colonel said nothing. Then with sudden harshness in his voice,

"Pringle, make a note to check on the mail delivery for

14

the prisoners in Warehouse B!"

"Yes, sir, I'll make a note, Sir."

"Do it now, Pringle!"

"Yes, sir, I'm making a note right now, Sir."

Pat spoke again, "Colonel, there's one other thing that I'd like to mention."

"What is it, Chaplain?"

"It's the food, Sir."

"What about the food? What are you getting at?"

Pat's temper flared. "We are just barely surviving, Colonel. That's what I am getting at."

"What do you expect us to do, Chaplain? We do the best we can. We live on what the supply depot sends us."

"With all due respect, Colonel, what the prisoners are getting is no more than hog swill. That slop that Hagan and those two men of his dish out to us hardly ever contains any solid food. There are days when it won't have a single bean or kernel of corn in it. It's hardly more than greasy water."

Pat's voice hardened a bit. "And while I'm speaking, Sir, I can't remember the last time we were given any clean bandages for the wounded. That drunken doctor of yours never sets foot in Warehouse B."

"Now, if the Colonel will excuse me, I have dying men inside that hell-hole of a building that need some attention." Pat turned abruptly, walked toward the entrance to the compound, and never looked back.

As the Colonel looked thoughtfully at the departing chaplain, his face hardened. Just for an instant, anger flashed in his eyes, like steel striking flint. There was just a hint of the battlefield commander that he used to be. Without another word, he turned and walked away at a rather determined gait for a man with a bad leg and only one arm. Lieutenant Pringle followed on the Colonel's left, two paces behind him.

As Pat headed toward the prison compound gate, Jud and Deke were lagging behind.

15

Jud spoke softly to Deke. "Wonder what got into the chaplain?"

"Looks like he's got a burr under his saddle,"

"I dunno about the Chaplain's saddle, Deke, but he sure as hell put one under the Colonel's saddle, and it ain't no little one either. I betcha that burr's got Hagan's name on it too."

"Why do you say that?"

Jud replied, "I don't think the way Hagan handles things sets too well with the Colonel. I've heard tell he'd like to get shed of him, but no outfit's willing to take him."

"I'll tell you what I think," responded Deke. "I think that both the Colonel and the Chaplain are about fed up with Hagan."

"Well, it may be as you say, but lemme tell you something else. I don't know what it is with the Chaplain, but it seems like he's gittin' kinda bitter all of a sudden. Could be this place is gittin' to 'im. I've been watching him lately. It appears to me that the fire for his preacher work is burning on the low side. It might be 'cause he ain't heard from his wife in a while. It's been nigh on to two months, I believe."

"Don't know nothing 'bout his preaching fire, but some kinda fire is burning in his gut, and it's burning mighty fierce, too," commented Deke.

# 3

When Pat reached the compound gate, he submitted to the obligatory search by the guards stationed there. Their search completed, the guards opened the gate and motioned for him to enter, then they turned their attention to Jud and Deke. Before going inside the warehouse, Pat took several deep breaths and reminded himself not to breathe through his mouth once he got on the inside. The stench was terrible, and you could almost taste the filth. The living conditions were indescribable, especially for the wounded. Pat wanted to be of some assistance to them, yet he felt completely helpless. Never had he felt so inadequate. He was also troubled by all-too-frequent pangs of doubt about his own faith, yet he wasn't going to ignore his obligation to those wounded men in Warehouse B and to their families.

Once inside, Pat made his way to his pallet, which was located near the corner of the building where the wounded were housed. After gathering up a few pages of writing paper, two pencils, and a small board that he used as a desk, he began making his rounds. He stopped beside young Jimmy Pitts from Blue Springs, Georgia. His face, upper body, and arms were shrouded in dirty bandages that had not been changed in days. Only his eyes showed that he was alive. His mouth and jaw had been shattered, which meant that he had to be spoon-fed. Had not Bracewell assumed that responsibility, Pitts likely would have starved to death. Pat wondered if feeding him was only delaying the inevitable.

"Hello, Pitts," Pat said, "remember what I've told you? Talk to me with your eyes. One blink means yes. Two blinks mean no. Do you understand?"

Blink.

"Do you want me to write a letter to your family?"

Blink.

"Do you want me to write them about your wounds?"

Blink... Blink.

"Tell you what, Pitts, why don't I write what I think is in your heart. When I've finished, I'll read it to you, and we'll take out what you don't want your ma and pa to read. Is that fair enough?"

Blink.

Pat had some reservations concerning the letter he was about to write. What could he possibly say to this young man's parents? Pitts was nineteen years old and would never make it out of this filthy hell-hole. Pat knew writing a letter to Pitt's parents was a waste of time, but something compelled him to do it anyway. He had to let them know that someone who cared was at their son's side, even though it was obvious that Pitts would not last much longer. When he died, no family members would weep at his grave. In fact, they probably would never know the location of his grave.

As Pat began to write, Pitts watched him with teary eyes, longing to speak, longing to add to the letter's contents, but all he could do was blink yes or no or try to blink away the tears from his eyes. Sitting on the dirt floor beside him, Pat silently composed the letter to Pitts' parents. As he wrote, he sensed the emotional trauma in the eyes of young Jimmy Pitts, eyes that reflected a question that was on Pat's mind, "What kind of life would he have even if he managed to survive?"

When Pat finished writing the letter to Pitts' parents, he sat for a moment with his hand on the bandaged shoulder of the young soldier. Finally he forced himself to read the letter aloud to Pitts. It was a difficult thing to do.

*Dear Mr. and Mrs. Pitts,*

*I take pencil and paper in hand to write you at the request of your son, Pvt. James Pitts, of the 27th Georgia Infantry Regiment of the Confederate Army of Tennessee. He was wounded and taken prisoner by Union Forces in The Battle of Peachtree Creek near Atlanta. He is now receiving treatment in the medical section of Clonnerville Prison north of Atlanta.*

*I am at his bedside now, and he has requested that I tell you of his love for you and that he misses you very much. He says that he longs to be back home.*

*From my personal association with your son, I can tell you that he is a very brave young man, and you have every right to be proud of him. He is a fine soldier.*

*Your faithful servant,*
*Patrick Ravenwood*
*Chaplain, C. S. A.*

When the letter was read to Pitts, the young soldier blinked his approval. Pat then knelt on the packed earthen floor beside Pitts' stained pallet and prayed. When he had finished, he gathered up his writing material, stood up, and moved on to write another letter, trying not to look Pitts in the eye.

As he slowly walked away, he prayed again. This time, he prayed for himself. "O God, forgive me for the false hope that I have given this young man's parents."

As he continued to make his way among the prisoners under his care, the colonel's question also came to mind again, "Where is God in all of this?"

He had to admit to himself that he didn't have a good answer. When he sought to dredge up comforting words from the Scriptures, he found nothing that was meaningful. The only words that ever came to mind were those that Jesus spoke while hanging on the cross, "My God, my God, why hast thou forsaken me?"

He was brought back to reality by a request from a soldier on pallet to his left, "Preacher, would you pray for me?" It was Billy Johnson, a young man who was a member of the Pine Creek Methodist Church. Pat knew him and his parents well.

When Pat finished his rounds, he made his way back to his own pallet, sat down, and began a letter to Molly Ann and Johnny. He tried not to speculate on why he had not received any mail from her in over two months. While he was trying to compose his letter, a burst of activity outside attracted his attention. He got to his feet and moved over to one of the shuttered windows. As he peered through a crack between two of the shutter boards, he was elated at what he saw. Beyond the fenced in area of the compound was a horse and rider. Mail was being delivered. Maybe there would be letter from Molly Ann. Pat watched as the rider handed a mail bag to Hagan. With the bag in hand, Hagan turned and walked back inside the guard shack and out of Pat's line of sight.

Once inside, Hagan closed the door and dumped the contents of the bag on a table. He pulled up a chair, sat down, and began to meticulously examine each piece of mail, supposedly searching for any forbidden items. Actually, he was looking for anything of value to keep for himself. As he examined each envelope, he pocketed a small gold cross from one and a child's silver bracelet from another. Finally, Hagan came to a letter addressed to Chaplain Patrick Ravenwood. It was from Molly Ann. Enclosed in the letter was her picture.

On the back of the picture she had written, "To my dear husband." It was signed, "Molly Ann, your loving wife."

Hagan thought to himself, "That's a mighty fine lookin' woman, mighty fine!"

The letter from Molly Ann was beautifully written and spoke of her love for Pat and how much she and Johnny missed him. When Hagan finished reading it, he wadded it up and tossed it and its envelope in the shack's small pot-bellied stove. He was careful to keep the picture for himself. After examining the remaining letters, he dumped them back into the mail bag. Clutching the bag under his arm, he set out for the prison compound. Once inside, he walked over to Pat and dumped the bag's contents on the dirt floor at Pat's feet.

"Here's your mail, you damn preacher man. I guess you think all that whining to the Colonel paid off. Well, it didn't. There's nothing there for you. That woman of yores prob'ly don't want to write to you no how. More'n likely, she's done run off with somebody else and took that boy of yores with her. Yes sir, I'll betcha little ole Molly's done found herself somebody else to sleep with."

Jud and Deke, who were standing nearby, quickly stepped in between the two men and pushed Pat away. They dared not touch Hagan.

Hagan glared at Pat and said, "Anytime, Reb. Anytime, just you and me."

He then turned, grabbed the outgoing mail from its basket on the wall, bagged it, and walked out. Once out of the warehouse, he went directly to the guard shack where he burned every letter.

"Stinking Rebs, I'll show them it's me, not the Colonel, who's in charge here."

Back in the warehouse Pat's face was blood-red with anger. "Jud, Deke, how did he know her name? I've never even mentioned it around him, and how did he know about my son?

Have y'all said anything about them to anybody?"

"We ain't said a word to nobody, Chaplain," answered Jud.

Jud paused a moment and added, "I'll tell you what's happened. That critter's been reading yore mail and not passing it on to you. That's the reason you ain't heard nothing from yore wife."

"God forgive me," said Pat, "but I could kill'im."

"Chaplain," said Jud, "I could kill'im too and not lose a minute's sleep thinkin' about forgiveness. The way I figure it, I'd be doing God a favor."

Deke spoke up, "Jud, the line for them that wanna kill Hagan starts behind me. If you wanna kill'im, then you gonna hafta git in line and wait your turn."

Deke started to walk away, but stopped, turned back and said, "Beggin' the Chaplain's pardon, I don't want to speak ill of anybody in front of a man of the cloth, but I'm gonna say it anyway. I know the Good Book says God sent his Son to save us 'cause he loves us. Now I ain't got much Bible learning, but I just don't see how God could love somebody like Buck Hagan."

Pat managed a trace of a smile, "I know what you're saying."

"Don't know whether it's true or not," Jud injected, "but I heard from some of the prisoners in Warehouse A that he used to be a lawman somewhere and nearly beat a prisoner to death. He claimed the prisoner was trying to escape, but when Hagan couldn't explain how a prisoner wearing handcuffs and shackles could escape, the Judge gave him a choice of jail or the army, so he joined the army."

# 4

Following his encounter with Hagan, Pat went to his pallet and sat down. Once his emotions were under control, his thoughts turned from his current situation to Molly Ann. He smiled as he remembered the time that he asked her to go to the Methodist Church picnic with him. He was sixteen years old and she was fifteen.

Pat and his pa, Dan, had hitched up the team and driven the two miles from their farm to Pine Creek, a little rural South Georgia town fifty miles south of Macon. It had a population of about two hundred fifty people. In spite of a relatively small population, Pine Creek had several small businesses that supplied the needs of the families in the surrounding area. Of those businesses, it was McDaniel's General Store that interested the father and son. Dan needed supplies for the farm, but Pat's sole purpose was to see Molly Ann, Sam McDaniel's daughter.

As the two-horse wagon rattled toward town, Pat sat silently on the seat beside his father. Dan gave the appearance of being totally focused on driving the team, but there was a trace of a smile on his face because he knew the reason for Pat's eagerness to accompany him into Pine Creek. Dan's wife, Leona, had shared with him that Pat had asked her how he should go about inviting Molly Ann to the picnic at the Methodist Church.

"Whoa now," said Dan to the team as he gently pulled back on the reins in front of Sam McDaniel's general store. Dan could sense the excitement in Pat as they climbed down from the wagon. At that point Molly Ann stepped out of the store with a broom in her hand.

"Morning, Miss Molly Ann," said Dan as he tipped his hat to her.

"Good morning to you, Mr. Ravenwood," she replied. "I was just about to sweep the front porch. Come on in. Daddy's inside."

Glancing back at Pat, Dan smiled and walked past Molly Ann into the store and shook hands with Sam. They both watched with more than a little amusement as Molly Ann and Pat greeted each other on the front porch of the store.

"Hello, Molly Ann," said Pat as he snatched off his hat.

"Well, I do declare. It's Pat Ravenwood, what a surprise!" she said as she resumed her sweeping.

"Molly Ann, I come to town—"

"I came to town," she interrupted.

"Where you been?"

"Patrick Ravenwood, what in the world do you mean, asking where I've been? You know I live right here in Pine Creek, and I haven't been anywhere."

"I mean," said Pat, "that you just said you had come to town, so I was just wondering where you'd been."

"I wasn't talking about me. I was talking about you. Why would I want to go to the church picnic with someone who talks like he's never been to school in his entire life?"

"But Molly Ann, I ain't even asked you yet."

"Well, you were going to ask me, weren't you?"

"Yeah, Molly Ann, what I've been trying to tell you all along is that I come to town to ask you to go to the picnic with me. Then you said you'd come to town too, but then you just said you hadn't been anywhere. Now, I'm all confused. What I'm trying to find out is, are you going to the picnic with me or not?"

"Well, I thought you'd never ask. Yes, I'd love to go with you. I hope I didn't hurt your feelings, but you need to do something about the way you talk. That's something you can

24

work on, and you're smart enough to do something about it. Now, your ma can help you, and Miss McCurdy at the school can help you. You are too big and too old to be in school, but she will be glad to help you every Saturday when you and your pa come to town for supplies. I know that she'll do it because she's already said she would."

Realizing that she had said something that she hadn't meant to say, Molly Ann clamped her hand over her mouth, turned, and darted back into the store.

The two fathers choked back their laughter.

Once inside the store she paused, looked back at Pat and said, "We can sit together in church Sunday and then go to the picnic." She added, "Please be on time!"

Sam and Dan looked at each other and smiled as she flounced on toward the back of the store. They had been friends for many years, and both had high hopes for Pat and Molly Ann, hopes that they had never discussed openly, but were always there.

Shaking his head, Dan said, "Love."

"Puppy love," chirped Susanna McDaniel who was stocking a shelf across the store.

"Maybe so, Susie," Sam responded, "but it's mighty real to puppies."

# 5

With their supplies loaded, Dan and Pat climbed on the wagon and headed home. Pat had hardly spoken a word since his rather one-sided conversation with Molly Ann.

Finally, Pat turned to his Pa and said, "Do you think I need more schoolin' Pa?"

"Yes I do, Son, and we'll talk to your ma about it when we get home. I know I don't have much formal schoolin' myself, but things were different then. Let me give you a little family history. Yore great-granddaddy was a doctor who came to America from Scotland and settled in the Carolinas. As I understand it, in Scotland there was the Scottish Highlanders and the Scottish Lowlanders. Yore great-granddaddy was a Highlander. The Highlanders was a fiercely independent lot, strong of character and very proud of their history. They believed in strong family ties. If you was a Highlander, you looked after yore family, and you always stood by yore neighbors. He passed those values on to yore granddaddy."

Dan continued. "Yore granddaddy had eight young'uns. I was the oldest of the whole bunch. Times was hard then, and it was a struggle for us to even put food on the table, but we done it without blaming somebody else for our troubles or begging from anybody. We done it because we had that Scotch Highlander blood in us, and we made it on just plain old determination and love for each other. You see, I couldn't go to school because I had to work and help feed the family. Now, my point is, determination will take you a long way, but these days, determination ain't enough. You need an education to go along with it."

"But how did you get from the Carolinas to the farm where we live now?" Pat inquired.

"It's sort of a long story," replied Dan. "I worked with Pa on the farm up in the Carolinas 'til I was might nigh grown. When the two brothers closest to me in age was growed up enough to help pa on the farm, I lit out for Georgia to make it on my own. I worked 'round in these parts for five years. Then, I married yore ma. With the little money I had saved and a loan from the bank, I bought the hundred acres where we live now for fifty dollars."

"Was I born there?" asked Pat.

"Yep" replied Dan, as he fired up his pipe, "right in that same house where we live now. We never told you, but when you was born, yore ma had such a rough time, she was never able to have any more children. Wouldn't mention that to her if I was you. She'll get all teary about it."

"Pa, do you think you would've had one of them big plantations if you'd had more schoolin'?"

Dan stopped the wagon, looked at Pat and replied, "Prob'ly not. You see, I don't have no use for slavery. Wouldn't want to be one myself, and I wouldn't want to make a slave out of somebody else. Besides, the way things are now, you couldn't run a plantation without slaves. Fact is, one reason I like living at Pine Creek is there ain't no plantations or slaves in the area. There's just small land owners like me."

Pat sat quietly for a while and then responded, "Pa, if you don't have much schoolin,' then why do you think I ought to have it? You ain't done so bad."

"Because," responded Dan, "I want you to be the kind of man that'll make a difference in this country, not just because of something you've done or said, but because of what you stand for and because people have respect for you and for the things you believe in. I want you to make a difference right here in Pine Creek. Every place needs somebody who'll stand for what is right and do what is right. An education'll help you do that.

"Mind you, times are changing, and what's more, I've got a feeling that there's going to be trouble over this slave situation. It's just a matter of time. You know I'm just an uneducated farmer from up in the Carolinas and I don't know much 'bout running a country, but to hold another man in bondage is wrong. The early settlers of this country come here to be free. Then they took freedom away from somebody else. This farm that we live on used to be Creek Indian country not too many years ago. Folks who come here before you and me took it away from 'em. They just packed them up and moved 'em out. It just don't make sense to me, Son."

It was late afternoon when Dan and Pat arrived back at the farm. Dan guided the horses over to the barn where he and Pat unloaded the supplies from McDaniel's store. When they had finished, they unhitched the team, rubbed them down, and put them in their stalls, where they were given a generous amount of grain for their hard day's work.

From the back porch of the house, Leona called, "You men better hurry up. Supper's 'bout ready, and I don't cook it just to let it sit there on the table and get cold."

"Yeah, Ma, we'll be there soon's we get the harnesses put up," replied Pat.

"Gabriel will blow his horn when those two aren't hungry," she thought as she went back into the kitchen to take the biscuits out of the oven.

After washing up on the back porch, Dan and Pat went into the kitchen where supper was on the table.

When they were seated and Dan had asked the blessing, Leona said, "What's the news from town? Is there anything that I need to know about?"

"No, Ma," Pat replied quickly before Dan could say anything. "Nothing much ever happens in Pine Creek. We just got our supplies at Mr. McDaniel's store, loaded 'em on the wagon, and come home. I mean we came home, just like we always do."

"Did you see Molly Ann?"

"Yes, ma'am, when we got to the store, she was sweepin' the front porch."

"Well, Pat, did y'all speak or talk about anything?"

"We just passed the time of day for a bit," Pat replied.

"Passed the time of day," Dan chuckled. "Pat, you're dancing 'round the truth like you were trying to win a dancing contest in some ballroom somewhere. Why don't you just go ahead and tell yore ma that you finally got around to asking Molly Ann to go the church picnic with you, and she said she would."

# 6

After a rather raucous time in the kitchen, Dan, Leona, and Pat moved into the sitting room in front of the fireplace. Things had calmed down quite a bit since Dan made his comments at the supper table.

Finally, Pat spoke, "Ma, do you think you could help me with some book learnin'?"

"Of course I'll help you, but I'm a little bit curious. Why do you have this sudden interest in improving your education? You're the one who rebelled and quit school a few years ago."

"I know, Ma, but on the way home from town, Pa was talkin' to me 'bout how times is changing. That kinda made me think that maybe I need to get more schoolin' if I'm gonna amount to anything."

"Amen to that," commented Dan, "and don't forget to tell yore ma that Molly Ann thinks you ought to git a better education too."

"Ah, Pa, whatcha you keep bringin' up what me and Molly Ann talked about? You must've been listenin' to every word we said."

Undeterred, Dan continued with a mischievous grin on his craggy face. "Leona, it was 'bout the funniest thing I ever seen. Now, you have to understand that Molly Ann said all this while our love-sick son here only managed to notice that she was sweeping the porch."

"All I did was ask her to the church picnic. How come you're making so much of it?"

"Yeah, I know, but when she said she would go with you,

a picnic wasn't all she had in mind. You mark my words, Patrick," Dan continued, "fried chicken ain't all that'll be in that picnic basket. There's a recipe for marryin' in there somewhere and I think you're one of the main ingredients."

"Dan, you lay off that boy. Quit ragging him so much about courting, marrying, and all kinds of falderal like that. If you don't stop it, I've a good mind to tell him all about our courtin' and how it was that you and me got married sort of sudden-like when I was just sixteen years old. You mind what I'm telling you. Do you hear me, Daniel John Ravenwood?"

"Hrumph!" Dan responded as he fired up his pipe with an ember from the fireplace.

Pat turned, poked at the coals in the fireplace and pretended that he didn't hear what he had just heard his ma say.

After Leona put an end to Dan's frivolity, she got up from her chair and said, "I'll be back in just a minute. I want to get something from the bedroom."

Dan and Pat gave each other puzzled looks and shrugged their shoulders, but they didn't say anything. Both of them knew that when Leona set her mind to something, you might as well let her be. When she returned, she held out two books for Dan and Pat to see.

"This here's a *McGuffey's Reader*, and I've had it since you were in school, Pat. You've probably forgotten about it, because you weren't too interested in books at that time. Well, I saved it, hoping you would come to your senses one day and see that you need to do some studying. Now, if you're really serious about an education, this little book is a good place to start, and you should read a little from it every day. Some of what's in here you already know, but it won't hurt you to read it again."

"Also, I got this other book for you. It's called *Ivanhoe*, and I want you to read a little from it every day, just like in regular school."

"Where'd you git that? I ain't never heard of no *Ivanhoe*

31

before."

"Well, I guess I'll have to confess. I got it from Miss Mc-Curdy about a month ago when I went into town with your pa. While he was getting supplies and jawing with Mr. Mc-Daniel, I met with Miss McCurdy, and we talked about how we might get you interested in reading. She thinks you need to read something that'll challenge you and make you use your imagination. She wants you to put yourself into whatever you're reading, and maybe see yourself as one of the characters in the book. She suggested *Ivanhoe*, so I borrowed it from her. I've been keeping it here at the house just hoping we could talk about it sometime."

"But Ma, all I wanted to do was ask Molly Ann to the church picnic. I didn't know I was startin' somethin' everybody was gonna get mixed up in."

"By jingo, I told you there'd be more in that picnic basket than fried chicken and biscuits," said Dan, as he slapped his leg in laughter. "Ain't it a sight what women can cook up and feed to a young man who's just plain too narrow 'tween the eyes to see how complicated love can be."

"Dan Ravenwood," said Leona, "you're gonna be sleeping in the barn with the cows and horses if you don't mind your tongue. It's for certain you won't be sleeping with me."

"Yes, ma'am," he said, as he saluted Leona.

Not to be deterred, Leona said to Pat, "You want to know why we are concerned about your education? I'll tell you why. Your body is growing and you're getting strong, and that's good, but I want what's inside that brain of yours to grow and be strong too. Now this is what we're going to do about it, so listen carefully, both of you. I'll work with Pat on his reading every evening. That's where the *McGuffey's Reader* and *Ivanhoe* come in."

"Dan, every Saturday, when you go to town, I want Pat to go with you. He can go to the school and Miss McCurdy will work with him on his writing and the way he talks while you get our supplies from Sam's store and get your drink at Otto's Bar. Now, don't you go acting so surprised. I've been knowing about your weekly toddy at Otto's Bar for a long time."

Much to Dan's relief, she changed the subject. "It's time to go to bed, fellers. The sun comes up early in the morning."

"Yore ma has a plan for everything," Dan whispered to Pat.

"But Pa, all I wanted to do was ask Molly Ann to the ..."

"I know. I know," interrupted Dan.

Pulling his chair a little closer to Pat, "Seriously, yore ma and me don't want nothing but the best for you, and we believe some more book learnin' will be good for you. Fact is, I wish I could've had more. It would've been good for me. A good education 'll be good for you, but don't put all yore trust in books. You can learn from a lot of things. Experience is a good teacher.

"Good experiences, as well as bad experiences, can teach you a lot. The main thing is to be sure that you learn something from every experience in life.

"You can learn from other people too, even people who ain't school teachers. I'm talking about folks like Reverend Troup at the church and Sam McDaniel over at the general store. Sam teaches by the way he lives. He lets a lot of folks have groceries even though he knows they can't pay him. He's not gonna let a family go hungry just because they don't have the money to pay for their groceries. Sam is a good man, and there's a lot to be learned from good folks.

"While we're talking about good men and good teachers, let me tell you something. My ole daddy, yore granddaddy, was a good man and a good teacher. I don't know how many times he told me, 'Always tell the truth. Always pay yore debts, and when you go to see somebody, don't wear out yore welcome.' Now, that was some good advice."

"Here's something else I want you to remember, and it's something from yore own daddy. You be careful what you

33

think's important in yore life."

Dan continued, "I'm telling you that because what you think is important is gonna make you what you are. And another thing, remember that yore good name is worth more than all the gold in the world."

Meanwhile, in the kitchen, Leona smiled to herself as she listened to Dan's advice to Pat.

"Now go to bed," Dan said. "Get a good night's sleep, and don't forget to say your prayers." Then he added, "And don't forget to thank God that you ain't married ... yet."

"Daniel John Ravenwood!"

"Yes, ma'am," Dan said as he and Pat grinned at each other.

"Go to bed, Son. Morning comes early on the Ravenwood farm." Dan said, as he got up from his chair and emptied his pipe into the fireplace.

"That's what you always say, Pa."

"Well, it always do, don't it?"

"Yeah, Pa, always."

Pat thought, "Just for one time in my life, I'd like to get up in the morning after the sun gets up."

As Pat climbed the ladder to the sleeping loft, Dan carefully banked the shimmering oak coals toward the rear of the fireplace. As he was sweeping off the hearth, Leona walked back into the room.

"Thank you for doing that. Now come over here and let's just sit for a while. It's been such a busy day."

"You should know. All that planning keeps a body busy."

"Oh Dan, can't you ever be serious?"

"I'm serious about you," he replied.

She reached over and squeezed his hand, "I know."

Silently, they sat holding hands and staring at the glowing oak coals in the fireplace.

It was a time to talk, their way of closing out the day.

Finally, he said, "We've got us a good boy."

"Yes, we do," she agreed, "and he's going to be a fine man one of these days."

"He already is," said Dan. "I just hope this country doesn't fall apart around him and cause him grief. I fear for him, Leona, and us too. Hatred and all this vile talk for and agin the right to own slaves can't lead to anything good."

"Do you really think it's that bad?"

"I think it's gonna be worse than we can imagine."

He continued, "When I was in Sam's store, he told me about an article he saw in that newspaper that comes from Macon. He said there'd been a meeting in Nashville, Tenn. to talk about some sort of deal between the North and the South on this slavery business. Nine states from the South had people there. He didn't say which states, but the main thing I wanted to tell you is, there was also some talk of Southern states breaking away from the Union if some sort of deal couldn't be worked out."

"What do you think's going to happen?"

"I don't know, but it's like I told Pat, there's trouble brewing. If we break away from the Union, it won't settle anything. Just as sure as I'm sittin' here next to you, some hot head'll get us into a shootin' war, and if there's a war, we'll all suffer from it, every one of us. There's no doubt about it."

"God help us."

"I hope so, Leona. I hope so, but I'm afraid there's folks on both sides of this slavery business that ain't gonna let God have a say in anything they do."

# 7

The next morning, Leona had breakfast on the table before the sun began to light up the eastern sky. Breakfast for Dan and Pat consisted of two eggs apiece, a generous serving of smoked sausage, cathead biscuits with cane syrup and steaming, black coffee. After Dan had asked "The Good Lord" to bless their food, he and Pat quickly ate the food that Leona had set before them. Leona, who ate much less, never ceased to be amazed at the amount of food her men could put away.

A little after daybreak, Dan and Pat were in the field plowing. Dan always made sure his two horses were well cared for. When he used the wagon to bring supplies from town, they were harnessed together, but when it came to plowing, they were hitched to individual plows, one for Dan and the other for Pat. His horses were accustomed to hard work and were as well trained for field work as show horses were trained for performing in the show ring at the county fair.

While the men worked in the field, Leona had her own responsibilities. After clearing away the breakfast dishes, she would go to the barn, milk the cow and then gather the eggs from the henhouse. Once she had completed her outside chores, she would return to the kitchen, rekindle the fire in the wood-burning cook stove, and prepare dinner for Dan and Pat. Dinner was the meal that was served in the middle of the day. Supper was served in the evening.

To Leona, the distinction between dinner and supper was simple. "When Jesus and his disciples gathered for a meal in

Jerusalem on the night before He was crucified, it was called The Last Supper, not The Last Dinner." That settled it so far as Leona was concerned.

When dinner was ready to put on the table, Leona would go out on the back porch and ring the farm bell, which was mounted on a post just beyond the railing of the porch. It was a signal to Dan and Pat that it was time to come to the house and eat. Afterwards, the men usually rested a few minutes in the cool shade of an oak tree in their front yard before returning to the field to plow until quitting time.

The men, with their horses in tow, always returned to the house before sundown because supper was served before dark since coal oil lamps were their only source light at night. After the horses were rubbed down and stabled, Dan and Pat would wash up at the washstand on the back porch and go into the kitchen more than ready to eat the supper that Leona had prepared. Supper often consisted of fried salt pork bacon, navy beans in a white sauce and cathead biscuits. If there was a dessert, it was a biscuit with some of Dan's home-made cane syrup. Occasionally Leona would serve one of her delicious apple pies.

After supper, Leona and Pat would usually sit at the kitchen table and read from the *McGuffey's Reader*, or from *Ivanhoe*.

One evening, as they read from *Ivanhoe*, Pat turned to Leona, "Ma, did people really live like it says here in this here book?"

"Well, maybe not exactly like it is in the book," she replied. "It's probably dressed up some to make it a little more interesting."

Leona continued. "Actually, things were pretty primitive in those days, much more so than the way we live today, but it does tell us about a way of life that was very different from ours. It lets us know that there's a world out there that's bigger than this county that we live in."

She pointed to the book. "Perhaps the best thing about this book is that it shows us how important words can be. It shows us how to paint pictures with our words. If people get a picture in their minds of what you're talking about, then you've done a good job of getting your point across to them."

Leona was amazed at the progress Pat made with his studies. It was as if he had suddenly realized books could open up a whole new world for him. The more he read, the more he wanted to read. In fact, he soon came to regret that he had rebelled at attending school when he was younger. Now, he seemed to want to make up for lost time. Even the time spent studying penmanship with Miss McCurdy became something that he looked forward to each Saturday. Of course, he was always eager to finish his sessions with her so he could spend some time with Molly Ann. His last visit to town was no exception. When he arrived at the general store, Molly Ann was sitting on a bench out front waiting for him, although she never would have admitted it.

He had just put his foot on the first step when she greeted him with her usual, "Well, I do declare. It's Pat Ravenwood, what a surprise!"

"How is your schooling going with Miss McCurdy over at the schoolhouse?" she asked.

Pat bristled. "It's not really schoolin'. I'm not sitting there all day at a desk like I was a child."

"Oh, for goodness' sake, Pat, you know what I mean. I'm just interested in what you're doing." Then she reached up and patted him on the cheek.

"Yeah, I know you are, and I'm sorry I spoke out of turn. All this studying is hard work, sort of like working in the field with Pa." Pat said as he reached out and hugged her.

Susie McDaniel noted from inside the store that it was more than just a casual hug. She was of the same opinion when Molly Ann returned the hug.

After they had stood for a moment holding hands, Molly

Ann said, "Was there something you wanted from the store?"

"No, Pa's got all the supplies loaded, so I thought I'd come by and speak to you before we go home."

"That's sweet of you. Are you going to church tomorrow?"

"I sure am. Could we sit together, maybe some place besides with your ma and pa? It ain't that I don't like'em, it's just that I sort of feel like your ma's watching us all the time."

Molly Ann laughed, "We'll sit anywhere you want to."

"Good! I'll see you tomorrow at church. Could I walk you home after church?"

"Of course, silly."

"By Jaybird Lake?"

"Maybe so," she replied coyly.

# 8

Pat found comfort in the memories of his life on his father's farm. He was dreaming of the meals that his ma always served after he had worked in the field all day when suddenly he was awakened by a hard kick to his side.

"Wake up you lazy, no good, stinking whiner," said Sergeant Buck Hagan. "You told the Colonel that you wanted better food for this bunch of sorry, shot-up Rebs. Well, here it is."

At that, Hagan had Perkins and Lawton place a small tub in front of Pat that contained the prisoner's morning ration of a broth that was practically colorless with the exception of a greasy film across the top. Once they had set the tub down, Hagan dumped in a bucket of food scraps that had come from the plates of the prison guards. Then, from under his arm, he took four loaves of hard, stale bread and threw them on the dirt floor at Pat's feet.

"There's the solid food you whined to the Colonel about," he said.

Pat glared at Hagan, but there was nothing he could do. A sense of hopelessness mingled with helplessness overwhelmed him. When he was captured, he stood six feet tall and weighed two hundred pounds. Now, he probably weighed no more than a hundred fifty.

After Hagan left, Cofer and Bracewell appeared and began distributing tin cups to the wounded so that they could have their morning meal. As they served the stale bread and the pitiful excuse for broth to the men, Pat continued to sit on his pallet. He began to think about his life and what had brought him to be a prisoner of war in this hell-hole called Clonnerville Prison. Was it worth it? Had his ministry really made a difference?

He remembered the Colonel's question, "Where is God in all this?" There seemed to be no answer, for the Colonel or for himself.

He had just stretched out on his pallet with his face toward the wall, when he felt a hand on his shoulder. It was Jud.

"Pardon me, Chaplain," he said. "Pitts has died. I thought you'd want to know."

"Thank you, Jud," said Pat as he sat up on his pallet.

After Jud left, Pat put his head in his hands and thought, "God, what can I write his folks this time?"

As discouraged as he was, Pat vowed to do whatever was needed for the men in Warehouse B. In spite of his bitterness, he was still their chaplain, and he would do his best to minister to them even in death. Somehow, he had to pull himself together and conduct a service for Private Pitts. After the service, he would write a comforting letter to the bereaved family, even though he knew in his heart that Pitts was better off dead than alive.

Once again, Jud and Deke had to go through the ordeal of getting a shovel from Hagan.

As in previous funerals, they dug the grave under the watchful eyes of Rat Perkins and Jake Lawton, both of whom were under orders to shoot to kill if Jud or Deke gave them what they perceived to be any thought of escape. Keenly aware of this, Jud and Deke were very careful and made no sudden moves as they dug the grave for Pitts.

When they had finished digging, Jud and Deke went back to the warehouse, and notified Pat that they were ready for the burial. They shrouded Pitts's frail body in the pallet on which he had died. With Pat leading the way, they carried the body up the hill and placed it in the freshly dug grave. Reverently, the two of them stood aside as Pat conducted the service.

Pat was well aware of the meaning of death. A soldier's death was always a loss to someone. Even though Pitts' funeral was attended only by Jud, Deke, and two prison guards, he was determined that the service be conducted with a sense of reverence. He also felt that it was his sacred responsibility to make each service personal. These young prisoners were his flock and they needed to be treated as such, even in death. With Jud standing to his right and Deke to his left, Pat opened his Bible and began to read from Psalm 121. It was a scripture that he had carefully selected for a young soldier who could only communicate with his eyes.

*I will lift up mine eyes unto the hills, from whence cometh my help.*

*My help cometh from the Lord, which made heaven and earth.*

After a few comments, he prayed a brief prayer and stood aside as Jud and Deke filled the grave with dirt from the Clonnerville Prison graveyard. Pat, Jud, and Deke were returned under guard to warehouse B. Once inside, Pat went to his pallet, gathered up some paper, a pencil, and a writing board and began the heart-rending task of trying to write words of comfort to the parents of Private Jimmy Pitts.

*Dear Mr. and Mrs. Pitts,*
*It is with deepest regret that I write to inform you that your son, Private James Pitts, has died of wounds he received in combat near Atlanta.*
*He was a fine young man who, with no regard for his own safety, fought bravely against overwhelming odds for a cause he believed in. It is my prayer that you will find some degree of comfort in knowing that his last thoughts were of you.*
*Your Faithful Servant,*
*Patrick Ravenwood*
*Chaplain, C. S. A.*

When he had finished the letter, he placed it in an envelope, addressed it, and put it in the mail basket on the wall beside the warehouse door.

Turning around, he caught the eye of Jud who was trying to give a sip of water to one of the wounded prisoners. Jud responded with a wave as Pat signaled that he would be at his pallet if needed. He hoped that he could get at least an hour's rest, but his state of mind made it impossible to relax. He had never known such hopelessness. There had been hard times on the farm, but at no time did his family feel that they would lose everything. There was never a feeling of total despair. Nothing, absolutely nothing, had prepared him for that which he was experiencing in Clonnerville Prison. He had seen men die on the battlefield, some had even died in his arms, but this was different. Here, he and the other prisoners had no chance to fight back. Hopelessness tainted their every thought. No one knew what date it was nor did they know the day of the week. Only the rising and setting of the sun gave them some sense of time. There were no clocks nor calendars in Clonnerville Prison.

Pat was totally consumed by two overwhelming thoughts, his love for Molly Ann and his hatred for Buck Hagan. He marveled at how Jud and Deke held up in this hell-hole. They helped him care for the wounded and bury the dead. Their days were just like his, yet they seemed to be better able to take life one day at a time. Neither of them had a Molly Ann. She was his inspiration, his reason for living, but because of Hagan's sadistic nature, he had not heard from her in weeks. He had no doubts about her faithfulness. She was the one thing that kept him going. She was his hope for some kind of future. Yet he had been denied any contact with her. And what of Johnny, who reminded him so much of himself?

Always on Pat's mind was Hagan's merciless kicking of a young soldier whose only crime was calling out for his mama in his delirium. Pat was also convinced that the starvation rations that Hagan grudgingly provided had contributed to the death of other wounded prisoners. After an hour of just sitting on his pallet, Pat made a vow. He would endure his time in Clonnerville Prison. In spite of the hell that he was in, he would survive and return to his beloved Molly Ann and his son, Johnny. Somehow he would see that Hagan was held accountable for all that he had done to the prisoners. But Pat realized that, justice in a court of law was unlikely, so there would have to be some other way to make Buck Hagan pay. Pat vowed that he would assume that responsibility. He would make Hagan pay.

Again, he closed his eyes and tried to get some rest. After about twenty minutes of fitful sleep, Jud Cofer gently tapped him on the shoulder.

"Sorry to bother you Chaplain," Jud said, "but Corporal Daily just died."

"Just cover him up for now, Jud. We'll bury him tomorrow."

"Hagan was right about one thing," he thought. "No one leaves this place alive."

# 9

Pat turned his face to the wall again and tried to focus on the memories of his earlier years at Pine Creek, especially the Methodist Church picnic with Molly Ann.

He remembered what Reverend Troup said in his sermon that Sunday, "Fill yore life with good memories and good deeds. They'll carry you through some mighty hard times."

John Henry was an unusually gifted man who chose to serve smaller churches such as the one in Pine Creek. In fact, John Henry Troup was a "Circuit Rider," a term applied to a minister who served as pastor of two or more small churches and made the rounds of his pastorate on horseback. In John Henry's case, his circuit consisted of three churches: Pine Creek Church with services every Sunday morning and evening, Shiloh with services every first Sunday afternoon, and Friendship with services every fourth Sunday afternoon. On fifth Sundays, John Henry preached at a county-wide service at Sweet Water Methodist Campground.

Brother John, as his parishioners called him, was six feet four inches tall, weighed two hundred thirty-five pounds, and was known for his handlebar mustache and his long shock of white hair which many said likened him unto Moses, a comparison that some suspected originated with John Henry himself. He was known for his love for his parishioners, but he was perfectly willing to dangle them over the fiery pits of hell in his preaching if the spirit so moved him. With his Bible in his saddle bag and a .44 caliber Walker Colt revolver tucked in his belt, John Henry Troup was quite an imposing figure as he made the rounds of the Pine Creek Circuit. He was a teller of tales, a good fisherman, and one who could plow a field with the best of the farmers on his circuit. It was his fishing ability that appealed to Pat, and that was good because Brother John was known to have fished many a person into the church, and he had baited his hook for Pat.

It was not unusual for him to show up just as Leona was ringing the farm bell calling Dan and Pat in from the field for their noonday meal. It was said that John Henry could hear a dinner bell ringing five miles away. He was always welcomed at the Ravenwood table. After the meal, Dan would excuse Pat from his afternoon field work so that he could go fishing in Walden Creek with John Henry.

It was no secret among the parishioners on Brother John's circuit that his saddle bags contained fishing tackle for catching fish and his Bible for catching people. After several afternoons fishing on Walden Creek, Brother John "caught" Pat into the fellowship of Pine Creek Church. There was no doubt about it. John Henry knew how to fish for people. In fact, he often said, "I'm a fisher of men, but I practice by fishing for fish ever chance I get."

That afternoon, John Henry wasn't just fishing for fish. He was fishing for someone special. He was getting on up in years and realized that one day he would have to step aside and let someone else fill his pulpit. Sitting there on the banks of Walden Creek, John Henry began to have a vision, and that vision involved his fishing buddy, Pat Ravenwood.

As he lay on his pallet in Clonnerville Prison, Pat smiled as he remembered the Sunday on which he and Molly Ann sat together in church and afterwards enjoyed the fried chicken and home-made biscuits in Molly Ann's picnic basket. He almost laughed aloud when he remembered Brother John's closing prayer at the end of the service that had run about twenty minutes past the hour.

Molly Ann gave Pat a rather sharp jab in his ribs when he snickered while John Henry was praying.

*O God, we pray that you will bless the food that we are about to eat and the hands that have prepared it. Bless the tie that binds us together as friends and as families in this church and in this town. May husbands and wives grow in their love for each other. May the children obey their mamas and daddies. May the young ladies always be lady-like, and may the young men always behave themselves.*

*Amen*

As Brother John said, "Amen," the congregation joined in with their own enthusiastic "Amen," all except Pat, who snickered again and received another elbow jab.

When the service was over, Brother John mingled with the congregation. The children dashed out to play. The women scurried about getting the picnic lunch ready to be served from two picnic tables located in the shade of large pine trees on the east side of the church. Blankets and table clothes were spread on the ground so families could sit together and eat their lunches while fanning gnats and flies away. When lunch was served, Pat and Molly Ann quickly helped themselves and moved off to one side, slightly away from the other church people. In the shade of a giant pine tree, they sat holding hands and deftly eating fried chicken at the same time. They were totally unaware of the surveillance of their respective mothers.

That afternoon, everyone moved back inside the church for the customary hymn sing which was led by Josh Taylor, the Sunday School superintendent, and accompanied by Miss Minnie Dubbery on the pump organ. With sundown approaching, Reverend Troup called it a day at the Pine Creek Methodist Church and everybody headed home. Sam and Susie McDaniel joined Dan and Leona on the Ravenwood wagon for the short ride to the to the McDaniel home.

It was customary for the two families to share a "potluck" meal after an event at the church. Pat and Molly Ann chose to walk home by way of Jaybird Lake rather than ride in the wagon with their parents. They were late for supper because of the rather circuitous route they had taken to the McDaniel home.

"Took you long enough to get here," smirked Leona. "You must've stopped for a while."

"Oh, that's all right," Susie McDaniel interceded. "It's only leftovers and you know how young people are. They just seem to lose track of time."

"Yeah, Leona," Dan chimed in, "I can remember one time when ..."

"Dan Ravenwood, you mind your tongue, or you'll have to walk home, and when you get there, you'll have to sleep in the barn."

Sam McDaniel continued to stir the pot, "Now Leona, don't be too hard on Dan. He's already told me about your courting days."

"Dan, you didn't!"

"Well, not all of it," he replied.

# 10

Two gentle taps on his shoulder awakened Pat to the reality of Clonnerville Prison and the stench of Warehouse B.

"Sorry to bother you, Chaplain," said Jud Cofer, "but Hagan's two thugs are coming with that hog slop they call breakfast."

Pat managed a slight grin, "Don't make it any worse than it is, Jud."

"Now, you know I wouldn't do that, Chaplain. There's absolutely no way I could make it any worse'n it already is. If you don't believe me, taste it and see. By the way, don't forget that we have to bury Corporal Daily today. Remember, he died last night."

"Thanks for reminding me, Jud. Let's take care of it right after breakfast."

Sensing that Jud had something on his mind, Pat said, "Is there something else you want to talk about, Jud?"

"Not exactly, we can talk later," replied Jud.

"Now's as good a time as any to talk. What's bothering you?"

"Well, I might as well go ahead and say it, Chaplain. I don't know how much more of this place I can take. We was captured in July, and I don't even know what month it is now. Hell, I don't even know what day it is. 'Scuse my language, Chaplain, but what I'm tryin' to say is, how much longer do you think we'll be in this place? The weather's changing. It's gittin' cooler ever night. That means winter will be before long. If we're still alive when it gits here, we'll prob'ly freeze to death. Whatcha think, Chaplain? How much longer?

I know thinkin' about it just makes it worse, but this place is really gittin' to me. You asked Deke and me to help others, and we done that, but there's just nothing left inside me to give any more. Do you see what I mean Chaplain? We're having more and more funerals. The sick's getting sicker, and them prisoners that wasn't sick when they come here, is gittin' in bad shape. Just look at you and me. We ain't half the men we used to be."

Pat replied. "I know what you mean, Jud, but we have no way of knowing how long it will be. We can't get any news about the war. The Yankees won't tell us anything. You know as well as I do that so long as we are prisoners here, we're cut off from everything, but if the Battle of Peachtree Creek tells us anything, then we're in trouble. Look at it this way. They beat us right in the heart of Dixie. Now I'm just a Georgia preacher turned chaplain, but I think it looks bad for the Confederacy, real bad. Our armies are getting whipped. People are losing hope. Remember how the people looked when we were marched through Clonnerville? Either they didn't care or they were beyond feeling anything. Only one crippled Confederate soldier paid us any mind."

"Are you saying we done lost the war, Chaplain?"

"I'm afraid that's the way it looks. At any rate, the three of us lost our part of the war at Peachtree Creek. We're out of it for good. I just hope we can survive. I keep hoping there will be some sort of prisoner exchange, but I don't think that'll happen. By the way, where's Deke? Does he feel like you do?"

"He's in the back part of the building trying to help some pore feller that's talkin' about killin' hisself, but to answer your question, yeah, he feels the same way. It ain't nothing against you, Chaplain. You got us this far, but how much do you have left inside you?"

"There's not much left inside me, Jud. I've just about given all I can. This place has drained me dry. It makes me feel like a hypocrite when you and Deke call me Chaplain. If you really want to know the truth, there's just two things keep me going in this place, and that's Molly Ann and Buck Hagan."

"What do you mean?"

"I mean that it's not my faith that keeps me going. It's my love for Molly Ann and my hatred for Buck Hagan. I'm ashamed to say this to you, but somehow, somewhere, I'm going to see that he pays for what he's done to these prisoners, not just the wounded, but all of us."

Angrily, Pat continued. "A man like that just can't be allowed to go free. I've never seen a man so filled with the devil as he is."

"I hear what you're saying Chaplain, and I hate to remind you of somethin' that's disagreeable, but we still have that dee-licous breakfast to serve to the wounded."

"My God! I'd forgotten all about it. It's probably cold by now, not that it makes any difference. Let's dip the grease off the top and let the men eat, if they can stand it."

"You're right Chaplain, it won't make no difference, but it ain't gonna get no better. I'll get Deke, and we'll get started."

When the wounded had finished their meal, Jud and Deke collected their tin cups and brought them to the door of the warehouse where they would be picked up by Perkins and Lawton. When they finally showed up, Hagan was with them. He was carrying a packet of mail which he threw at the feet of Pat. "There's the mail, but there's nothing in it for you from that little hussy of yours. Course it's prob'ly hard for her to write when she's snuggled up to somebody else."

Laughing, he and his men gathered up the greasy buckets and cups and made their way out of Warehouse B.

"Don't let him get to you, Chaplain." Jud said.

"I know, Jud. I know he's just trying to make me to do something foolish, but I'm not going to take his bait. When I

51

deal with him, it'll be on my terms and in a place of my own choosing. I know it sounds bad coming from me, but there's something I have to tell you, Jud. When we get out of this hell-hole, if we ever do, I may turn in my ministerial credentials."

"What exactly do you mean, Chaplain?" Jud inquired. "Do you mean that you're going to quit being a chaplain?"

"It goes beyond that, Jud. It means that I may quit being a preacher, even if I make it back to Pine Creek. It'll be a tough decision because I'll be turning my back on the only thing I've ever done. I guess it all boils down to the fact that I don't have the faith that it takes to be a preacher any more. And on top of it all, I feel like I've let you and Deke down."

"You ain't let us down, Chaplain. A man's like a pack horse; he can only tote so much, and it seems to me that you've been totin' double lately."

"Yeah, I know it seems that way, but you and Deke have been doing more than your share too. I don't know what I would've done without you two."

"Appreciate you saying that, Chaplain. Truth is, neither one of us was church goers. But we was brought up knowing that we ought to help our neighbors out. So I guess we just sorta included these here pore souls on our neighbor list." Jud continued. "I guess the Good Lord's done figured out a way to get a little good out of us. Mind you, I ain't denying that me and Deke got a lot of catching up to do if we gonna get on the Lord's right side."

"Considering what y'all have done here, I'd say you're in pretty good shape. Of course, you know I'm not the judge," Pat said with a slight grin on his face.

"We know you ain't the judge, but you can put in a good word for us. Fact 'tis, both me and Deke's kinda counting on you. We ain't likely to find a better person than you to do it."

Pat continued the banter. "You know I'd stick up for you two any day, and it won't take a court order to get me on the witness stand either."

"I knowed you'd do it Chaplain. Course you know there's somethin' else that we ain't talked about that could work in our favor."

"What's that?"

Jud grinned. "I'm talking about the fact that you and the Judge have a pretty close relationship that goes way back yonder."

Pat's expression changed. "I'm not sure that's the case anymore. You know what this place has done to me, and you know how I feel about Hagan."

"I know, Chaplain. It's just that we don't want you to give up. If you give up, who can Deke and me turn to?"

"I don't know, Jud. I honestly don't know, and that bothers me. I'm not even sure who I can turn to."

# 11

Back home in Pine Creek, Pat had been so sure of his call to the ministry. Now, he was having serious doubts about it. Questions about his faith and his calling gnawed at him daily.

"What good is a call to the ministry if your faith crumbles when times get hard?"

"Did I misunderstand what God wants me to do?"

"Have I been living a lie all these years?"

Pat always felt that he was called to lead people on their faith journey. But now in Clonnerville Prison, where a strong faith was needed, he was grasping for something to hang onto, something to help him survive.

His home life had been as stable as anyone could ask for. His pa and ma were faithful members of the Pine Creek Church. They had instilled in him a strong sense of right and wrong.

He treasured the time when his pa shared his feeling about slavery. Then there was Leona, his ma. If there was ever a person with a backbone of steel, she was the one. His pa wanted him to get a good education, but his ma was the one who stepped in and did the actual teaching. There was no denying the fact that his home life had a lot to do with the development of his faith, but so did John Henry Troup there on the creek bank.

As Pat thought of the many times he had gone fishing with John Henry, one particular afternoon stood out above all the others.

"Boy, you ever thought much about being a preacher?" John Henry asked as he put a fresh worm on his hook.

"No, sir, I ain't. To tell you the truth, I prob'ly wouldn't like it very much. Standin' up there in the pulpit, talkin' in front of all those people, I just don't think I could do it. Why'd you ask me about that Brother John?"

"Well, I been sittin' here noticing you. For a young boy, you seem to have a pretty good passion for fishing. You do like fishing, don't you?"

"Yes, sir, I like fishing, Brother John, but what's that got to do with preaching?"

"Patrick, my boy, what I'm leadin' up to is, if you like fishing, then you'd like preachin'.

The two of them's a lot alike in many ways. Just look at it this way. When you go fishing, you always need to have good bait, and it has to be the right kind of bait. Fish ain't gonna bite something they ain't interested in. Another thing is, you always have to watch yore cork. When that cork starts bobbin', you need to set that there hook and bring'em in. That's just like preaching. If yore cork ain't bobbin', there ain't nobody paying attention. If nobody's paying attention, then you ain't gonna' catch anything. Understand what I'm saying?"

"Yes, sir ... I think so."

"Well, don't you worry about it, Sonny Boy. The Lord will help you understand it one day, but just to set the record straight, it'll be the Lord that calls you to preach and not me. If you don't remember anything else I say, you be sure to remember that. Hey! Look at yore cork! You're getting a bite! Looks like a good'en too!"

It was late afternoon when they got back to the house with their string of hand-sized bluegills. When they had cleaned their catch, Leona carefully sprinkled each fish with corn meal and fried them for supper along with a generous supply of hushpuppies flavored with onions. When she had put the food on the table and everyone had taken a seat, Dan asked Brother John to ask the blessing. After they had finished their meal, which was topped off with one of Leona's apple pies, Brother John was quick to be on his way home.

"The missus might be worried about me," he said.

That night, Pat tossed and tumbled all night long. What Brother John had talked to him about was stuck in his mind and wouldn't let him have a moment's rest. For the very first time, he was beginning to experience a sense of purpose in his life.

He had just dozed off when his ma called to him."Patrick, the sun's coming up. It's time for you to get up."

"Why does sunrise have to come so early?" He thought as he struggled to get out of bed. His sleepless night had sapped his energy, but somehow, he made it through the day without prodding from his pa. That evening at the supper table, Pat asked, "Have we ever had any preachers in our family?"

"Nope," Dan smiled, "most of our ancestors had to work for a living."

Leona was about to pour him another cup of coffee, but she stopped. "You can get your own coffee. Pat's got something on his mind, and I want to hear about it."

Turning her attention to Pat, "Why did you ask, Son? Whatcha got on your mind?"

"Ah, it's nothing. I was just thinking about something Brother John said the other day when we was fishin' down at the creek. He said preaching was kinda like fishing."

Pouring his own cup of coffee, Dan responded. "Well, I don't know about that. Brother John's a mighty good man, but you need to remember that it's the Lord that calls you to preach. Ain't nobody else. Keep in mind too, that Brother John has kind of a knack for tying fishing in with everything else he does."

"That's kinda what he told me, Pa ... I think."

The conversation that occurred that night at the supper table was not mentioned again, but like Mary's response to the message from the angel Gabriel, Leona treasured that conversation and thought about it often. As months passed, she was amazed at the way Pat worked at his studies, often reading a book supplied by Miss McCurdy until way after she and Dan had gone to bed. She also noted that he spent a great deal of time reading the family Bible, particularly passages suggested by John Henry Troup.

The next Wednesday, Dan, Leona, and Pat were having an early supper so they could attend the prayer meeting at the church that evening.

Pat surprised his ma and pa with, "If y'all don't mind, I'll walk home when prayer meeting is over."

Dan responded, "No need for that, we'll wait on you a few minutes."

"I may be a while, and I don't want to make y'all late."

"You must be going by to see Molly Ann."

"No, I'm supposed to meet with Brother John for a while. I'll tell y'all about it later."

Dan wouldn't quit. "It's no big secret, is it?"

Leona gave Dan a look that said rather emphatically, "Why don't you be quiet!" She followed the look with a kick to his shin.

Pat smiled at this interchange, but he remained silent. When they arrived at prayer meeting, he spoke to Brother John and sat with Molly Ann the rest of the evening.

# 12

After the prayer meeting was over, Pat visited a few minutes with Molly Ann before she walked out of the church and joined her parents, who were talking to Dan and Leona. In the course of the conversation, Sam and Susie invited Dan and Leona to drop by their house for a piece of Molly Ann's sweet potato pie. Dan accepted before Leona could say anything.

As the Ravenwoods were driving away in their wagon, Dan peered through one of the side windows of the church and saw Brother John and Pat kneeling in prayer right in front of the pulpit.

"Wonder what that's all about," he said.

"It's about prayer," snapped Leona. "That's what it's all about."

"Yeah, but what are they praying about?"

"Now, Dan, you're my husband, and I love you dearly, and I don't want to be cross, but there's a fine line between being interested and being nosy. Sometimes, I don't think you know the difference. Right now, we just we need to remember that we've got a fine boy who's becoming a man in a hurry."

Dan put his arm around her. "You must know something I don't know."

She grinned at him, "Most of the time I do, but not this time. We'll just have to wait and see what's going on."

Dan wasn't ready to drop the subject. "You don't think there's something going on with Pat and Molly Ann, do you? You know we ...... "

Leona responded emphatically. "Oh, hush up!"

Meanwhile at the church, John Henry and Pat had finished praying and were sitting on the front pew. They were involved in a very serious conversation. It appeared that Brother John was doing most of the talking as he thumbed through his Bible. Pat was listening attentively.

Finally, John Henry put his Bible aside and asked Pat to join him behind the pulpit.

"Pat, this pulpit is a sacred place, and it comes with a sacred responsibility. Don't ever take it for granted and don't ever walk up here unprepared. Always remember if you're standing behind this pulpit in the right spirit, then you ain't standing alone, and don't you ever get the idea that you're the most important person up here here, because you ain't, not in this pulpit or any other pulpit, not by a long shot."

He continued. "That's enough talking for tonight. You need to go on home and tell yore ma and pa what you've decided to do. I'll be seeing you later. We've got a lot more talking to do, and you've got plenty of work to do. God bless you, Son."

As Pat turned to leave, John Henry put his hand on his arm and stopped him, "I just thought of something. Instead of going home, why don't you go by Molly Ann's house and tell her what you've decided. In fact, yore folks may be there now. I'm pretty sure I caught a glimpse of them leaving together after prayer meeting. Now, get a move on and get yourself on over there."

Pat wasted no time making his way to Molly Ann's house. As he drew closer, he saw his pa's wagon and team of horses on the street in front of the house. He spoke fondly to both the horses, bounded up the steps, and knocked on the door.

Molly Ann answered the door. "Well, look who's here. I thought you might come by. Come on in. There's one piece of pie left."

She took Pat's hand, stood on her tiptoes, gave him a peck on the cheek, and ushered him into the sitting room. As she left to get his piece of pie from the kitchen. Dan nudged Leona with his elbow. She responded with one of her "behave yourself" looks.

When Molly Ann returned, she took a seat next to Pat. "Well, what brings you here, other than a piece of my sweet potato pie?"

Pat thanked her for the pie, gulped down a bite, and looked around at everybody in the room. "I've got something to tell y'all." He hurried on. "After talking with Brother John tonight, I've decided that I want to become a preacher."

"Oh, I'm so proud of you!" Molly Ann squealed as she hopped up and gave him a big kiss right smack on his sweet potato-flavored lips.

Dan leaned over close to Leona ear, "Remember what I said about that picnic basket?"

"Hush your mouth, Dan Ravenwood!"

"I knew something was working on you, but I didn't know exactly what it was." Leona said while giving Pat a big hug.

Dan was standing right behind her grinning from ear to ear."Doesn't surprise me one bit."

# 13

The following Sunday, as the church sang all six stanzas of *Just As I Am*, Pat walked down the aisle of the church and, in a symbolic statement of his commitment, shook hands with John Henry.

The silver-haired patriarch asked the congregation to be seated. "Brothers and sisters, standing before y'all today is Pat Ravenwood. He's asking for yore approval for him to be a minister in The Methodist Episcopal Church, South. There'll be a church conference two weeks from today for us to approve Pat's request. On that Sunday, after y'all have approved Pat for the ministry, we'll have an old-fashioned celebration dinner out in the picnic area."

Two weeks later, during the morning worship service, John Henry announced, "We're gonna omit the final hymn and move right into the church conference. Reverend Jackson Hardy, the Presiding Elder of the Macon District, will guide us through this process. Brother Jack, come down front and start us off with a prayer. While Brother Jack is coming forward, let me remind y'all that we'll have dinner on the grounds right after the service."

After his prayer, Reverend Hardy took a seat behind a table at the front of the sanctuary. "Let the conference come to order. Miss Minnie, will you act as our secretary while you're over there at the organ? Thank you, ma'am. Brother John, please state the purpose of this conference."

John Henry came back to the pulpit. "The purpose of this here conference is to approve Pat Ravenwood's request to become a minister in The Methodist Episcopal Church, South.

Mind you, this is only the first of many steps that he'll have to take to become a minister, so it's very important that he gits yore approval."

"Thank you, Brother Pastor. Let me remind you that only church members are allowed to vote, and we will deal with only one issue in this conference, that of approving Pat Ravenwood as a candidate for the ministry in the Methodist Episcopal Church, South."

Hardy, who was not only a stickler for details but was also very efficient, carefully ushered Pat's approval through the conference in a little more than ten minutes. At the conclusion of the conference, he asked Pat to give the benediction and bless the food.

After Pat had stumbled through his assigned duties, Dan looked at his pocket watch and showed it to Leona. "That whole thing took just eleven minutes. Now that's the way church meetings ought to work."

"Dan Ravenwood, you are truly one of a kind."

"Ain't you glad!"

"Well … maybe sometimes."

Outside, the men stood around, smoked, and discussed crops, and politics, while the women saw to it that the tables were covered with an abundance of fried chicken with all the trimmings.

It was mid-afternoon by the time all the festivities ended at Pine Creek Methodist Church. It had been a long, eventful day and everyone was tired, but it was a good tired. Pat was the first person ever to go into the ministry from that church. No one could be more proud than his parents and Molly Ann and her parents. Even John Henry was showing just a little pride, but that didn't bother him. He always said there was nothing wrong with pride so long as it was a holy pride, as he called it.

Both Dan and Sam expressed the need for an afternoon nap, so each family went their separate ways, with the exception of Pat and Molly Ann who said that they preferred to walk back to her home by way of Jaybird Lake.

Dan slapped the reins on the rumps of the two horses and headed home. "I just hope they keep walking. Jaybird Lake is a mighty romantic place."

Leona looked at him. "Dan, I do believe that you have a guilty conscience after all these many years.

"It's not a guilty conscience. I just have a good memory, even after all these years."

"Hush your mouth, Dan Ravenwood!"

"Yes, ma'am."

Later, Susie looked at the clock on their sitting room wall. "It sure is taking Molly Ann and Pat a long time to get home from church. I hope nothing's happened to them."

Sam stirred a little from his nap, "Me too, Mama."

He was snoring gently and Susie was still fidgeting when the door opened and in walked Pat and Molly Ann.

With just a little sarcasm, Susie said, "Well, my goodness, back so soon, you two must have hurried."

"We didn't exactly hurry. We just had some things to talk about. In fact there's something that Pat wants to talk to Pa about, but it can wait until he wakes up."

Suddenly, Sam was awake and alert as a mouse in a room full of cats.

Pat shook his hand, "Good afternoon, Mr. McDaniel. We didn't mean to wake you up."

"I was just resting a little. Whatcha want?"

"Well, I'll just go right ahead and say it, Mr. McDaniel. I'd like to marry your daughter and I want your permission to do it, and yours, too, Mrs. McDaniel."

"What do you think, Susie? Do they have our permission to get married or not?"

"Sam, you know they do. Pat, come over here and give me a hug. Molly Ann, you give your daddy a hug too."

"Not so fast now," Sam said sternly. "You have my permission on one condition."

He paused briefly, and then continued. "Pat, I take it you haven't told your folks about this marrying business."

"No, sir, I haven't."

"Well, here's my condition. I wanna be there when you tell your folks that you wanna marry Molly Ann."

Susie looked at him wide eyed. "Sam, why on earth would you want to do that?"

"Because I wanna see the expression on Dan's face when Pat tells him that they wanna get married. Ole Dan'll be a sight to see!"

When the four of them arrived at the Ravenwood home, Sam stopped their one-horse wagon in the shade of an oak tree in front of the house and hopped down.

Susie watched with amusement. "What's the hurry? You act just like you might miss something."

"I wouldn't miss this for the world. Molly Ann, you and Pat let me and your Ma go in first. I wanna get me a good seat."

They were met at the door by Leona, "My goodness, look who's here. Y'all come on in. Dan! Look who's here."

Dan got up from the rocker beside the fireplace. "Well, what brings y'all to the country?"

Sam deadpanned, "Pat and Molly Ann have something real serious to tell y'all."

"Oh? What seems to be the problem?"

Susie gave Leona a sly wink that the men didn't see.

Sam took a seat. "I told them they'd have to tell you. It's not up to me to do it."

Once everyone was seated, Pat fidgeted forward in his chair. "Pa, there's no problem. What we want to tell you is we want to get married just as soon as we can work out a few things."

Leona clapped her hands and cried, "Praise the Lord." Then she and Susie hugged each other, totally oblivious to everybody else in the room.

Much to Sam's chagrin, Dan's expression didn't change one bit. He just sat there and rocked.

Only after he had taken two or three puffs from his pipe did he say anything. "Well, it's about time. When's this big wedding gonna take place?"

"We've talked about that Pa, and there are two things that I need to get done before we marry. I need to meet all the requirements to get ordained, and I also need to build a cabin for Molly Ann and me."

"That sounds like a good plan. Now, about that cabin, I'll tell you what I'll do. I'll furnish the logs and help you build it if you can get yore future pa-in-law over there to furnish the nails, all the doors and all the windows, and also any paint we may need."

The crestfallen Sam merely nodded his approval of Dan's plan.

"Pa, there's one other thing."

"What's that, Son?"

"If you think you and Ma would agree, Molly and and me were kinda hoping you and Mr. Sam would help us buy a small piece of land in Pine Creek where we could build us a house."

"Son, if that's where y'all want to live, you know yore ma and me will help y'all any way we can. How about you, Sam?"

"Why, Susie and me wouldn't have it any other way, but first, let me tell you about something that you may be interested in. You know Mrs. Cochran that lives down by the school? Well, she was in the store the other day and said that she might move up to Dykesboro and live with her son and his wife. She lives alone and is getting on up in years. Seems her boy has been after her to move up there with him, so if she decides to move, you might want to think about buying her house. It's a small house, but it's in good shape, and it would save building a house. Just a suggestion, that's all."

Dan said to Pat, "That sounds to me like it's something you and Molly Ann ought to think about. I've already told you that I would help you build, and I will, if that's what you want. However, you need to remember that any help I give you will depend on how much I can be away from the farm."

Leona spoke up, "I think that's a wonderful little house. Don't you think so, Susie?"

"Well, nobody asked our opinion, but I agree with you, Leona. Of course, they'd probably have to add on to it after a while."

Leona beamed. "Wouldn't that be nice!"

"This is gonna take some more talking between Molly Ann and me," responded Pat. "We hadn't counted on buying house, but it sounds mighty interesting."

Dan stood up. "Enough of this marrying talk. Ma, let's celebrate! I'll build a fire in the stove if you'll put on a pot of coffee and serve us some of yore good ole apple pie."

After the pie was demolished, Sam and Susie climbed in their wagon and began the two-mile ride back to Pine Creek. Pat and Molly Ann decided they would walk. In their frame of mind, two miles really didn't matter. It just gave them more time together. Once in Pine Creek, it was no accident that they walked past Mrs. Cochran's house. After looking it over, they decided that they liked what they saw, but wouldn't be sure that it was what they wanted until they saw the inside. They were unaware that Sam and Susie had already driven by and given it their approval.

The next day, Mrs. Cochran walked into Sam's store. "Good morning Mrs. Cochran, it's good to see you. Can I help you with something?"

"I just need a pound of coffee."

"Coming right up. Is there anything else I could get for you?"

"No, that's all. Would you put that on my ticket, please?"

"I'll be glad to. By the way, Mrs. Cochran, are you still thinking about moving up to Dykesboro to live with your son?"

"Well, actually, we've gone beyond the thinking stage. I'll be moving just as soon as I can sell my house. You don't happen to know of anyone that might be interested in it, do you?"

"As a matter of fact, I do. You know my daughter, Molly Ann. Well, her and young Pat Ravenwood are planning to get married, and I think they might be interested in it when you're of a mind to sell."

"Those two are going to get married! How wonderful! I know you and Susie are thrilled. That Pat is a fine young man, and Molly Ann's such a delightful young lady."

She was about to leave when she remembered Sam's question about her house. "My goodness, you got me so excited, I nearly forgot about the house. I'd love to talk to them about it."

She was nearly beside herself. "We haven't had a wedding in Pine Creek in goodness knows when. You'll have everybody in town there."

"And you'll invite them." Sam thought as he opened the door and stepped out on the porch with her.

"When could Molly Ann and Pat come by and look at the house. I know they'd like to see it. That goes for Susie and me too."

"Any time after today will be just fine. I just need some time to spruce it up a bit. I'll do that today, after I've had my coffee, of course."

As he turned to go back into the store, he realized that Susie was standing just inside with a grin on her face. "Well, Sam, that takes care of inviting folks to the wedding."

"I messed up again, huh?"

"Right," she said.

Pat was in town later in the day to talk to John Henry

about getting ordained. When their meeting was over, he left the church and went directly to the store to see Molly Ann. She saw him coming and ran to meet him.

After giving him with a hug, she said, "Let's go sit on the steps in front of the store and talk for a minute before we go inside."

He put his arm around her waist. "That's fine with me because there's something that I want to talk to you about."

She didn't let him continue. "Let me tell you this first. It's for certain that Mrs. Cochran does want to sell her house, and she said we could go by and see the inside any time. What do you think?"

"That kinda goes along with what I wanted to talk to you about."

"What are you talking about?"

"When we told our folks that we wanted to get married, I said there were two things that I would have to do before we got married. The first thing I would have to do is build a house and the second is get my ordination work done. Do you remember that?"

"I remember, and we also said it would take about two years to do both, but what are you leading up to?"

Excitedly, Pat continued, "I was thinking if we can manage to buy Mrs. Cochran's house, then why don't we just go ahead and get married. Of course, I would still have to work on my ordination, but I could do that after we're married. I'd have to get a job, too."

She jumped up, gave Pat a hug, and squealed, "I can't believe it! That is exactly what I wanted to talk to you about! Let's go inside and tell Mama and Daddy. Then, we'll take the horse and wagon and go out to your folk's house and tell them. The next thing will be to set a date for the wedding. I've been thinking about that, too."

After telling Sam and Susie about the change in wedding plans, Pat and Molly Ann, with Sam's help, hitched Sam's horse to the wagon. When they finished, Pat shook Sam's hand. Molly Ann gave her daddy a hug. Then, she and Pat climbed into the wagon and drove away toward the Ravenwood farm. They graciously rejected Sam's offer to accompany them this time.

When he went back inside the store, Susie greeted him with with raised eyebrows.

"I wish Dan had been here to see the expression on your face when they told us that they wanted to get married soon and not wait two years."

Smugly, he responded, "Why that didn't surprise me one bit. In fact, if the truth be told, it's a wonder to me that you hadn't already thought of it."

# 14

Pat, Molly Ann, and their two families, went to see the house on Wednesday afternoon before prayer meeting. When the tour was over, everybody gathered with Mrs. Cochran and her son, Joe, in the small sitting room. After a brief discussion, they agreed on the sale price, shook hands, and the deal was struck. There were no papers to sign. A hand shake was all that was necessary. The next morning, Mrs. Cochran and Joe met Pat, Dan and Sam at the bank in Dykesboro to finalize the sale. Pat signed the note with Dan and Sam co-signing with him. Mrs. Cochran signed the deed, gave it to Mr. Paul, the bank president. In return, she received a check from the bank for the prescribed amount. It was agreed that she would move out within a week and give the keys to Pat at the time she moved. The next step on the agenda would be the wedding, which would be far more complicated than buying a house.

On the way back to Pine Creek in Dan's two-horse wagon, nothing was said for a while. There was only an occasional snort from one of the horses.

Finally, Dan spoke, "You know, I think we made two real good decisions today."

That got Sam's attention. "What do you mean, two real good decisions? Did I miss something somewhere?"

"I mean it was a good decision to buy that house. That was the first thing. The second good decision we made was to leave the women folks at home to deal with all them wedding plans. Talk about complicated, there's no doubt about it. That's gonna be the most complicated wedding you've ever seen."

Sam agreed, "I'll say 'Amen' to that several times over." He turned back to Pat who was seated behind them with his legs hanging off the rear of the wagon. "Boy, you're mighty quiet back there. Whatcha thinking about? You ain't gone to sleep on us have you?'

"No, sir, Mr. Sam, I ain't asleep, not by a long shot. I was just thinking about how I'm gonna have to get me a real job to pay for that house I just bought."

Sam howled with laughter as Dan bristled, "What do you mean a real job. Just exactly what do you think farming is? You wait till I get you in the field in the morning about thirty minutes after sunup. I'll show you what a real job is."

Sam looked at Dan, "Tell me something, Dan, when are you gonna get a real job?"

Dan looked at him and smirked, "Maybe right after I knock yore rear end right off this wagon, you lazy no-good storekeeper. Then, you can walk home, if you're able. Of course, that would require a little energy, which you ain't got too much of."

Pat snickered, "There y'all go again. I'm just glad y'all are good friends else we might never get home, at least, not all of us."

"If y'all want to talk about something besides each other, y'all can talk about how I can make some money so I can pay back what I borrowed at the bank today. You know, both of y'all signed that note with me. Y'all are not forgetting about that, are you?"

Sam grinned at Dan. "That boy learns fast, don't he? You didn't raise no fool after all."

"I don't know, Sam. He's foolish enough to want to get married. Nothing against Molly Ann, you understand."

After traveling about a mile, they stopped their good-natured bantering and began to discuss the matter of Pat's employment. Although he had some rudimentary skills, he had never been employed anywhere except on the family farm.

71

The fact that Pine Creek was small and didn't offer many avenues of employment was another factor to be considered. The nearest town larger than Pine Creek was Dykesboro, eight miles to the north, so Pat's opportunities for employment were somewhat limited.

Finally, they came up with what they thought was a good plan. Pat would work on the farm with Dan through the week and share in the income of the farm. On Fridays and Saturdays, he would help out at Sam's general store. Any spare time that the three of them had would be devoted to work on the newly purchased house.

Sam looked back over his shoulder at Pat. "What do you think about that, Son?"

"I'm thinking that I didn't know marrying was gonna mean so much work. It's no wonder you two look so old and worn out."

"You watch yore mouth, boy."

The rest of the trip back to Pine Creek was fairly uneventful. When they pulled up in front of Sam's general store, Molly Ann rushed out, gave Pat a big hug, grabbed him by the hand and tugged him inside. "Let me show you what we did today while y'all were gone."

The three men followed Molly Ann into the store where Leona and Susie were busily discussing every detail of the upcoming wedding. On the counter in front of them were scraps of material for a wedding dress and a note pad filled with several pages of wedding plans.

"I told y'all this wedding was going to get complicated." Dan muttered to Sam and Pat.

"Good afternoon, y'all. I got word y'all wanted to see me about Pat and Molly Ann wanting to get married." It was John Henry who always seemed to have a flair for the dramatic.

After hugging Molly Ann, he shook hands with everyone else and said, "All right, tell me what y'all have planned for this big event."

Susie responded, "We would like for the wedding to be on June 16th. Are you free?"

"I'll be free. That wedding's more important than anything else in this town."

"That's wonderful. It will be at four o'clock in the afternoon. Afterwards, we will serve refreshments outside in the picnic area. If it's raining, we'll serve them inside. By the way, there's one thing that'll be a little different. Sam and I will stand with Molly Ann, and Dan and Leona will stand with Pat. Is that permissible?"

"Miss Susie, you can do anything you want to with the music, marching folks in, telling them where to stand, and marching them out, but once they get down at that altar in front of me, they're mine until I turn 'em loose. Of course, we'll have a rehearsal the night before. Now, do y'all have any more questions?"

Bowing slightly to the group, John Henry said, "Forgive me for rushing off, but I have an appointment to visit with Mr. and Mrs. Bream this afternoon."

Leona looked at Dan. "Who are Mr. and Mrs. Bream? I don't believe I've met them."

"They're fish, Leona! He's going fishing."

"Oh yeah ..." Still not quite getting it.

On the night of June 15th, the two families met with John Henry at the church for a brief rehearsal. Since Pine Creek was a small town, many of the townspeople were also in attendance.

Mrs. Cochran and her son were there, having driven down from Dykesboro in his buggy. It was the social event of the summer for the little town of Pine Creek.

Pat and Molly Ann were married the next day. The church was packed. Those who could not find seats stood outside and listened to the service through the church's open windows. The weather was beautiful and the refreshments were superb. An aura of happiness seemed to surround the newlyweds.

After the reception, Pat and Molly Ann were seated in a borrowed buggy ready to leave the church when Dan walked over and with a big smile on his face said to both of them,

"We're really happy for y'all." Then looking directly at Pat, he added, "See you at the barn in the morning about six thirty. We've got a lot of work to do."

Having said that, he walked away several steps, stopped, turned back to the bewildered newlyweds and said, "Ah, I was just funnin' y'all. Pat, you don't have to start yore real job until after dinner tomorrow. Y'all go on home now. I'll stop by your house as soon as we get through here and return that horse and buggy for you."

Half way back to the crowd, Leona met him. "Dan Ravenwood, what in the world have you been up to now?

"Nothing, Ma, I was just telling Pat and Molly Ann that I'd return the Johnsons' horse and buggy for them."

"Why Dan, that's real sweet of you."

"I thought so, too."

# 15

In spite of all the kidding about a real job, Pat had plenty of work to do. His days were consumed with work on the farm with Dan and work at Sam's store on the weekends. Many an evening was spent working on his ordination studies by lamplight. Of course, all of his studying was done with the encouragement of Molly Ann. She did not resent the time that he spent on his studies. To her, the diligence that he showed as he pursued his studies was just another measure of the man she loved. She even enjoyed those evenings when Brother John came by to review his work and give him some guidance as he began to preach. John Henry was good for Pat. Behind his "old country preacher" façade was an effective preacher and an excellent student of the Bible, and he genuinely cared for Pat.

Admittedly, Pat needed a lot of help in the area of his preaching. John Henry would occasionally call on Pat to speak at a Wednesday evening prayer service. Pat would fumble his way through the service and then go home knowing that he had not done a very good job. Molly Ann knew that his speaking ability left a lot to be desired, but she never made a negative comment about it. She believed with all her heart that if anyone could help Pat become a good preacher, it was Brother John. He was no seminary graduate. In fact he had gone through the same course of study that Pat was working on. He was proof that you did not have to be a seminary graduate to be a good preacher. John Henry could preach, and there was no question about the source of his inspiration. Molly Ann loved that old preacher. He had been her pastor as long as she could remember.

John Henry loved Molly Ann's sweet potato pie, so there was a freshly baked one on the table awaiting John Henry's session with Pat. As the time for John Henry's arrival drew near, Molly Ann began cutting the pie into six generous slices. As she made the last cut, three loud raps echoed from the front door. John Henry was right on time. Whether he was there for a meeting with Pat or for a slice of her sweet potato pie was somewhat debatable.

Pat answered the door. "Good evening, Brother John. Come on in. We were thinking it was about time for you to be here."

"Pat, Molly Ann, it's good to be in yore home. I see that pie over there. Lordy, I could smell it all the way down at the church!"

He was already headed for the table when Molly Ann said, "Would you like a slice while you and Pat talk, and how about a glass of cool milk to go with it?"

"Both would be fine. When you get the pie and milk, we'll sit at here the table, so we can eat while we talk."

After they were seated and John Henry had taken a bite of his pie, he said, "Patrick, let's talk about last week's message. What did you want to tell the people last week?"

"Let me get my Bible and my notes and I'll tell you," Brother John.

John Henry was eating his second slice of pie when Pat placed his Bible and notes on the table and began laboriously reading the scripture and his handwritten notes.

"That's what I thought," commented John Henry.

"What do you mean, Brother John?"

"You don't remember what you wanted the people to remember."

"But I had to write it down. It's too complicated to remember."

"Now, we're getting somewhere, Boy!"

John Henry took another bite of pie followed by a drink of milk.

Then, with a gentle, fatherly touch, John Henry reached over and put his hand on Pat's shoulder. "I know I've been kinda rough on you, Boy, but it's because I love you, and you are the first minister ever to come out of Pine Creek Church. I want to proud of you. The Church wants to be proud of you, and The Lord wants to be proud of you. Now I want you to speak at the prayer service a week from this coming Wednesday. That'll give you plenty of time to prepare. Here's what I want you to do to get ready."

"Let the Spirit help you choose yore scripture and and what the subject's gonna be. Then you write down in one sentence what you want the people to remember. Mind you, no more than one sentence. You get in your mind what you want the people to remember, and you drive it home like you was driving a nail into a board."

He shifted his chair a little closer to Pat and continued, "You see, preaching's sorta like driving a nail. If you ain't hitting the nail on the head, you ain't getting the job done. Do you hear what I'm saying Pat?"

"Yes, sir, I think I do, but I thought preaching was kinda like fishin'."

John Henry chuckled and said, "Either way, my boy, you still have to get the job done, Let me put it another way, and it's a good example of what I'm talking about. Molly Ann, you listen to this, because it involves you too."

She gave Pat a puzzled look.

He turned to Pat."Why did you marry Molly Ann?"

"Because I love her."

Turning to Molly Ann, "Why did you marry Pat?"

"Because I love him."

"There you go. Both of you hit the nail right on the head."

"Do you get my point? You see, you didn't have to write a book or quote the marriage vows. You didn't have to give yore family history. Y'all just said right up front that y'all got married because you love each other."

"That's kinda the way preaching is. Don't make it complicated. Pat, you remember that, and you'll do just fine."

Pat continued his work at the farm and at the general store. Both were time consuming, but not nearly as much as his studies. As if he didn't have enough to do, Molly Ann suggested that he take on another project.

"You want me to do what?"

Grinning, she said, "You heard what I said. It's time we added another room onto this house. You remember, we talked about how easy it would be when we first bought it."

"But why in this world would you want me to add a room onto the house? We had plenty of room when we got married, and there's still only two of ... ! It finally dawned on him. "You mean we're going to have a baby?"

Smugly she replied, "Can you think of any other good reason for adding a room?"

He was beside himself as he rushed across the room and gave her a big but gentle hug.

With the help of the two fathers, the room was added to accommodate the expected child.

The baby was born on July 19, in the second year of their marriage. They named him Daniel John Ravenwood II, after Pat's father. They called him "Johnny."

Pat responded to the birth of Johnny with a greater sense of urgency to complete his ordination requirements and to improve his preaching. His hard work paid off. He completed his ordination studies ahead of schedule and improved greatly in his preaching ability. John Henry was amazed and also very proud of his protégé. One Sunday morning when Pat was preaching at the Pine Creek Church, John Henry was in the pulpit during the first part of the service, but when it was time for Pat to preach, he came down from the pulpit and took a seat in the congregation right next to Dan, Pat's father.

During the sermon, John Henry became so enthralled by Pat's preaching ability that he leaned over to Dan and said in a not-too-soft stage whisper, "Dang! That boy's good!"

Pat was doing an excellent job, but after that comment, it took a while for the congregation to settle down and for Pat to regain his composure.

Oblivious to the chaos that he had created, John Henry continued his commentary on Pat's preaching, "You know, I taught him everything he knows about preaching." John Henry's holy pride had asserted itself once again.

The following June, Pat was ordained a minister in the Methodist Episcopal Church, South at the meeting of the South Georgia Conference in Macon. At the request of the three churches on the Pine Creek Circuit: Shiloh, Friendship and Pine Creek, Pat was assigned as an associate pastor to work with John Henry.

As Pat grew in his preaching ability, so did his responsibilities. He and John Henry were a team, and their teamwork was reflected in the growth of all three churches. Each year when the ministerial appointments were read at meeting of the South Georgia Annual Conference, there was never any question about who would be appointed to the Pine Creek Circuit. It was John Henry Troup and Daniel Patrick Ravenwood. John Henry couldn't have been prouder. Pat and Molly Ann couldn't have been happier. But an uneasy wind was blowing across the land, a wind that would be followed by a storm of chaos, hatred, and bloodshed. Pat Ravenwood would find himself right in the middle of it.

# 16

On the morning of April 12, 1861, the people of Charleston, South Carolina were awakened by the sound of cannon fire as Confederate forces, under the command of General Beauregard, began shelling Fort Sumter. The Union fort was located in Charleston's harbor. Its purpose was to guard the seaward approach to the city. Two days before the attack, Beauregard sent a message to the commandant of the fort requesting that he surrender. When the request was denied, Beauregard ordered the Confederates to launch their attack. There was little doubt about the outcome of the battle. The Union forces were outnumbered and outgunned. Their defeat was inevitable.

After thirty-four hours of intense shelling by the Confederates and with the fort's food supplies and ammunition running low, the commandant struck the American flag, ran up a white flag and surrendered the fort. The Civil War had begun. No one could have imagined the dire consequences that would follow.

Not a single life was lost inside the fort as a result of the Confederate bombardment. However, this bloodless battle marked the beginning of a war that would result in the deaths of 625,000 Americans. It would divide a country, turn state against state, family against family, and brother against brother. It would strike at the heart of cities, towns and villages in the North and especially in the South. The little town of Pine Creek would not escape its wrath or its heartache. The news that the South was at war came to Pine Creek by telegraph and then by the newspaper from Macon. Dan was in Sam's store when they heard the news.

With his face red with anger, Dan slammed his fist down on the counter. "I knew it! I knew it was going to happen. I've said all along that some hothead was gonna get us into a shooting war. Now it's happened. We've got ourselves in a damn war."

"Yep, you're right." Sam responded. "We've spent a lot of time working ourselves into this mess, but what did you expect? Even our own church split over the slavery issue. It's a sad state of affairs when churches can't work together."

Dan agreed and added, "We've let this slavery issue tear us apart."

Rapping his knuckles on the counter to emphasize his point, "Now if that ain't self- righteousness in the church, I don't know what is. It's just plain ole hypocrisy. Where are the peacemakers we're supposed to have in the church, and what about loving your neighbors? Has the church done forgot what the Bible teaches?"

Dan continued. "I know there are a lot of good folks in the church, and John Henry is a good man, and I believe he's God's man, but the way I see it, the higher up you go in the church the more political and hypocritical it gets."

"I agree with you, Dan. Sometimes it seems like the Lord has to get his work done in spite of the church, don't it?"

A half a mile down the road at Otto's Bar, the news of the war was received with a mixture of anger, bar room rhetoric, and alcohol-enhanced bravado. Tom Gunter had a Walker Colt pistol tucked in his belt. Zeke Thompson stood beside him with a double-barreled shotgun cradled in his arms.

"They want to fight us, by God we're ready." Tom asserted, hitching up his pants from beneath his overhanging gut.

"Dang right we are. Ole Betsy here has a double load of buckshot just waiting for a Yankee target," Zeke added.

"I'm worried about what might happen to our women and children," muttered Lonzo Brantley. "Who's gonna protect them if we're off somewhere fighting Yanks?"

"Hell, Lonzo, we won't be gone thirty days," chided Tom Gunter.

Big Jake Sizemore bellowed, "I tell you what I think we ought to do. We ought to march right into Washington and blow them Yankee politicians to kingdom come."

An entirely different mood prevailed at the Pine Creek Methodist Church that night. John Henry had called his flock together to pray for peace and a quick and just resolution to the war.

It was at this meeting that Pat, with Molly Ann and Johnny at his side, announced that he was planning to enlist as a chaplain in the Army of the Confederacy.

John Henry spoke to the crowd. "Today, I spent most of the afternoon with Pat and Molly Ann. We talked and prayed about this decision Pat has made. You know how I feel about Pat.

He's like a son to me, and I hate to see him leave his work here at Pine Creek. You also know how I feel about killing other people, but our young men who are at war need spiritual comfort and guidance. If I had a son fighting in this war that we've gotten ourselves into, I'd want somebody like Pat to be his chaplain, so I agree with his decision. Molly Ann agrees with it, but in order for Pat to enlist as a chaplain, he'll need the approval of the three churches on the Pine Creek Circuit as well as the presiding elder and the bishop. Therefore, I am announcing that a church conference will be held one week from this coming Sunday right after our morning service. The purpose of that meeting will be to give our approval for Pat to serve as a chaplain in the Army. I'll see that the other churches on the circuit are invited."

# 17

The church conference convened with John Henry presiding. After the purpose of the conference was stated, a motion to approve Pat's enlistment as a chaplain was made and seconded. John Henry opened the floor for discussion. There was a brief period of silence, and he was about to call for the vote when Jonas Dunlap stood.

"Now just hold on a minute. Let's not rush into this thing. I like Pat as much as any you, and I want it understood that what I'm about to say is not about Pat. I'm just concerned that we are mixing the church with politics. If we approve Pat to become a chaplain, are we saying we approve of a war where a lot of folks are gonna get kilt?"

Without waiting to be recognized, Josh Taylor, Sunday School Superintendent, spoke to the crowd, "I don't like politics in the church any more than you do, Brother Jonas, but like it or not, it's there.

However, we're not talking politics this morning. We're talking about meeting the spiritual needs of men in uniform. If a soldier had come here to worship with us this morning, would we have denied him that privilege? Of course we wouldn't. If we wouldn't deny a soldier the privilege of worshiping with us in our church, then why should we deny him the privilege of hearing the Gospel on the battlefield? Let's not forget that we are here for one purpose and that's to approve Pat going into a new ministry."

"Amen!" The congregation responded in unison. John Henry recognized Dan Ravenwood. "Y'all know how I feel about the church and politics, so I'm with Brother Jonas on that. Y'all also know how I feel about slavery. I believe it's wrong, and I don't believe our country ought to be divided over it. What's more, I don't believe God's church ought to be divided. Y'all know Pat's our only child and we love him. Leona and me don't want him to leave home, but if this is the way he wants to spread God's word, then I'm all for him."

Jonas Dunlap immediately sprang to his feet, "What's good enough for Dan Ravenwood is good enough for me. I say let's vote and let's make it unanimous!" And so it was that Pat was approved for the chaplaincy by the Pine Creek Circuit, the Presiding Elder of the Macon District and the Bishop of the South Georgia Conference.

Two weeks later, two Confederate soldiers, one a lieutenant and the other a sergeant, rode into Pine Creek. They were following a recruiting schedule that had been printed in the Macon newspaper. They were recruiting volunteers to serve in the 27th Georgia Infantry Regiment of the Confederate Army of Tennessee. The lieutenant spoke to Will Emory at the railroad station and received permission to conduct their recruiting on the loading dock of the railroad station. As soon as Will provided them with a table and two chairs, the lieutenant and the sergeant began processing the nineteen young men who had lined up in front of the table. All but one of the enthusiastic volunteers had been processed when Pat arrived.

The braggarts from Otto's Bar were nowhere to be seen.

When the last man was signed up, Pat handed the sergeant his authorization papers from the church.

"What's this?" asked the sergeant.

"I want to volunteer as a chaplain, and that's the authorization from my church which shows that the church approves of what I'm doing. I had understood that it was needed in order to enter the chaplaincy."

The lieutenant reached over the sergeant's shoulder and took Pat's authorization papers. "Sergeant, I'm familiar with that, so I'll sign the Reverend up. You take care of these two men that just walked up."

The sergeant acknowledged the two newcomers with, "State your names please."

"Jud Cofer," responded the first..

"Deke Bracewell," added the second.

Once the enlistment papers were completed, the lieutenant addressed all the new recruits. "Welcome to the Army of the Confederacy, gentlemen. Be here at the station one week from today. You will board the noonday train for Macon, where you will join your assigned units."

Turning to Pat, he said, "Welcome aboard, Chaplain. We're going to need your prayers."

As a chaplain in the Confederate Army, Pat would receive no special training, nor would he be provided with any ministerial supplies. He would have no direct ministerial or military supervision. However, he was indirectly responsible to the commanding officer of the unit to which he was assigned. In Pat's case, this officer was the company commander.

Pat would have no rank, nor would he wear a uniform. He would be paid approximately half the salary of a first lieutenant when funds were available. Chaplains in higher positions were paid more. Standards for the chaplaincy in the Confederacy varied. To be a chaplain, all one had to do was meet certain standards within one's own denomination.

Under the strict tutelage of his pastor, John Henry Troup, Pat had become an ordained minister in the Methodist Episcopal Church, South. With the church's authorization, he was now a chaplain and would report for duty in one week.

Early on the morning of his departure date, Dan and Leona were at Pat's house.

Molly Ann was teary. Johnny was fussy and clinging to Pat. When Pat got a chance to speak to Dan alone, he said, "Did you get everything?"

"Yep, everything we talked about. It's over at Sam's

house now. They're waiting on us to come over."

Pat grabbed an apple from the kitchen table, stuck it in his pocket and then reached down and grabbed Johnny's hand. "Come on, Little Buddy, let's go over and see your granddaddy Sam and your grandma Susie."

When they arrived, Sam and Susie greeted them with hugs. With Johnny still clinging to him, Pat led the procession of the three families through the house and out to the back yard.

There tied to a post was a beautiful blaze-faced gelding with four white stocking feet.

Johnny was totally bewildered."That's not Granddaddy Sam's horse!"

"Nope, he sure isn't." Pat said as he took the apple from his pocket and quartered it.

"He's your horse. Now take these apple slices over there and make friends with him. His name is Stormy, and I think he likes you."

Johnny was apprehensive at first, but pretty soon he was all giggles as Stormy nuzzled him in search of more apples.

"My very own horse," he said.

"He sure is, Son, and you're going to have to take care of him while I'm gone. I know you'll do a good job. Now, listen to me, Johnny. He's going to spend most of his time out at Granddaddy Dan's farm where he'll have plenty of room to run and frolic, but your mama will see that y'all get to spend a lot of time together."

Nearly everyone in town was at the depot to see the Confederate volunteers to depart from Pine Creek. As the train pulled into the station and squealed to a stop, many of the volunteers eagerly jumped aboard. Pat was is no hurry to leave. He continued to hold Molly Ann and Johnny in his arms until the conductor made his last "All aboard!" call. Only then, did he climb on board.

As the train began to inch forward, Molly Ann stood apart

86

from the rest of the crowd. She could see Pat waving from an open window of the last passenger car. Totally oblivious to the engine's billowing smoke and soot, she returned Pat's waves until the train was out of sight, then she cried.

# 18

It was in the fall of '64 that John Henry Troup stomped into McDaniel's store. He was a man on a mission. It was a cool morning outside, and John Henry knew that Sam McDaniel always had a good pot of coffee on the pot-bellied stove in the rear part of the store.

"Morning Sam, Susie, and good morning to you, Miss Molly Ann. Almost didn't see you  over there behind the counter. How y'all doing?"

"I guess we're doing as as well as could be expected under the circumstances." said Sam as he poured John Henry a cup of coffee and one for himself. "You know we haven't heard a word from Pat since he wrote that he had been captured. Let's see now, when did we get that letter? Susie, do you remember when we got that last letter from Pat?"

"It was the second week in August, and we haven't heard a word since then. All we know is that after he was captured, he was taken to someplace called Clonnerville. That's all we've heard. It looks like somebody would tell us something."

"We don't know what to do, Reverend." Molly Ann said as she dabbed her eyes with the corner of her apron.

"I write him two or three times a week. I even sent him a picture of me, but I never hear anything back from him. He was always so good to write, but now I never hear anything from'im. I try not to think about it, but something's got to be wrong. I know he'd write if he could."

John Henry reached out and tenderly took Molly Ann's hands in his. "Now, now, Molly Ann, don't you go thinking such thoughts. Pat'll find a way back home to you. You know he's kinda special to me ever since he walked down that aisle at church and told me he wanted to be a preacher. He was just a good ole farm boy with no education. Of course, you know what I told him Molly Ann. You was there and heard ever word of what I said."

Susie rolled her eyes at Sam whose only response was to take another sip from his coffee cup. Molly Ann managed a trace of a smile. She had heard the story many times, but she didn't mind hearing it again. It brought back fond memories of Pat.

John Henry took a slurp of his coffee, set the cup down on the counter, and began to repeat his story. "I said to him, 'Boy, you may have religion, but you still got a whole bunch of studying to do 'cause you ain't got no education.' Well, danged if he didn't set his mind to studyin' and become an ordained Methodist preacher."

"Now, y'all know he didn't go off to school at some place like that Methodist school up there at Oxford, Georgia or that Baptist school in Macon. No sir. He took that church correspondence courses, just like I did. I'm telling you the straight of it. Them correspondence courses is a whole lot harder'n sitting there in some classroom where all you hafta to do is 'gurgitate back whatever the teacher dishes out. Yes, sir, old Pat jumped on it like a dog on a pork chop. Course he had a little help from me from time to time. Now, the reason I'm tellin' you all this is to remind you that Pat's got gumption. That boy's gonna come home."

"Now, let's get back to the subject of finding out something about Pat. Tell you what I'm gonna do. I'm gonna leave right now and go straight to the telegraph office and send a telegram to the pastor of the Clonnerville Methodist Church." He paused long enough to pour himself another cup of coffee. "I'll ask him to go over to the prison and see what he can find out something about Pat. Of course, a lot depends on whether or not the telegraph lines are are still up and working, but I'll let y'all know just as soon's I hear anything."

In spite of his seemingly cheerful mood, John Henry was worried. He knew that there was a good chance Pat would never come back home. The war was not going well for the South. Atlanta had fallen. That meant that Union forces were less than a hundred fifty miles north of Pine Creek. The last word they had from Pat was that he was in Clonnerville Prison Camp north of Atlanta. That hardly made any difference so far as his survival was concerned. There was little difference in the mortality rate of soldiers in prison and those on the battlefield. It was merely a question of dying in a prison camp or dying on the battlefield. While there might be little hope for Pat's survival, hope was something John Henry believed in.

He finished his coffee and was about to walk out the door when he stopped, turned, smiled, and said, "By the way, that was some mighty good coffee. The only thing that would have improved it is one of Miss Molly Ann's sweet potato pies. I'll see y'all later." With his coat tail flying in the breeze, he was at the telegraph office in a matter of minutes.

"Brother Will, do you have time to send a telegram for me before you go to dinner?"

"I'll do my best. You know how it is. Service sorta comes and goes. The Yankees have been playing hell with the lines lately, so I never know when the system is gonna work."

"Well, let's give it a try. Gimme one of them pads over there so I can write it out for you. Of course, the way I write, I may have to read for you."

Will pitched a pad and a pencil up on the counter and John Henry began to write, wondering if it was all in vain.

*To: Pastor Clonnerville Methodist Episcopal*
*Church South Clonnerville, Georgia*
*Please check Clonnerville POW Camp for*

*Chaplain Patrick Ravenwood, a captured Confeder-*
*ate chaplain. Advise me of status. Rev. John Henry*
*Troup, Esq. Pine Creek Methodist Episcopal Church,*
*South Pine Creek, Georgia*

"While you're sendin', Brother Will, send a copy of that same message to the commander of the Clonnerville Prisoner of War Camp. Maybe we can get some information from him. I appreciate you doin' that. Now, if you'll figure up how much I owe you for both of'em, I'll pay up and be on my way. I know yore missus and mine's prob'ly waitin' dinner on us."

"John Henry, for this, you don't owe me anything, not one penny. I'm glad to do it, and I'll be sure to let you know if and when I hear something."

"Bless you, Brother! Bless you!" And John Henry was on his way.

At closing time, there was still no response to John Henry's telegrams. Finally, Will pulled down the shades and locked the door from the inside. To the casual observer, it would appear that the office was closed and that Will Emory had gone home for the day, but Will had watched Pat and Molly Ann grow up. If there was an answer to John Henry's telegrams, he wanted to be there when it came in. A little after nine o'clock in the evening, he gave up and went home with nothing to report to John Henry.

He had been at work about a half an hour the next morning when his equipment chattered out a message from the commandant of the prison where Pat was being held. There was also a message from the Methodist minister in Clonnerville. Both confirmed that Pat was alive.

Will Emory tore out of the telegraph office like a house afire yelling to the top of his lungs, "PAT RAVENWOOD'S ALIVE!"

John Henry and Will both reached Sam's store at about

the same time. Will shoved the telegrams into John Henry's hands urging him to hurry and tell Molly Ann the good news. But John Henry just shoved him through the door and on into the store. With a big grin on his face he said, "You tell'em, Will. You've told everybody else in town, so you might as well tell these folks too."

Molly Ann could hardly believe what she was hearing. She immediately grabbed John Henry and gave him a big hug. Then, she hugged Will Emory and thanked him several times for the good news.

Suddenly she cried out, "Johnny! Nobody's told Johnny!"

She rushed out the front door of the store and ran all the way to the school. Miss McCurdy was teaching math when Molly Ann burst through the door of the one-room school and screamed, "Johnny! Your daddy's alive!"

The entire class erupted in a loud, chaotic cheer led by the normally stoic Miss McCurdy!

# 19

At Clonnerville Prison, there was no euphoria in Warehouse B. Winter was rapidly approaching, and the nights were already unseasonably cold. Inside, the prisoners had no blankets, nor was there any heat in any of the buildings. The prisoners had been promised blankets and stoves but neither had materialized. Pat wondered how much Sergeant Hagan had to do with that situation. As it turned out, Hagan had nothing to do with it. Colonel Randolph had requested blankets and heaters in preparation for the coming winter, but the Union supply depot had simply failed to ship them on time. When succeeding requests were either denied or ignored, Randolph became furious and vowed to do something about the situation. His prisoners were the enemy, but they were also human beings and deserved to be treated as such.

Determined to remedy the situation, Colonel Randolph, accompanied by Lieutenant Pringle and two armed guards, rode into Clonnerville seeking help from the people of Clonnerville. His first stop was to visit Otis Clonner, the mayor of Clonnerville and also the owner of the local lumber and grain warehouse. It was his cousin, Purvis, who had sold the three cotton warehouses to Union Forces for use as a prison to house Confederate captives.

The Colonel tied his horse to a hitching post and walked into the warehouse accompanied by Lieutenant Pringle. "Good morning, Mr. Mayor."

"Colonel," nodded Clonner as he warmed himself in front of a small wood-burning stove in his makeshift office.

"Mr. Mayor, I wonder if I could speak with you privately

on a matter of extreme importance."

"You can say your piece right here, Colonel."

"As you wish, I'll get right to the point. I have approximately seven hundred fifty Confederates in Clonnerville Prison. Due to the bungling of our military supply post, they have no blankets nor do they have any heat. They are beginning to suffer from the cold weather that is upon us. So I am requesting that you ask the town council and the citizens of Clonnerville to do whatever they can to provide some comfort for these prisoners."

"I ain't doing nothing to help none of you blue bellies."

"Clonner, these are men who fought for the Confederacy. Do you mean to tell me that you are not willing to help them? You are much less a man than I thought. I could requisition the needed items from the citizens, but I don't want to do that. I'm asking for help."

"You heard me right! Ain't no gimpy, one-armed Yankee devil gonna come in here and make me do anything, no matter how much you threaten and insult me."

"Lieutenant Pringle, would you leave us alone for a moment."

"Yes, sir, Colonel!"

The instant the warehouse door closed behind Pringle, the Colonel reached across his body, unsnapped his holster and pulled out his Remington revolver. Clonner had taken one step toward his desk when he heard the distinctive cocking of the Colonel's weapon.

The authoritative resolve of a battlefield commander was about to surface. "Clonner, I have not even begun to insult you or threaten you, but to be sure that you are not disappointed, you listen carefully, you worthless bucket of hog slop."

Colonel Randolph continued, "If you so much as move a muscle toward that desk of yours. I will put a bullet right between your eyes. Furthermore, since we don't have blankets for the prisoners, you're going to provide some of your burlap grain bags as a substitute, and you're going to donate lumber so that we can plug up the air leaks in those buildings."

"But, Colonel …!"

"Clonner, I'm not through. When I get back to the compound, I'm going to send two wagons here to pick up what you are going to donate so generously. The first wagon will be empty. That's the one in which you will load the material for the compound. The second will contain eight of the most physically fit Confederate prisoners in the compound. They will have been told that you initially refused to do anything to help them, so I would advise you to be very gracious and cooperative toward them.".

"Do you understand me, Mr. Mayor?".

His honor nodded meekly

"Lieutenant, get in here!"

Pringle immediately sprang through the door with his own Remington .44 in his hand, cocked and ready.

"You won't need that, Lieutenant. Mr. Mayor was just about to give you a list of things he's going to donate to the compound."

"But while you're in here, Lieutenant, you might as well go to Clonner's desk and remove whatever weapon he might be tempted to use.

Pringle examined the contents of the desk and replied, "All he's got is an old pepperbox pistol, Sir. What shall I do with it?"

"Bring it with us. I wouldn't want the man to get hurt."

From Clonner's lumber and grain business, Colonel Randolph went to the town's two general stores and also to the three churches. They all offered to do whatever they could to help the prisoners cope with the adverse weather conditions. Although the Colonel was generally pleased with their response, he was taken aback when he learned that Sergeant Hagan was in one of the stores the week before with an unauthorized requisition for food.

95

As they rode back to the compound, the Colonel turned in his saddle toward Pringle.

"Lieutenant, would you have shot Clonner?"

"That would've been for him to find out, Sir."

"Can you actually shoot that gun you're carrying on your hip?"

"Yes, sir, I won first place in marksmanship at the Point, Sir, Class of '59, although the .44 caliber I was shooting then did seem to shoot just a tad high."

The Colonel didn't reply, but as they rode he wondered if there might be qualities in Pringle that he had missed.

"Perhaps now is a good time to find out," he said to himself.

As they neared the compound, he said, "Lieutenant, I want you to take four of our best men and go tell Hagan that he is relieved of his stripes and confined to his quarters for thirty days for his unauthorized requisition of food from one of the merchants in town."

"Furthermore," continued the Colonel, "See to it that the heater in his quarters is removed and placed in warehouse B near the wounded captives. It is to remain there permanently. Notice that I said permanently, Lieutenant."

"Yes, sir, I'll see to it right away, Sir."

Within the hour, Pringle laid Hagan's stripes on the Colonel's desk. The first thing the Colonel saw was that the knuckles on both his hands were bruised. Then he saw that Pringle's top lip was slightly puffy and one cheek showed a hint of discoloration.

"What happened, Pringle?"

"Hagan didn't want to give up his stripes, Sir."

"You mean that it took you and four guards to take his stripes?"

"The guards didn't get involved, Sir. I took 'em off myself."

"Where is Hagan now?"

"The guards took him to see Doc Clayton to get him patched up. He was doing kind of poorly when I removed his stripes."

"How in the world did you manage that, Lieutenant?"

"I was school champion in boxing at the Point, Sir, Class of '59."

"Where did you stand in your class when you graduated? You were first, I presume, in the Class of '59 of course."

"I was last, Sir."

"Would you be kind enough to explain that to me?"

"I was first place with the girls, Sir."

The Colonel allowed a slight smile on his face. "Lieutenant Pringle, we just might make a soldier out of you yet."

"I hope it'll be without the help of my Uncle, the Senator, Sir."

"You're dismissed, Pringle. Now go get cleaned up."

Salutes were exchanged and Pringle departed leaving a slightly bemused Colonel Randolph still seated at his desk.

After a moment, he said aloud, "Yes, sir, we just might make a soldier out of you yet and perhaps even a good officer."

News of the war was hard to come by for the Confederates in Clonnerville Prison, but the the bits of information that they managed to glean from the guards made it clear the Confederacy was doomed. Atlanta surrendered to Union forces on September 2nd. Following the surrender, Sherman sacked the town, burning most of the public buildings even though city officials pleaded with him not to do so. On November 14, he began burning his way to Savannah.

When the Union supply train finally arrived in Clonnerville, it delivered the long-awaited supplies for the prison. The shipment consisted of burlap bags filled with giant navy beans, bags of corn meal, and numerous slabs of salt pork. In addition to the food there were three wood-burning stoves and four hundred blankets for the approximately seven hundred fifty prisoners.

There are times when the quality of a soldier is measured not by his bravery but by his ingenuity in dealing with the flawed wisdom of the army. When Colonel Randolph learned of the blanket situation, he ordered that each blanket be split into two pieces which created more than enough blankets for the seven hundred fifty prisoners.

After the blankets were distributed to the prisoners, Pat called Jud and Deke to one side and gave them some up-to-date news.

"I have some interesting news for you. First of all, Hagan will return to his regular duties tomorrow, so that means that things will be rough for us. I'm sure he'll be meaner than ever, but let's remember not to let him get the best of us."

"The second thing is, Colonel Randolph sent word by Sergeant Nelson that we will have some kind of dinner on what he's calling a Day of Thanksgiving."

"Is that some sort of special holiday, Chaplain?" Jud asked. "I ain't never heard of it before."

Pat replied, "I asked the Sergeant Nelson about that. He said that in '63 President Lincoln set aside the last Thursday in November as a national Day of Thanksgiving for the Union. So the Colonel has picked that day for the guards and prisoners to eat together. I don't know what we'll eat. It probably won't be nò more than beans and salt pork, but it's bound to be better than that slop that Hagan and his crew have been serving."

"Anything'll beat that. No matter what day it is." quipped Jud.

Deke grinned and nodded in agreement.

Pat continued. "I think it's pretty well guaranteed to be better. I also heard that the colonel has posted an order stating that the guards will be eating the same thing as the prisoners.

I also understand that he will eat with the prisoners in one of the three warehouses. Nobody knows which as of right now."

Jud elbowed Deke in the ribs. "Man! That colonel's on a tear lately, ain't he?"

"Yeah, and from what I hear that Lieutenant put a Saturday night bar room whuppin' on ole Sarge." Deke said as he feigned extreme discomfort in the ribs.

As promised, the Day of Thanksgiving meal was served with guards and prisoners sharing the same fare, which consisted of a small serving of beans, a piece of cornbread and a small slice of salt pork. It was no surprise that the Colonel chose to eat with the prisoners in Warehouse B. It was how he and the guards ate that surprised everyone.

"Where're we gonna sit?" growled Hagan.

"That's a good question, Sergeant. Since there are no chairs, it looks like we'll have to sit on the floor. At that the Colonel, in spite of his gimpy leg, took a seat on the hardened dirt floor.

Lieutenant Pringle handed the Colonel his plate, turned to Hagan and pointed to the floor.

"May I help you to your seat, Sergeant?"

The Colonel shot Pringle a sharp "don't push it" look which Pringle acknowledged with an expressionless nod. In the meantime, Pat enjoyed what was, under the circumstances, an excellent meal. Meanwhile Jud and Deke cleaned their plates and choked back any evidence of mirth at the sergeant's misery.

As the days plodded on toward Christmas, things returned to normal inside the prison compound. Hagan regained his stripes and returned to his old ways, needing little or no excuse to vent his feelings on the prisoners in Warehouse B.

The lack of food remained a problem in spite of the efforts of Colonel Randolph. Union supply trains were still unreliable. The availability of supplies at supply depots was unpredictable. His telegrams requesting food were usually answered with a curt, "Supplies unavailable due to needs of Union troops who are still in combat."

Three more prisoners died and were buried on the cold hillside cemetery. There was little change at Clonnerville Prison except the weather, which changed from cold to colder. Those prisoners who were able to move around were afraid to venture outside because the deadline was covered with snow.

Pat, Jud, and Deke would spend Christmas in prison. General Sherman and his army would spend Christmas in the port city of Savannah. From Atlanta to Savannah, the victims of Sherman's march to the sea would spend Christmas cold and hungry.

# 20

Christmas was hardly a festive occasion in Pine Creek. The young men of the community simply were not there. They were at war. Some were in combat, others were in prisoner of war camps, and others were in graves, many of which were unmarked and in unknown places.

History provides no accurate records of the size of the Confederate army. It was estimated to be about 750,000. Of that number, an estimated 250,000 died. Approximately 195,000 were wounded. The exact numbers are unknown. Accurate records are difficult to maintain in the heat of battle and are of little use to the defeated. Battlefield casualties are of no comfort to the bereaved on either side.

The main street in Pine Creek presented a vivid commentary on the war between the North and the South. From the east came those fleeing from the destruction left by Sherman's march to the sea. They came with expressionless, vacant stares. It could not be said that they were seeking hope. They had forgotten what hope was. They were simply trying to flee from the horror of a war that had cost them everything. There was nothing to go back to and nothing to go to.

The slaves who remained in the wake of Sherman's march to the sea were facing equally hard times. Like their former owners, they found themselves homeless and bewildered. They had heard reports that Mr. Lincoln's Army was coming to set them free. When General Sherman's army appeared, they were indeed set free from their original owners. Yet, at the discretion of Union commanders, able-bodied slaves could be pressed into service according to the needs of a particular unit. Others were simply left to fend for themselves.

In Pine Creek, the people still had their homes. Ironically, they could thank Sherman for that. After a careful study of all the resources available to him, he had determined that an army that was going to live off the land needed to go where the land was most productive. The rich river bottoms and the presence of a number of large plantations to the east of Pine Creek were the deciding factors. Pine Creek was spared, but they still felt the impact of war.

If there was an element of hope in Pine Creek, it was to be found in the person of one John Henry Troup. He was a source of inspiration, information, comfort, and compassion. Unfortunately, he was often called on to be the bearer of tragic news. That was the purpose of his visit to the home of Cliff and Faye Johnson. He had learned that their son, Billy, had died in Clonnerville Prison.

As he neared the home of the Johnsons, he was driven more by sheer determination than devotion to his calling. The war was taking its toll on John Henry, and it was beginning to show. Trying to brace himself for the task that lay before him, he stepped up on the porch of the home of Billy's parents, and rapped on the door three times.

Cliff opened the door. "Why, hello, John Henry, it's good to see you. Come on in."

"Faye!" he called, "John Henry is here."

She came from the kitchen wiping her hands on her apron. "Gracious me, Cliff, where are your manners. Let Brother John sit down. Don't let him just stand there.

"Brother John, could I get you a cup of coffee?" She continued.

"No thank you, Miss Faye. Please have a seat. I need to talk to y'all."

She knotted her apron up in her hands as she sat down. "It's about Billy isn't it?"

"Yes, ma'am, I'm afraid it is. There's no easy way to say this, but I've come to tell you that Billy died two days ago in Clonnerville Prison. If it's any comfort to you, Pat conducted his funeral. In fact Pat was with him when he died. I thought you'd want to know that Billy was not alone. A friend was there with him."

After John Henry had spent some time trying to comfort the distraught parents, Cliff walked John Henry to the door. "Thank you for coming by John Henry. If we had to hear that kind of news, we'd rather hear it from you than anybody else. We know you care. We hadn't heard from him in so long. I guess we knew deep down inside it would turn out this way."

Fighting back the tears, Cliff hugged John Henry. "We'll see you in church Sunday, Brother John. We'll need to be there."

When he was out of sight of the Johnson home, John Henry took his handkerchief out of the breast pocket of his coat, wiped his eyes, and hurried on to Sam's general store. There were no customers in the store when he arrived. He was thankful for that. Susie and Molly Ann were there with Sam. Little Johnny was in school. John Henry didn't waste any time getting to the point. "Susie and Molly Ann, I need y'all to get some folks from the church to go over and see about Cliff and Faye. I just told them that Billy was dead. He died at Clonnerville Prison."

They were shocked at the news. Susie was the first to speak. "I don't know what I can do, but I'll get over there right now."

Molly Ann came from behind the counter. "I'm going too, Mama."

"No, I need you to get some folks from the church to take some food over there, and while you're out, get in touch with Josh Taylor. Ask him to get some folks to sit with the Johnsons tonight."

In those days and in years to come, it was the custom for

103

people to sit all night with the grieving family. It was a country way of saying to the family that they were not alone.

After the two women left, John Henry, with his shoulders sagging, leaned against the counter. His fatigue was clearly evident.

Sam reached over and put a hand on his shoulder. "You look like you could use a cup of coffee. I was just about to pour a cup for myself."

"I sure could use one, Sam, and fix it like you fix yours."

After Sam had poured a little whiskey in both cups, he added coffee then handed a cup to John Henry. "They're just alike, John Henry."

"I appreciate it, Sam."

Sam raised his cup and acknowledged John Henry's gratitude, "Anytime, old friend."

"By the way," Sam continued, "How did you find out about Billy?"

"By telegram from the Methodist preacher in Clonnerville. He said he had taken some clothing and food to the prison. By chance, he encountered Pat who was about to conduct Billy's funeral. Pat told him to get word to me that Billy had died. Why did you ask how I knew?"

"Because Will Emory was in here just a few minutes ago and said he couldn't reach anybody by telegraph. Evidently your telegram about Billy dying must have been the last one that Will received. It looks like the whole system is down again."

That afternoon, John Henry saddled up his circuit riding horse, Rambler, and set out to call on some folks in the Shiloh and Friendship churches. With Pat in the chaplaincy, John Henry had sole responsibility for all three churches on the Pine Creek Circuit. It was an eight-mile ride to Shiloh. From there he would ride on to Friendship, spend the night with some church members and return to Pine Creek the following day.

He was about four miles out of Pine Creek and was dozing in the saddle when he sensed that Rambler had stopped and was very skittish. Just barely cracking his eyes, John Henry saw two men in the road in front of him. One was lying down, the other was kneeling over him.

John Henry spoke to the kneeling man. "What's going on here?"

The kneeler responded, "Mister, my buddy has done took sick. Could you help me out?"

Both men wore tattered Confederate uniforms, and each had a Springfield rifle. John Henry thought it strange that the sick man had a cocked rifle across his belly.

As the kneeler rose with his cocked rifle in his hand, he found himself looking at the business end of John Henry's Walker Colt.

"Sonny Boy," John Henry said, "that trick ain't worked since Blue was a pup. Now you just ease that hammer down and tell yore sick buddy to do the same with his gun."

The man on the ground didn't move.

"Gentlemen, the name's John Henry Troup. I'm pastor of Pine Creek Methodist Church. I do healing services and I also do funerals. Now either that sickly fellow gets healed in a hurry and lets the hammer down on that gun real slow and careful-like or we gonna have us two funerals. I'm available for either one right now. What's it gonna be?"

Slowly and deliberately, the man lying on the ground lowered the hammer on his Springfield and sat up. "Reverend, we wus just on our way home from the war, and we thought we'd have a little fun with you. We didn't mean no harm."

"Don't know that I believe that, Sonny. I think y'all are deserters and you ain't on the road home. Y'all are on the road to perdition, and I couldn't sleep tonight if I didn't try to change yore wicked ways."

"You that was kneeling, you take both them guns by the business end of the barrel, one in each hand and you walk

105

over here to my right and lean'em against that tree. And you, Lazarus, since you've been raised up, you walk with him so I can keep and eye on the both of you. Lazarus, you keep your hands up high. I won't shoot a man who lifts his hands to the heavens, but if you let'em down or even think about it, I'll blow the hell out of you. Now move!"

"Please don't shoot us, Reverend. All we want to do is go home."

"Oh, I ain't gonna shoot you. We gonna have us a baptizing, an old-fashioned Baptist baptizing. You boys walk right out in the middle of that creek over there."

"But Reverend, it's freezing. That water's cold."

"And Hell's hot. Now make your choice. By the way, since you need to keep your powder dry, hand me those shot pouches and powder horns."

John Henry watched as the young culprits waded out toward the middle of the creek. "When the water is deep enough, I want y'all to start ducking each other, and don't stop until you can't hear me singing no more. Then Y'all can come out on the creek bank. By the way, you better keep in mind that y'all ain't Baptists until they vote you in."

He then nudged Rambler over to the tree where the rifles were. With an eye still on the two in the creek, John Henry picked up the rifles and rode off singing at the top of his voice.

*Amazing Grace, how sweet the sound,*
*That saved a wretch like me.*
*I once was lost, but now am found,*
*Was blind, but now I see.*   -John Newton-1835

When the two hooligans could no longer hear John Henry, they sloshed out of the creek.

Shivering, the kneeler said to Lazarus, "That old coot would have shot both of us dead."

106

"Ain't no doubt in my mind." said Lazarus. "He would have shot us, and then preached our funerals right here on the creek bank. I tell ya sumpin' else. I done come of a mind that I ain't cut out to be no road agent."

Back in town Johnny walked into Sam's store. "Grandpa Sam, have you seen mama?"

"She'll be back in a little while. She's helping your grandma over at the Johnsons.

They just got word that Billy died. He was at the same prison where your daddy is."

"Is my daddy all right?"

"As far as we know. We really haven't heard anything about him other than that he conducted Billy's funeral."

"Grandpa Sam, is he ever coming home?"

"We all hope so, Son, and when he does come home, it'll be a happy time here, won't it.""Yeah! Me and him can go riding together, just the two of us. I'll ride Stormy and he could ride ... Could he ride your horse, Grandpa?"

"He sure could."

# 21

Before the war, Pine Creek had been a peaceful little settlement. People went about their daily routines with little concern for their safety and the security of their homes. There was no crime to speak of. Occasionally a watermelon or a stalk of sugar cane would go missing from a farmer's field. Most folk responded to these shenanigans with a "boys will be boys" attitude.

There were no abandoned children, no neglected elderly people, and no one went hungry.

People looked after themselves and their loved ones and kept a watchful eye on their children and those of their neighbors. No one ever bothered to lock their doors. There was no need to. It was that kind of community. There were a few scuffles at Otto's Bar, but they were usually settled quickly by Otto and his hickory ax handle. Pine Creek did not even have a peace officer.

Although the shelling of Fort Sumter and the beginning of the war were topics of discussion in Pine Creek, still, there was little concern for the community's welfare. However, when a Confederate officer and a sergeant rode into Pine Creek and recruited nearly all their young men to fight the Yankees, the war became a reality. Suddenly their tranquil little community became a part of the war as young men were captured and others killed in battles that were occurring closer and closer with each new day.

It was about two o'clock in the afternoon when John Henry rode back into town from his visits in the Shiloh and Friendship communities. As was his custom, he stopped by

Sam's general store to catch up on the latest news before going home.

He tied Rambler to the rail out front and walked in. "Gentlemen, how y'all doing?"

Surprised at the number of men there, he turned to Sam, "Lord, have mercy, Sam. You've got a good crowd here. Wish I could have this many at prayer meeting tomorrow night."

Sam returned the greeting. "Good afternoon to you, Brother John. Before we talk about why these gentlemen are here, tell us what went on yesterday on your way to Shiloh."

"Let me tell you why I'm asking. A couple of young fellers came in here this morning asking about you. They wanted to know if I knew you. When I told them that you were my pastor, they said to tell you that the baptism took."

John Henry smiled. "Yes, we did have a little prayer meeting on the road to Shiloh. I tried to show them the danger of their wicked ways, and they turned out to be right agreeable. I didn't want to put any undue pressure on them, but I did have to dangle them over the fires of hell before I made believers out of them. Are they still around town or have they moved on?"

"I think they've moved on. At least I haven't seen them around for a while. They came in here begging for food. Since they looked so pitiful and hungry, I just couldn't refuse giving them something to eat, especially after they said you had baptized them.

"What did you give them?"

"Some cheese, an apple apiece and a couple of cans of beans."

"Well, that was good of you, Sam, since you don't have all that much to give these days. That reminds me, I've got some things tied to my saddle for you. I'll be right back."

When John Henry returned, he had in his arms two Springfield Rifles, two shot pouches and two powder horns, all of which he laid on the counter in front of Sam.

109

"Those two fellows made a little contribution to the Lord's work when I met them on the road yesterday. I want you to have their contribution in payment for the food you gave them."

"John Henry, I figured there was more to that story than what those two beggars were telling me."

"There usually is, but what's going on here? Looks like y'all are havin' a town meeting."

Josh Taylor, one of the three members of the town council, spoke up. "You're mighty close, Brother John. Actually, we were talking about calling a town meeting for Wednesday night. Now that you're here, we'd like to ask if we could have it at the church after prayer meeting Wednesday night. Would that be all right with you?"

"You know you can meet there, but what's going on?"

Sam responded. "We feel that we need a law enforcement officer in Pine Creek. In fact the Mayor is on his way to Hawkinsville right now to ask the Sheriff to meet with us. He left it up to us to find a place to meet, so we thought of the church."

"Could I say something?" It was Dan Ravenwood who spoke. "Y'all know that I don't live in town, but I've got a daughter-in-law and a grandson who live here. And I hope and pray that one day my son will be able to come back and live here. What I want to say is that Pine Creek is not the same little town it used to be. We've had break-ins, violence has increased, and people are being harassed for handouts."

Dan moved so that he could look everybody in the eye. "Many of these people that we see here are perfectly good people who are suffering because of the war, but there are others mingled in with them who are deserters and still others who are nothing but criminals. I don't want to say anything against good folks who are suffering, but both the good and bad are desperate and that makes for a bad situation. Desperate folks will do desperate things. That's the problem as I see it, and I think we need some law here in town, not fifteen miles away in Hawkinsville."

Josh Taylor got to his feet. "I think we're all in agreement. There's a problem, and it needs fixing, but we can't take any action here. That'll be up to the town meeting."

"Brother John, what time can we meet?"

John Henry didn't believe in beating around the bush. "Prayer meeting is at seven o'clock, but you go ahead and call your meeting for that hour. I'll open the meeting with prayer, and we'll deal with concerns of this community. I can't think of any better way to have a prayer meeting than to deal with what's bothering people. See y'all in church. I'm tired, and I'm going home."

John Henry had his hand on the door know and was about to leave when he turned and said, "Y'all be sure to let Brother Rayburn at the Baptist Church and Brother White over at the Pentecostal Church know about the town meeting."

The news of the Wednesday town meeting spread rapidly throughout Pine Creek. The church was packed. John Henry got everyone's attention and called on Brother Rayburn to open the meeting with prayer. Afterwards, John Henry welcomed everyone and turned the meeting over to Mayor Fred Davis.

"Thank you, Brother John, for allowing us to have this meeting here, and I want to thank y'all for coming. Y'all know why we're here. We're concerned about the safety of our town. Yesterday, I rode over to Hawkinsville and asked Sheriff Dunn to meet with us tonight and talk to us about what can be done to keep Pine Creek safe. Sheriff, please come down front and talk to us about our safety."

Sheriff Dunn stood before the town meeting and offered the usual safety precautions. Always lock your doors. Don't go out alone at night, and don't open your door to anyone unless you know them, and don't leave your children at home alone.

Then he made a recommendation, one that he and Mayor

Davis had discussed.

"As you know, my deputies and I are fifteen miles from you. Even when the telegraph is working, if you needed us, it would take us a half a day to get here. So this is what I am willing to do. If you can come up with two volunteers who are willing to give of their time and do the work, I will appoint them as deputies. This would be the first step in getting law enforcement here in Pine Creek."

The crowd began to murmur. "Let me finish. If you will find two men who are willing to be deputized, then I will send my best deputy over here to work with them for at least a week.

Obviously, I can't put a deputy here full time, but at least you'll have a peace officer visible on the street for a short period of time."

From the crowd came a question. "Sheriff, if this deputy plan that you're suggesting is just the first step as you call it, then what would be the next step?"

"I suggest that the town council employ a town marshal."

Sheriff Dunn then turned the meeting back over to Mayor Davis.

With the Mayor presiding, the crowd approved the appointment of two volunteer deputies. Tom Corley, the town blacksmith, and Jeff Frazier, who ran a feed and seed warehouse, volunteered and were approved by the town meeting. The sheriff deputized both men that night before the meeting adjourned with a prayer by Brother White from the Pentecostal Church.

The mayor and council met briefly after the town meeting and agreed that lodging for the deputy would be provided. Sheriff Dunn, who spent the night at the Mayor's house, left for Hawkinsville early the next morning with the promise that a deputy would arrive in Pine Creek the following day.

# 22

At about two o'clock on Friday afternoon a dappled gray mare came high-stepping into Pine Creek. Sitting real easy in her saddle was the deputy that Sheriff Dunn promised. He wore a slightly faded blue shirt, tucked into black pants that were tucked into well-worn, polished, black boots. In the collar of his shirt was a neatly tied black string tie. His black wide-brimmed hat was pulled low over his eyes. His neatly-trimmed hair and mustache were salt and pepper gray. For warmth, he wore a loose fitting sheep skin coat which was unbuttoned. He was dressed for the weather and for the job. On his left hip was a model 1858 .44 caliber Remington revolver, butt forward. In a saddle scabbard under his left leg was a .52 caliber Spencer repeating carbine. Beneath his right leg was a similar but shorter scabbard holding a sawed- off double-barreled shotgun loaded with the new solid brass shells filled with double-ought buckshot. He walked the mare up to the front of Sam's general store, pulled the shotgun from its scabbard, dismounted and draped the reins of the mare over the hitching rail. He never dismounted without his scatter gun in his hand. Keeping the gun to his right hand, he walked up the steps and walked into the store. Sam, Susie, Mayor Dunn, and the two newly appointed deputies were inside.

Touching his fingers to the brim of his hat, he nodded to Susie, "Ma'am."

Then he spoke to the men. "Gentlemen, the name's Jim Bob Patterson, chief deputy, from Hawkinsville. Sheriff Dunn sent me over here to help y'all out for a few days. Now, where might I find Mayor Davis?"

The Mayor spoke up. "I'm Fred Davis, the Mayor. Most folks here just call me Mayor.

We're mighty pleased to make your acquaintance. What should we call you?"

"Deputy will be just fine, Mr. Mayor."

"Fine, fine, let me introduce you to the two gentlemen who have volunteered to be deputies. This fella on my left is Tom Corley, our blacksmith. Over there, leaning against the counter, is Jeff Frazier. He owns the feed and grain warehouse here."

Jim Bob shifted the shotgun to his left hand, shook hands with the two men, then turned his attention back to the Mayor.

"I was told by the sheriff that y'all would provide lodging for me."

"Yes, we were about to discuss that when you arrived."

Jim Bob responded. "I'd be pleased if you'd hold off on that discussion for a while. I may be able to acquire lodging myself."

He turned and spoke to Corley and Frazier. "I'll meet you back here in one hour. We've got some work to do."

Again, he nodded to Susie, touched the brim of his hat with his fingers, and said, "Ma'am."

He was at the door, about to walk out when he turned to Sam. "By the way, Sir, would you be kind enough to tell me where John Henry Troup lives?"

After receiving directions to John Henry's house, Jim Bob walked out to his horse, put the shotgun in its scabbard, and deftly swung into the saddle. No one in the store said a word for a while. They all moved to the front of the store and watched him ride away.

Mayor Davis was the first to speak. "He ain't a very sociable old geezer, is he?"

Sam McDaniel replied, "You're right. He may not be very sociable, but the Sheriff said he would send us his best deputy. I guess we'll have to take him at his word."

Jeff Frazier, still rubbing his right hand, commented, "I'll tell you one thing about him. He may look like an old geezer, but he's got a grip like a bulldog chomping down on a bone. Lordy, he just about broke my hand. What about you, Tom?"

"Well, I've been blacksmithing for nigh on to thirty years and I have pretty strong hands, but me and him 'bout squoze to a draw."

Susie spoke up. "I thought he was right nice and very courteous, to tell you the truth. You can call him an old geezer if you'd like, but none of you ... gentlemen tipped your hat to me when you came in today."

There was far more to this "old geezer" than the men in Sam's store realized. He had ridden with Sam Houston when Houston defeated Santa Anna in the battle for Texas independence in '36. Twelve years later, he was in the army of General Winfield Scott when Scott's outnumbered army defeated Santa Anna in the battle for Mexico City during the Mexican-American war. Also serving in Scott's army were two West Point graduates of historical significance. One was an engineering captain by the name of Robert E. Lee. The other was an artillery lieutenant named Ulysses S. Grant.

Jim Bob had no trouble finding John Henry's house.

John Henry answered his knock on the front door. "Good afternoon, Sir, can I help you?"

"Good afternoon, John Henry," Jim Bob responded.

John Henry squinted at Jim Bob's face. "Do I know you?"

"You ought to, you old coot. My old daddy tried to teach you how to preach a long time ago when you were just a boy preacher."

John Henry squinted at the face again, then bellowed, "Jim Bob Patterson!"

After a bear hug of grizzly proportions, he continued, "Come in. Come on in! My soul, Jim Bob, what's it been, thirty years? Let me tell the missus you're here."

115

"Marthee! Marthee! Come here quick, Joe Frank's boy, Jim Bob, is here!"

"What brings you to Pine Creek, Boy?"

When Jim Bob explained why he was in Pine Creek, there was no question about where he would stay. Although the reunion could have lasted all afternoon, Jim Bob was back at Sam's store on time. He left his horse at John Henry's house and walked back to Sam's store with his constant companion, his sawed-off shotgun. The two volunteer deputies were just walking up the steps of the store when he arrived. They allowed him to enter the store first.

Jim Bob tipped his hat to Susie, then turned and spoke to the Mayor and council members. "Gentlemen, I'm glad to see y'all here. This meeting is primarily for the two deputies; however, I realize that it is your town and you're interested in its safety, so you're free to listen in. By the way, Mr. Mayor, I've made my own arrangements for lodging. I'll be staying at John Henry Troup's house."

Pointing toward an area in the rear of the store, Jim Bob said, "Let's meet over there so we won't interfere with Mr. McDaniel's store business."

Jim Bob leaned against the counter as Corley and Frazier stood before him.

Only when the Mayor and Council had taken their places off to the side did he speak. "All right, gentlemen, I need a little information. Do you two volunteers own any firearms?"

Both confirmed that they each had a muzzle-loading rifle.

"That's not satisfactory. A rifle is no good in the middle of a crowd inside a building."

Jim Bob explained. "Those long muzzle-loaders would likely get you killed. You need something effective in close quarters. Excuse me just a minute."

He returned with two ax handles, one in each hand. "Mr. McDaniel, charge these ax handles to the town council."

"Let's not go too fast here," popped off Councilman

116

Jonas Dunlap. "The council has to approve all expenditures."

Noting the cold, piercing look that he received from Deputy Patterson, he immediately added, "What I meant to say is that since the council has to approve all expenditures, I move that the town council pay for the two ax handles." The motion carried with no discussion.

Jim Bob spoke again. "Now, if we could continue with our session. Here are some things that you need to remember.

"The first thing is, know your territory. By that I mean know all the nooks and crannies in town where trouble might start.

The second is, pick your battles and your battleground carefully.

The third is, if you're not willing to back up what you say, then don't say it.

The fourth is, watch your back. Don't let your adversary's buddies get behind you.

Number five is, if you have to hit somebody with one of these ax handles, be sure to hit'em first, hit'em with authority and be ready to hit'em again.

Finally, the sixth thing that I want you to remember is don't be afraid to ask for help. We don't need any dead heroes in town."

"Mister Mayor and members of the council, these two deputies and me are gonna take us a little walk around town. Thank you, Councilman Dunlap, for making the motion to pay for the ax handles."

"I'm always happy to do my civic duty, Deputy. However, I do have one question."

"I'll be happy to answer it, if I can."

"Do you always carry that sawed-off shotgun with you? That seems like you might be saying that you're anxious to shoot somebody."

"Mr. Councilman, a mule locked up in the barn don't do no plowing." Without another word, Jim Bob turned and

117

walked out of the store with Corley and Frazier following him.

The three men walked the entire length of town with Jim Bob pointing out some possible trouble spots. They finally wound up in front of Otto's Bar.

"Let's go in here for a minute." Jim Bob said as he headed for the door, followed by Tom Corley. Jeff Frazier held back. "Y'all go ahead. I'm a deacon in my church and I gave a pledge that I wouldn't go in such a place."

"I understand Mr. Frazier, but I am not trying to lead you astray. I'm just trying to head off trouble. Now, let's go inside."

Otto spoke as the three men entered his bar. "Why hello, Deputy, I haven't seen you since you run me out of Cedarville."

"Otto, if you remember, I didn't run you out. I just suggested that you leave for the sake of your good health."

"If I hadn't left, Deputy, it could have gotten real interesting."

"I would have made it so." Replied Jim Bob.

"Probably so, Jim Bob. I heard you were in town, but what brings you to my place?"

"I'll get right to the point, Otto. I know you run a pretty tight ship here, and you don't allow your customers to create any problems. I want you to keep on doing that. If somebody starts getting all liquored up in here and wants to start something that might spread to the rest of town, stop it right here. That's all I'm asking. You do that and you won't have any problems from me or these two fellers with me."

"You've got a deal, Deputy."

After they shook hands, Jim Bob and the other two men continued their walk through town. As they moved back toward McDaniel's store, Jim Bob pointed out other areas which could be troublesome after dark. Tom Corley dropped out of the tour at his blacksmith shop, and Jeff Frazier stopped at his warehouse. Jim Bob continued alone to McDaniel's store. The plan was for Jim Bob to make a round with one deputy the next morning and another tour with the second deputy in the afternoon.

He entered Sam's store just in time to hear John Henry's booming voice put the final touches on the story of his relationship with Jim Bob and his father, Joe Frank Patterson.

"Yes sir! That boy's daddy taught me everything I know about preaching. Y'all are in good hands with Jim Bob walking the streets."

Jim Bob nodded to Susie, "Ma'am." Then turning to the people in the store, he said, "Don't believe everything this old coot tells you. My ole daddy always said that John Henry was better at fishing than he was preaching."

John Henry just stood there basking in all the attention he was getting.

Fulfilling the sheriff's commitment, Jim Bob spent a week in Pine Creek working with the two volunteer deputies. As he rode out of Pine Creek toward Hawkinsville, he left behind a town that felt more secure than when he came. The presence of a peace officer in town did have its effect. Although he was leaving, the people had grown to have confidence in the two volunteers who had gained a measure of confidence in themselves.

# 23

Four weeks after Jim Bob's return to Hawkinsville the peaceful atmosphere of Pine Creek was disrupted by twelve-year-old Bobby Claymore. Several men of the town were gathered in Sam's store when Bobby, who lived on the north end of town, burst through the door.

"Pa sent me to tell you there's Yankees a coming!"

Sam stepped out from behind the counter and knelt down in front of Bobby. "Whoa now, just calm down, take a deep breath, and tell us what you're talking about."

"Pa was out at the wood pile cutting some stove wood when we seen this big bunch of soldiers riding down the road. He knowed right off they was Yankees, so he told me to high-tail it into town and tell y'all they was coming. Are y'all gonna shoot'em?"

"No, Bobby, we're not going to start a war here. We'll just wait and see what they want. Now you stay inside here and stay out of trouble. You can go back home to your folks when we find out what this is all about."

As Bobby moved over beside Susie, a Union captain walked in, flanked by two of his men, one a sergeant, the other a private. After tipping his hat to Susie, he turned his attention to the men. "Good morning, gentlemen. I'm Captain Luke Wesley and I represent Major General James H. Wilson, Commander of the Union Cavalry Corps, and I would like to speak to the Mayor."

Fred Davis stepped forward. "I'm the mayor. What can we do for you, Captain?"

The captain pulled the glove off his right hand and shook

hands with the mayor. "Please to meet you, Mr. Mayor. I wonder if we could talk privately for a few minutes."

Moving to the rear of the store and out of the hearing of the others, Captain Wesley said,

"Sir, I respectfully request that I be given an opportunity to speak with you and your town council about the safety and welfare of your town."

"Is this some kind of threat Captain?"

"No, sir, it's anything but that. I am here at General Wilson's orders, to try to save lives, not take them. Now, when could I meet with the council?"

Fred thought it over for a minute and then responded, "Actually, Captain, all of them are here but one and I can have him here shortly."

About that time, Jonas Dunlap, the missing councilman, walked through the door. "Here he is now, Captain," said the mayor.

Fred turned to Sam. "Could we use your storage room for a quick council meeting?"

After Sam had given his consent, the Captain turned to his sergeant, who had accompanied him into the store.

"Sergeant, ask Lieutenants Jones and Simmons to have their units dismount and rest for a while. Also, ask them to post guards on the horses and the supply wagons."

The Sergeant was about to carry out the Captain's orders when he turned and said,

"Sir, at least two of these men are armed. Would the Captain like me to be in the meeting also?"

"That won't be necessary, Sergeant."

When the Captain, the Mayor, and the three councilmen were assembled in Sam's storage room, the Captain spoke. "Gentlemen, you have a nice little town here and I'm sure you are proud of it, and I do not want to belittle you or the town in any way, but the fact is, you are of little military significance to the Union Army. However, we know there are

121

Rebel guerilla units, as well as bands of deserters, both Union and Rebel, operating in the area between the Oconee River and the Ocmulgee River. Telegraph lines have been pulled down. Railroad tracks have been ripped up, and God only knows what else they've done. You are isolated, and these renegade units could cause problems for you as well as for the Union forces. To counteract this threat, my troops and I will be bivouacked here three to four weeks while we do reconnaissance patrols in the area between the two rivers. I have been instructed to get your word of honor that you will cause us no trouble while we are here, and I give you my word that we will cause you no trouble."

"This is highly unusual," said a flustered Jonas Dunlap.

Josh Taylor responded. "Jonas, will you just be quiet!"

Surprisingly calm, the Mayor spoke, "Sir, are you asking us to surrender the town?"

"Not at all, Sir, General Wilson has no desire to take any military action against the people of Pine Creek. The word surrender implies conflict and defeat. Conflict is something we wish to avoid. As I have already said, Pine Creek is of little military significance to Union Forces. However, there are some conditions that must be met."

"First, no firearms are to be carried in town by anyone at any time. You may keep them in your homes, but they are not to be carried in public, openly or concealed."

"Second, I am requesting that everyone stay off the streets between the hours of sunset and sunrise, with the exception of those evenings when your churches are open for worship. This is only a request. I am not authorized to declare martial law in your town. I am requesting this for the safety of your people as well as the safety my troops."

"Third, you are to enforce the law among your people and my men will answer to me if they present a problem."

"Finally, I understand that you have a bar here in Pine Creek. It, like all other businesses, will close at sundown.

Needless to say, it is off limits to my men at all times."

Mayor Davis asked, "Do we have a choice?"

"No, sir, you do not. I'm merely trying to make it easier on both of us. Now, I know this is difficult for you, but here are the facts. The war will soon be over. Atlanta has fallen. General Sherman has gutted the Confederacy from Atlanta to Savannah. Macon, just fifty miles north of here, has also fallen. Right now there is no operational telegraph or rail service south of Macon.

I cannot estimate how many men, Union and Confederate forces combined, have died fighting in this war. I am from a little town in Ohio about this size, and I wouldn't want bloodshed there, nor do I want it here. I'm going to give you few minutes to make up your minds whether to accept or reject General Wilson's offer. Keep this in mind. I am neither a politician nor a diplomat. I am a combat trained soldier and under my command are one hundred trained cavalrymen all armed with .52 caliber Spencer repeating carbines. If there is trouble here, we will respond immediately and accurately. As I said, Pine Creek is of no military importance. We would like to keep it that way. Let me know what you decide."

Mayor Davis spoke, "Stay where you are, Captain. We'll vote with you in here."

"I want to go on record as saying, this is all very unusual," piped up Jonas Dunlap.

Josh Taylor tersely responded, "Jonas, will you just shut up. Mayor, you can put that on record too."

The mayor ignored the exchange between the two council members. "Do I hear a motion that we accept the Captain's plan?"

A motion to accept the Captain's plan was made by Will Embry and seconded by Josh Taylor. The vote was unanimous with Jonas Dunlap declaring that, for the record, his vote for the Captain's plan was being made under protest and only in the best interest of the town. The council adjourned and the Captain bade farewell to the men. On the way out he tipped his hat to Susie and simply said, "Ma'am."

In spite of the initial hysteria caused by the news that the Yankees were in town, the people soon calmed down and began to go about their daily routines with a fair degree of normality. The Captain's men patrolled the town in pairs, sometimes on horseback but primarily on foot. No firearms were carried by the citizens of Pine Creek. However, John Henry did get permission to carry his Walker Colt when traveling to his churches out of town.

The lawless element that had begun to trouble Pine Creek soon disappeared, but the evidence of war was still there. The trains no longer ran, and the telegraph lines were still inoperable. Young men of the town were still missing from the streets. The town was patrolled by Yankees, and the Ravenwoods continued to worry about Pat's welfare in Clonnerville Prison.

Death has a way of reminding people of the horror of war. Cliff and Faye Johnson experienced it when John Henry told them that their son, Billy, had died in Clonnerville Prison. Captain Wesley's patrols also served as reminders of the horror of war. In the course of the next two weeks that Wesley's troops patrolled out of Pine Creek, they returned with a total of fifteen bodies. Four of them were Wesley's own men. Of the remaining eleven, two were Union deserters and nine were Rebel guerillas who also might have been deserters. John Henry conducted the funerals for all the deceased.

# 24

After running reconnaissance patrols out of Pine Creek for four weeks, Captain Wesley received orders by courier to move west and assist General Wilson's Cavalry Corps, which was on its way to Columbus after capturing Montgomery. Specifically, Wesley's orders were to join up with a detachment of Wilson's forces that had crossed the Chattahoochee from Alabama into Georgia near West Point, Georgia. Strengthened by Wesley's troops, they were to move toward Columbus from the north and at the same time protect Wilson's left flank.

The departure of Captain Wesley and his cavalry troop was met with mixed emotions by the people of Pine Creek. They had felt relatively safe during the time Wesley's men were in town. There were townspeople who actually preferred that the Union soldiers stay, even though their presence was a constant reminder that they were a town occupied by the enemy.

In spite of the town's initial anxiety, life was rather uneventful as Pine Creek returned to its normal way of life. Captain Wesley's curfew was lifted and the restriction on carrying firearms was rescinded. Businesses were no longer required to close at sundown. Life was rather pleasant and peaceful, but elsewhere, the war continued and more young men died.

For the men in Clonnerville Prison, nothing changed. Each day brought with it the same boredom, the same abuse, and the same hopelessness. Pat longed to hear from Molly Ann, but her letters never came. The thoughts of her prompted him to get his pencil and paper and begin writing her another letter. He had written only a few words when the doors of the warehouse opened. In walked Sergeant Nelson accompanied by two additional prison guards. Pat was surprised to see them since they were not assigned to Warehouse B. Pat thought it rather strange that Hagan and his two henchmen were nowhere to be seen.

Looking directly at Pat, the Sergeant spoke, "Good afternoon Chaplain Ravenwood."

"Good afternoon, Sergeant. What can I do for you?"

"Colonel Randolph sends his regards and requests that you join him in his quarters.

I'm Sergeant Nelson and I'm to escort you there."

"Do you mean right now?"

"That's my understanding, Chaplain."

Pat put his writing material away and got up from his pallet. The two guards who accompanied Sergeant Nelson stepped aside and let the Sergeant and Pat walk through the warehouse door.

As they passed through the gate of the prison yard, Pat noted the absence of Hagan and his two thugs."Sergeant Nelson, where is Sergeant Hagan? Is he not here?"

"That would be for the Colonel to say, Chaplain."

They walked up a slight rise to the Colonel's quarters. The Sergeant knocked on the door.

"Enter," responded the Colonel.

The Colonel's quarters were nondescript, sparsely furnished, and hardly what Pat had expected.

While he was still seated Colonel Randoph dismissed the sergeant. Only when the sergeant had closed the door did the Colonel acknowledge Pat's presence.

"Good afternoon, Chaplain, please have a seat."

The Colonel got up from his chair and moved so that he could sit on the corner of his desk in front of Pat.

"Chaplain, this conversation is confidential. You may discuss it with Cofer and Bracewell but not with anyone else. Do I have your word on that?"

"Of course, Colonel, though I don't know what this is all about."

"Let me explain, this terrible war is going to be over in a matter of weeks, perhaps even in a matter of days. General Sherman has literally burned his way across Georgia from Atlanta to Savannah. General Wilson is moving down through Alabama toward Columbus. I could go on and on, but my point is, even when this war is over we will still have some serious problems here at Clonnerville Prison. We cannot possibly turn nearly eight hundred prisoners free by just opening the gates to the prison. I'm afraid they would totally destroy the surrounding communities. Then there's the wounded. We cannot leave them without care."

"But how does that involve me?"

"It doesn't have to involve you at all unless you are willing to be involved. Let me explain. When the war ends, we will release the prisoners in numbers that can be safely transported by rail as close to their homes as possible. We will give each one a pass for rail passage. However, that will not solve the problem of the wounded captives that you, Cofer, and Bracewell have been caring for. That is where you three can help us."

"What exactly do you have in mind, Colonel?"

"To be absolutely honest, I need you three to continue caring for the wounded until we can arrange transportation for them. Please understand, Chaplain, I am not telling you to do this. I am asking for your voluntary assistance."

"How long would this take?"

"It should not take more than a week or two. In return, we will make every effort to get a message to your family and the families of Cofer and Bracewell and let them know what you are doing and that you should be home shortly. Also, with supplies becoming more available, we should be able to improve the food situation for you and the wounded. I don't expect an answer from you until you have talked it over with the other two men, but I do need an answer shortly."

"I appreciate your concern for the wounded, Sir. I will discuss your request with Cofer and Bracewell as soon as I see them. My personal feelings are that I want to help you, but I can't answer for them. I'll see what their response is."

"That's all I'm asking, Chaplain."

"Colonel, there is another matter that I need to discuss with you before I leave. What about Sergeant Hagan?"

"I was going to talk to you about that. For a long time, I had no choice but to put up with Hagan, but I was finally able to get him transferred to another unit. His two cronies, Perkins and Lawton, were also transferred. The three of them have been assigned to the burial detail in General Wilson's Cavalry Corps. They left yesterday."

Pat responded, "I'm glad to hear that he has been transferred, but to be honest, I would like to have seen him transferred to a combat unit."

"Why do you say that?"

"Because he is a depraved, degenerate, evil man who should be put to death. I have been a Chaplain since '61, and I have never fired a gun at anyone. But if I had Hagan in my gun sights, I would have no problem pulling the trigger."

"I'm sure there are others who share your feelings, Chaplain. How do you think I feel? We were so proud of our son, not just because he graduated third in his class at The Point, but because he was a man of character and high ideals with so much to offer life. Yet, he was killed at the age of twenty-three, but Hagan, a miserable excuse for a human being, is still alive. What kind of god will let things like that happen? As I have asked you before, Chaplain, Where is your God in all of this?"

"I cannot answer that, Colonel, because I feel the same

way. So far as Hagan is concerned, I will not rest until he is dead. I feel that he is personally responsible for the death of at least one prisoner and for the inhumane treatment of many others."

"Chaplain, it sounds to me like you're willing to trade your Bible for a gun, but Hagan is not our main concern. What we have to focus on right now is care for the wounded. They will continue to need our help after the fighting stops and this war is finally over. Meanwhile, think about my request. I'll expect an answer from you in the morning."

At that point the Colonel got up from the corner of the desk where he had been sitting, opened the door and spoke to the Sergeant who was in the next room.

"Sergeant, escort Chaplain Ravenwood back to warehouse B."

He turned back to Pat, "Good day, Chaplain."

Pat nodded his response and was escorted back to Warehouse B in the company of the Sergeant and two guards.

Once inside, the first to greet him was Jud Cofer, "Glad to see you back Chaplain.

Deke and me wuz kinda worried about you. What's going on?"

"Get Deke and I'll tell you."

Jud left and returned momentarily with Deke, who was as curious as Jud.

The three of them walked outside the warehouse so they could talk privately.

Pat recounted his conversation with the Colonel. "That's what the Colonel wants, and I'm telling you because it also involves you. However, you must promise me that you will not discuss it with anyone. In fact, I was surprised the Colonel told me as much as he did."

Both Cofer and Bracewell agreed to keep the discussion confidential.

Pat continued, "The Colonel says all indications are the

war will be over in just a matter of weeks, perhaps even days. That means the prisoners will be released in groups that the railroad can safely handle. The situation with the wounded is another matter entirely. Special arrangements will have to be made for them. Some are unable to travel and may never recover. So, it all boils down to the fact that the Colonel wants us to care for them for a week or two after the war is over so that travel arrangements can be made for them."

Jud responded immediately. "What are you going to do, Chaplain?"

Deke added, "Yeah, that's what I was going to ask. What about you?"

"I'm staying, but whether or not you two stay is up to you."

Jud gave his answer. "If you're staying, then I'm staying. We've been through too much to split up now. How about you, Deke?"

"I ain't really got nobody to go home to, and you fellers are the best friends I've got, so count me in. I'm staying."

Pat shook their hands. "That's what I thought you'd say, but I didn't want to answer for you. I'm supposed to see the Colonel in the morning and tell him what we decided."

Two days' ride south of Clonnerville Prison, three men hunkered down around a fire, eating food they had taken from an elderly farmer and his wife. "I thought we was gonna have to kill that old Reb to get something to eat," said Rat Perkins as he chewed on a piece of sow belly.

Jake Lawton responded, "What we got ain't worth killing for. They didn't have nothing in the first place, just this here maggot-infested sow belly, no money, no whiskey, no nothing."

Buck Hagan chided both of them. "You two must be getting soft in the head. Don't feel sorry for that old buzzard. He's a Reb, and him and his old woman are lucky we didn't kill'em."

Rat looked at Hagan. "I ain't getting soft. I just hate to

waste all that energy for such a little bit of food."

Jake poured himself a cup of coffee. "Maybe the food in our new outfit will be a little better, though I ain't too happy about digging graves all day." He slurped another swallow of coffee, "How about y'all, what do y'all think about what the Colonel did to us, making us grave diggers?"

Hagan spoke up, "Now I know y'all have gone soft in the head. Me, I ain't digging no graves, though I'd prob'ly dig one for that gimpy-legged colonel or that troublesome chaplain."

"What do you mean?" Jake asked. "Are you counting on Rat and me to dig all the graves?"

Hagan snorted! "Y'all can dig graves if you want to, but I have other plans. I ain't gonna report to that grave diggin' outfit. I'm gonna strike out and just enjoy being out of the army. If Sherman can live off the land, I can too. Now, y'all can dig graves if you're of a mind to, but me, I plan to ride over and see the sights around a little place called Pine Creek."

It didn't take Rat and Jake long to decide to ride with him.

Rat said, "I guess that'll make us deserters. They'll hang us if we're caught."

"Listen," responded Hagan, "this war is causing so much confusion, they'll never miss us, and when it is over, there'll be even more confusion."

The next morning, Hagan, Perkins, and Lawton mounted up and continued riding in a southerly direction. About the same time, back at Clonnerville Prison, a sergeant and two enlisted men were escorting Pat to the colonel's quarters.

After hearing that Pat, Jud, and Deke would honor his request to care for the wounded, the Colonel responded, "Thank you, Chaplain. That's the answer I thought you'd give me. I know you, Cofer, and Bracewell are here against your will, but I want you to know that I appreciate your attitude about caring for the wounded. In the meantime, I'll try

131

to keep you up-to-date on the war and how it affects us here. You may return to your quarters."

As Pat was about to leave the colonel's office, he noticed a calendar on the wall.

"What is today's date, Colonel?" Pat asked.

"April eighth."

# 25

Palm Sunday, April 9, 1865 began as just another ordinary day, but it ended with an extraordinary event. In Clonnerville Prison, Pat, Jud, and Deke began their day by tending to the needs of the wounded prisoners in Warehouse B. Colonel Randolph faced the frustration of getting dressed with only one arm. To the southwest, Hagan, Perkins, and Lawton remained committed in their decision not to report to the burial unit in General Wilson's Cavalry Corps. In Pine Creek, Molly Ann and Johnny attended the morning worship service at the Methodist church and heard John Henry preach. That afternoon in the McLean home in Appomattox Court House, Virginia, Confederate General Robert E. Lee surrendered the Army of Virginia to Union General Ulysses S. Grant.

The ordinary day that ended extraordinarily marked the beginning of a week that ended in tragedy. President Abraham Lincoln was assassinated while attending a play at Ford's Theater in Washington on April fourteenth, Good Friday.

On Monday morning, April 10, Sergeant Nelson entered Warehouse B and sought out Pat. This time the sergeant was alone. No guards accompanied him. Pat thought this was very unusual. He had never seen a guard enter the warehouse alone.

"Chaplain, The colonel sends his regards and requests your presence in his quarters, sir."

When the two of them entered the colonel's quarters, Colonel Randolph arose from his desk and greeted Pat with a handshake.

"Good morning, Chaplain, please have a seat.

"Thank you, Sergeant,that'll be all."

"As you wish, Sir. I'll be right outside."

The Colonel, with a telegram in his hand, turned to Pat, "Well, Chaplain, the day has finally come. General Lee has surrendered. Depending on how effective communications are to other Confederate forces in the field, all hostilities should cease within a week."

"I'm glad it's over, Sir. When will you start releasing the men?"

"It will probably be a week from today. A lot depends on the availability of transportation."

"When will the men be told, Colonel?"

"I plan to make the announcement this afternoon, but you must understand there are still a lot of skirmishes going on, some of them not far to the west of us. However, for all practical purposes, the war is over, even though a number of Confederate forces have not surrendered."

That same day, Captain Luke Wesley, unaware of Lee's surrender, was leading his troops westward to join General Wilson's Cavalry Corps, when one of his outriders came galloping in and pulled up beside the Captain.

"You're riding that horse mighty hard, Sergeant. What's the rush?"

"Captain, there are three men in Union uniforms camped just over the hill to your right. They have horses with Union blankets and saddles on them. It may not be anything out of kilter, Sir, but it just didn't look right to me."

"Did they see you?"

"Don't think so, Sir. I was real careful. I spotted their smoke first, so I kinda snuck up on'em."

"Good work, Sergeant, ask Lieutenant Wayne to report to me, and you come back with him. I'm going to need you to guide the Lieutenant back to those men you spotted."

The sergeant did as ordered, and the Lieutenant appeared shortly.

Captain Wesley briefed the Lieutenant and gave him an order. "Lieutenant, take a squad of men and go get those three that the sergeant found and bring them back to me. The sergeant will show you where they are camped."

"Yes, sir!" said the lieutenant.

"One more thing, Lieutenant, when you ride in, ride in ready."

"Yes, sir, I wouldn't have it any other way, Sir."

A slight smile creased the captain's face as he dismissed the Lieutenant.

Hagan, Perkins, and Lawton were quite surprised when a squad of cavalrymen suddenly appeared in their camp.

As the lieutenant's men surrounded them, Hagan spoke softly to his cronies. "Don't do nothing foolish. Just let me handle this."

He had hardly finished speaking when he realized that the Cavalry had them surrounded and that he, Perkins and Lawton were looking at the business end of ten .52 caliber Spencer carbines.

Hagan spoke first. "Good morning, Lieutenant. Is there some kind of problem?"

The lieutenant replied, "Sergeant, this is how we are going to handle our little meeting out here in the middle of nowhere. I'll ask the questions and you'll give the answers. Now let's begin with you three moving away from your rifles. Sergeant, you take your finger and thumb and lift that sidearm of yours out of its holster and put it real gentle-like on the ground."

"Lieutenant, we ain't giving up our guns to nobody."

It was then that the three men on the ground heard ten Spencer rifles being cocked. From the Lieutenant's right hand came the unmistakable sound of the cocking of the Lieutenant's Remington revolver.

135

"Ah now, Lieutenant, there ain't no call for all of this. We're all on the same side, and besides that, we have our orders from Colonel Randolph at Clonnerville P. O. W. camp ordering us to report to General Wilson's Cavalry Corps. That's where we were headed when you and your men jumped us. I got'em right here."

"I said drop those guns. I mean now! You do that, and then I'll look at your orders."

Hagan realized that the lieutenant meant business, so he, Perkins, and Lawton complied with the lieutenant's orders. They were escorted back to the main body of the troop where they were questioned by Captain Wesley. After thoroughly examining their orders, Wesley had to admit that they appeared authentic, but there was something in his gut that told him something was amiss with these three.

He turned and spoke to Hagan. "Sergeant, your orders appear to be legitimate. I'm going to permit you and the other two to ride with us."

"Can I have our orders back?" Hagan asked.

"As you wish. We are a part of General Wilson's Corps. You are now riding with us, so therefore you have fulfilled your orders."

"What about our guns?"

"Your pistols will be returned to you, but they will be unloaded. They are to remain that way until further notice. The same thing goes for your rifles. You will have six of my men escorting you, and it will make them very unhappy if any of you attempt to reload them.

"What if we run into some Rebs," queried Hagan, "What are we s'posed to do?"

The captain ignored the question.

"When we get to an operational telegraph, I will send a telegram to Colonel Randolph and verify your story. Then you will be allowed to reload your weapons. In the meantime, if you give me any trouble at all, I'll have you chained behind one of the supply wagons."

Hagan, Perkins, and Lawton were assigned to ride at the tail end of the troop. They were accompanied by six of Captain Wesley's men. After riding a full day, the troop found themselves on the banks of the Flint River south of Oglethorpe, Georgia. Captain Wesley decided that they would make camp and cross the river the next morning. As the troops made preparation to camp for the night, Wesley sent riders to the north and to the south in search of a place to ford the river. The scouts riding to the north were ordered to steer clear of Oglethorpe because the town was still reeling from the devastation of a malaria and smallpox epidemic.

The next morning, as the captain was eating breakfast, Lieutenant Wayne rode up. He dismounted from his horse and apologized to the captain for interrupting his breakfast.

"Looks like we were right, Captain. They left us sometime during the night. Want us to go after them?"

"No, we've more important things to do, but when we find a telegraph office where the lines are operational, I'm going to send a telegram to Colonel Randolph and advise him that those three have deserted."

Captain Wesley did not find an operational telegraph office until he arrived in Columbus. Only then did he learn that Lee had surrendered. He also learned that President Lincoln had been assassinated. Compared with the magnitude of those two events, the desertion of three union soldiers seemed trivial, but he sent the telegram to Colonel Randolph anyway.

# 26

Due to the intermittent nature of the telegraph service, Colonel Randolph did not learn of the assassination of President Lincoln until mid-morning, on Monday, April 17, whereupon he immediately requested that Pat be brought to his office. This was done with dispatch, and Pat was seated in the Colonel's office within minutes.

Pat could feel the tension in the air as he entered the Colonel's office. No pleasantries were exchanged. It was evident that something had changed since their last visit together.

"Sit down, Chaplain. I have some terrible news for you!"

"What are you talking about? Has something happened to my family?"

"No, Chaplain, so far as I know your family is all right, but I can only assume that."

Pat relaxed a little. "Is it something that involves me?"

"Not just you," the Colonel replied, "but all of us, you, me, and this entire country. I have just learned that President Lincoln has been assassinated."

"My God! How did it happen?"

The Colonel took a seat behind his desk. "Evidently he was attending a play at a theater in Washington when a Confederate sympathizer with a derringer managed to get close enough to fire a .44 caliber bullet into the President's head."

"Colonel, what effect do you think this will have on the war?"

"God only knows, if there is a god in the midst of all this bloodshed. It could cause the South to keep on fighting, or it could cause the Union to retaliate and bring about more bloodshed. The President wanted to preserve the Union and restore peace to our land. Who knows what will happen now?"

"I hate to keep repeating myself Colonel, but how does that affect me?"

"Chaplain, I honestly don't know. As you can imagine, the Union is in a state of panic right now. I fear for the people of the Confederacy, and I fear for the Confederate prisoners. I thought they would be released in a few weeks. Now, I just don't know."

The Colonel had just finished speaking when there was a knock at the door.

"Enter!" The Colonel responded sharply as if he objected to the interruption.

The sergeant who had escorted Pat to the Colonel's office opened the door and stepped inside.

"Begging the Colonel's pardon, Sir, but this telegram just arrived. I thought I should show it to you immediately."

Colonel Randolph took the telegram. As he read it, his shoulders sagged. He took a deep breath, placed the telegram on his desk and flattened it out with his good hand.

Finally, he turned to the sergeant, "You did the right thing, Sergeant. You may go now."

He sat in silence for a moment. Then he began to bare his soul to Pat.

"Chaplain, you have rendered a tremendous service to the wounded prisoners that we have here, and regrettably, it has been against overwhelming odds."

Pat started to say something, but the Colonel motioned for him to remain silent.

The Colonel continued, "I have had to maintain this prison with little or no resources. The conditions under which the prisoners have been forced to live is deplorable. I was given only three or four good men under my command here.

139

Lieutenant Pringle is one, and the sergeant outside that door is another. Most of the others have been dregs, outcasts from other units, and Sergeant Hagan was the worst of them. Sometimes I feel that I am no better that they are, because this prison is under my command. I feel responsible for the conditions here."

"Colonel, you cannot blame yourself for ..."

"Let me finish, Chaplain. In the name of whatever god there happens to be, let me finish, because I want to ask for your forgiveness for all that has happened here. I see in you the kind of man that I wanted my son to become. I am ashamed of what happened to you here at the hands of Hagan, and you have every right to hate him as I have a right to do the same."

"Let me say something, Colonel. You are a far better man than Hagan. You have compassion. He has none. You have a conscience, but he does not. I hold no ill will toward you, but I cannot say the same for Hagan."

"Thank you, Chaplain. Your words are very comforting, and I regret with all my heart that you were exposed to a man like Hagan. Now, I must tell you some distressing news. You have no idea how much effort I put into getting rid of Hagan. Finally, I was able to transfer him out of here and into another unit. I transferred him as far away as I possibly could."

He picked up the telegram. "Now I have this, and it says that Hagan, Perkins, and Lawton never reported to their new assignment. They have become deserters, and no one knows where they are."

"Colonel, I promised you that I would stay here and look after the wounded until they could be sent home, but I have to be concerned about my family. Hagan knows my wife's name. He knows where she lives. The only way he could have gotten that information is by reading my mail. Given the kind of man he is, Sir, I beg of you to release me from my promise to care for the wounded and release me from this prison. Let me go home to see about my family."

"You have placed me in a difficult position, Chaplain. My orders are that I am not to release any prisoners until I am told to do so. I need time, Chaplain, time to think."

At this point, the colonel called the sergeant back into the room. "Sergeant, please escort the chaplain back to Warehouse B."

When Pat entered the warehouse, Jud knew immediately that something was wrong.

"Why the hound-dog look, Chaplain?"

"Hagan, Perkins, and Lawton never reported to their new assignment. They've deserted, and nobody knows where they are."

"Is anybody gonna do anything about it? Are they looking for 'em?"

"No, Jud, I'm afraid that three deserters are the least of the Union's worries right now.

The Colonel also told me that President Lincoln has been assassinated. I don't really know what's going to happen now. The Colonel's concerned about it. He's afraid of some sort of retaliation from Union forces."

In his office, the Colonel sat at his desk staring out the window at the three warehouses that lay before him. As if awakened from a dream, he slammed his hand down on his desk and said aloud, "To hell with orders!"

"Sergeant!" He tersely called.

The sergeant responded immediately, "You called me, Sir?"

"Yes, Sergeant, see that my horse is saddled and out front as quickly as possible. And Sergeant, don't use a Union saddle blanket. Find a plain one and use it. Also I want a bedroll and rain slicker, and get me whatever provisions you can come up with. Put them in a saddle bag. I want that horse ready for several days travel. Do you understand what I want, Sergeant?"

141

"Yes, sir, I know exactly what you want. You want the horse saddled and prepared for several days in the field."

"That is correct, Sergeant. One more thing, please send the quartermaster to my office as soon as possible."

Within minutes, there was a knock at his door. "Enter." He responded.

The quartermaster entered. "You sent for me, Sir?"

"Yes, I did, I need you to do something for me. I want it done quickly with no questions asked. Do you understand?"

"Yes, sir, I understand completely, Sir."

"Good, in a few minutes I'm going to send a man to you. I want you to see that he gets a bath. When he gets cleaned up, I want you to outfit him in some decent clothing, complete with a hat and boots. When you've finished, bring him back to me, and bring one of those Spencer carbines and some ammunition with you. Understand?"

"Yes, sir!"

"Good, now get to it, and send the sergeant back in here."

The sergeant overheard the conversation and appeared immediately. "You need me again, Colonel?"

"Yes, Sergeant, get the chaplain back up here as soon as you can."

"I anticipated that, Sir. I've already sent someone after him."

"You're a good man, Sergeant. I suppose you know I could get into trouble for what I'm about to do."

"I don't know what you're talking about, Sir. The way I see it, we have three Union deserters who are dangerous, and you're trying to see that they do not harm any citizens."

"You are exactly right, Sergeant, but if I do get into trouble, you don't know anything."

With a smile the sergeant said. "I'm mighty forgetful, Sir."

He had just finished speaking when a corporal appeared with Pat.

At the Colonel's invitation, Pat entered the room. The Colonel asked him to be seated.

"Chaplain, I'm going to put myself on the line, because I feel I owe you so much."

"What do you mean, Colonel?"

"Hagan and his two henchmen have deserted. With the fixation that Hagan seems to have on your wife, I'm very concerned because we don't know where they are or what they're going to do."

"I understand the situation, Colonel, and I'm concerned about it, but what can be done?"

The Colonel responded, "What I'm going to do, Chaplain, is this. I'm going to give you my horse. His name is Raven, and he will be completely outfitted for travel. After you've cleaned up, you will be given some clean clothes to change into. I will see that you are armed with a rifle and my personal .44 caliber Remington revolver with two extra cylinders already loaded. If you are not familiar with that model, Sergeant Nelson will brief you on how it works. I will also see that you have a pass that should get you past any Union patrols. You will be given money for travel and a map, which I have drawn, indicating what I believe is the best route for you to take. I suggest that you ride as hard as you can and get home as quickly as possible. One other thing, I believe it would be better if you bypassed Atlanta."

"Colonel, I don't know how to thank you."

"You can thank me by seeing that your wife and family are safe. Now, go back and tell Cofer and Bracewell what's going on, then come back here and get cleaned up and be on your way."

"I'll do that, Sir," replied Pat as he flew out the door, almost forgetting that he needed to be in the company of an escort.

The Colonel yelled after him, "Chaplain, take good care of that horse!"

Pat quickly told Jud and Deke of the colonel's decision to set him free. He grabbed few personal items and the Bible that the colonel had lent him; then he and his escort rushed back to the colonel's office. After returning the Bible to the colonel, Pat shook his hand and thanked him once again. Within thirty minutes he had taken a bath, put on clean clothes, and was in the saddle headed home. The Colonel's .44 Remington was holstered on his left hip.

Standing dangerously close to the deadline, Jud and Deke watched him ride away.

"Thank God," said Jud.

"Amen to that," added Deke.

# 27

After learning of Lee's surrender, there was an air of uncertainty among the guards as well as the prisoners. Colonel Randolph sensed this and wanted to do whatever possible to relieve the tension on both sides of the fence. As he watched Pat's departure, he saw that Jud and Deke were also watching from a place very close to the deadline. He shifted his eyes to the guard towers where two of the guards had their rifles trained on the two prisoners. They didn't fire, but they were ready should they feel the need to do so.

He thought to himself, "If someone got shot, it would surely start a riot."

"Sergeant," he called!

"Yes, Colonel."

"Sergeant, have Lieutenant Pringle report to me."

Within five minutes, Pringle was standing in the Colonel's office.

"Lieutenant, I want you to see that the deadline is removed. Notify all guards of what is taking place and tell them that all prisoners will have the use of the entire prison yard all the way to the fence. There is to be no more deadline."

Yes, sir, as you wish, Sir."

Within a few minutes, Lieutenant Pringle had informed the guards of the Colonel's decision and had begun the task of removing the deadline posts. As the removal of the posts continued, there was less anxiety among the prisoners, as well as the guards. The colonel surmised that, so far as the prisoners were concerned, it was the first visible proof that they were actually going to be set free. The guards seemed more at ease simply because they surmised that removal of the posts was an indication that the war would soon be over.

As Colonel Randolph watched Pringle and his crew work in the prison yard, there was a knock on his door. He gave his usual one word response, "Enter," then moved around behind his desk and took a seat.

"Sir, there are two men from Warehouse B out here who'd like a word with you."

"I was watching Lieutenant Pringle's crew work when these two came up to me and requested to see you. I took the liberty of bringing them up here. I hope I didn't overstep my bounds, Sir."

"Not at all, Sergeant. What are their names?"

"Privates Jud Cofer and Deke Bracewell, Sir. They worked with the Chaplain in taking care of the wounded prisoners."

"Yes, I'm familiar with them. They're good men. Send them on in, and get another chair in here so both of them can sit down."

Jud and Deke came in, followed by the sergeant with a second chair.

"Good morning, gentlemen, please be seated."

"Thank you, Sir," they responded in unison.

"Now what is it that you wish to see me about?"

Jud moved to the edge of his seat, "Sir, me and Deke wanted to talk to you about Chaplain Ravenwood."

"What about him?"

"Sir, we, that is me and Deke, figure that he's riding into a hornet's nest, and we was wondering if anything could be done to help him out."

"What did you have in mind? If you have a suggestion, I'd like to hear it."

"Well, Sir, I don't know exactly how to say it. I ain't never talked to no colonel before."

"Don't worry about that. You're doing fine. Now, tell me

146

what's on your mind."

"Colonel, Sir, what I want to say is that me and Deke would like to go help the Chaplain out. We've been through a lot together. He's helped us out many times, so we kinda feel like we owe it to him to help him out."

"I know how you feel, Private. I feel the same way. Are you asking me to release you two as I did the chaplain?"

"Yes, sir, that's about what it amounts to, though I don't know how we would catch up with him."

The colonel thought for a moment, then got up from his desk and began studying a map on the wall. He turned and faced Jud. "Private, evidently you and I have been thinking the same thoughts."

That said, the Colonel opened the door of his office and spoke to the sergeant in the other room. "Sergeant, how many mules do we have?"

"We have ten, Sir, but We can spare two, if I know what the Colonel is thinking."

"Saddles?"

"We have two that we could spare although they not in very good shape, and before the Colonel asks, we have two Spencer Rifles that we can spare."

"Sergeant, don't you know that thinking like a colonel can get you in trouble?"

"The way things are going, Sir, I'd be in good company," he replied with a grin.

The Colonel returned to his seat behind his desk and said to Jud and Deke, "All right privates, this is what I can do. I cannot spare another horse, but I can spare two mules with saddles and enough provisions for you to get to Pine Creek. I can also provide two Spencer carbines with adequate ammunition."

Jud spoke up, "That's good news Colonel, but what about the wounded down in Warehouse B? Who's going to look after them?"

"I'm putting Sergeant Nelson in charge of the wounded and the sick. I can assure you that he and his squad will do a good job."

The Colonel returned to his chair behind his desk. "What you need to do now is go back to Warehouse B, get whatever you need, then report back here in no less than thirty minutes. I'll have someone get some different clothes and a hat for each of you. When you have cleaned up and changed clothes, report back here ready to ride."

Both men jumped to their feet. "We'll be back in less time than that." Jud responded as they headed for the door.

True to their word, they were back in less than thirty minutes. The sergeant was waiting for them in front of the the colonel's office with two saddled mules outfitted with bedrolls, slickers, and provisions. Attached to each saddle was a saddle scabbard that contained a .52 caliber Spencer repeating carbines.

As the men were examining their mounts, Colonel Randolph stepped down from the front porch of his office. "Gentlemen, I believe we have outfitted you as well as we can under the circumstances. You have a map that I've drawn that shows the same route that I suggested to Chaplain Ravenwood, and you also have two passes that should get you past any Union patrols. One final thing, you may not be familiar with those Spencer carbines, so I have asked Sergeant Nelson to show you how they operate."

He shook their hands and said, "Good luck, gentlemen. You've got a hard ride ahead of you. I hope it's a successful one. Please give Chaplain Ravenwood and his family my regards."

"Sergeant Nelson, you may proceed with your instructions on firing those rifles."

"Thank you Colonel. You men listen carefully, because you need to be on your way."

Pulling one of the rifles from its scabbard, he said, "This

rifle is a .52 caliber Spencer, lever-action, repeating carbine. It holds seven rounds in the magazine and one in the chamber. Under the circumstances that you are facing, I recommend that you always have a round in the chamber and a full magazine."

The sergeant demonstrated the loading procedure and how the lever action worked. He then gave each of them an ample supply of ammunition in a leather pouch, and they were soon on their way.

# 28

Pat had been on the road south for three hours when Jud and Deke left Clonnerville Prison. There was no question about it. The colonel had put him astride a fine horse. Raven was an eight-year-old, solid black Missouri Fox Trotter gelding that stood about 15.5 hands tall. He was bred for endurance and craved opportunities to prove it. Pat, who had grown up with horses, soon discovered that he was on a horse that was intelligent and strong-willed. He also learned that Raven was willing to be cooperative, but never subservient.

They had not traveled far before Pat realized that they could cover more ground if he let Raven set his own pace. Strange as it might seem, Raven seemed to sense Pat's urgency and quickly established a routine of pacing himself by mixing rapid gaits with slower ones. There were times when Pat would slow him to a walk, only to have him move into a faster gait after a hundred yards or so. Nevertheless, Pat was concerned about Raven's welfare because it was a hundred and sixty miles from Clonnerville Prison to Pine Creek.

It did not bother Jud or Deke to be given mules to ride. Both of them were South Georgia farm boys and had worked with mules ever since they were old enough to walk behind a plow.

They knew that mules were neither stubborn nor stupid, as is generally perceived. A mule is an intelligent animal who can cover a lot of ground in one day, whether it's pulling a plow or carrying a saddle and rider. Both Jud and Deke knew mules have very good memories. They will remember kindness as well as cruelty and respond accordingly.

Jud and Deke were not on the trail long before they realized that they had a couple of good mounts beneath them. However, one situation that they did not expect was the competitive nature of the two mules. Neither one wanted the other one to get ahead. While this enabled them to cover a lot of ground, Jud and Deke were faced with the problem of getting their mounts to pace themselves.

At the same time, Hagan, Perkins, and Lawton were riding hard, trying to put as much distance as possible between themselves and Captain Wesley's troops. In order to avoid contact with any other Union military units, they bypassed towns and stuck to the less traveled roads. Unknown to Pat, they were headed in the general direction of Pine Creek.

In Pine Creek, Molly Ann walked into Sam's store. "Good morning Papa. Do you have anything for me to do while Johnny's in school?"

"Not really, we're running low on supplies, so there's no restocking to be done. You could do a little dusting and sweeping if you'd like."

"I'll be glad to help out," Molly Ann replied. "Where's Mama?"

"She's at the house fixing us something to eat. I'm sure there will be enough for all of us, so why don't you stay and eat with us?"

"I'd love to do that, but I'll need to be home when Johnny gets out of school."

"How's my favorite grandson doing in school?"

"He's doing fine, Papa, although he does like to daydream a lot. I think sometimes he has his mind on his horse more than he does on his studies."

Sam responded "Maybe I can take him out to the farm this afternoon if you and your ma could watch the store."

"That would be so nice." Then she gave him a peck on the cheek.

Hesitantly, she continued, "Papa, I know I ask the same

151

thing every day, but are the telegraph lines still down? I don't see Mr. Emory in the telegraph office."

Sam put his arms around her. "The lines are still down. We have no telegraph and no train service. With no telegraph and no trains, there's no reason for Mr. Emory to be there all day, but he does check every hour just to see if by chance the telegraph is working again."

"When you see him, would you ask him to let us know if he hears anything about Pat?"

"Honey, I've already done that."

To the north, Pat and Raven topped a hill and saw a small cabin and a dilapidated barn in the distance. An old mule and a milk cow were grazing in a small pasture nearby. Pat was tired and so was Raven, so he decided it was time for them to call it a day.

Pat rode down to the house and stopped at the remnants of a rail fence in front of the house. He could see a wisp of smoke twirling up from the chimney.

"Hello, the house!" he called.

At first there was no response. Then, the front door of the house opened slightly. Through the crack in the door appeared the barrel of a muzzle loading rifle. It was followed by an elderly, rather stooped old farmer with his thin, equally stooped wife right behind him.

Gesturing the gun toward Pat, the old farmer said, "State yore business, stranger."

"Sir, ma'am, I'd like your permission to water my horse, and if you don't mind, I would like to spend the night in your barn."

"Step a little closer so I can see you." At that point, the old man's wife stuck her hand in her pocket and fished out a pair of badly scratched glasses and put them on the old man.

"Air you Yankee or Reb young feller?"

Pat explained, "I am a Confederate Chaplain, I was just released from a Yankee prison camp and I am on my way home."

"Did you say you was a captain?"

"I said chaplain. I was a chaplain for the Confederates until I got captured. I've been released. Now, I'm on my way home."

The old farmer turned to his wife. "What's a chap-lin?"

She leaned toward his right ear and said, "preacher."

"Hee, Hee, Hee, a preacher! Well I'll be danged." Leaning the gun against the house, he waved to Pat. "Come on in, Preacher."

Pointing to the old muzzle-loader, "That thang ain't loaded no how. Ain't got no powder."

"I appreciate the invitation, Sir, but I'd like to see to my horse first."

"Good fer you, young feller. They's a well around back with a water trough right next to it. Take yore hoss 'round there and draw him some good, cool water. He can drink all he wants. You kin come in the back door."

His wife elbowed him and whispered in his ear. "Ma says preachers come in the front door."

Pat watered Raven, brought him back around front and tied him to one of the posts on the front porch. The old farmer met him at the door. "We was just fixin' to eat supper when you rode up. We'd be obliged if you'd set and eat with us."

Pat walked in the house, took off his hat, and looked around the room. On the table were two plates. Each plate contained two biscuits and two small slices of fried sow belly and a serving of beans in some white sauce. The old lady motioned him to a chair and placed an empty plate on the table in front of him. He was startled at the way she served his meal. She took a biscuit and a slice of meat from each of their plates and gave them to Pat. Then from each of their plates, she spooned some beans and white sauce into his plate. He started to protest, but didn't. To refuse what they offered would be an insult to their hospitality.

When the old lady had poured Pat a cup of slightly tinted

153

water which they called coffee, they asked Pat to say the blessing.

After the blessing, Pat said to the farmer, "I would like to buy some grain from you for my horse."

"Ain't got no grain, but you're welcome to some hay that's out there in the barn."

After they had finished eating, Pat took Raven to the barn and gave him some hay.

As Raven was munching on the hay, Pat removed the saddle and rubbed him down thoroughly.

When he had completed the rubdown, he removed a slab of smoked bacon and some hard biscuits from his saddle bags. He sliced off half of the bacon, counted out half his biscuits and took them to the house.

He gave both items to the farmer's wife. "I would like to provide breakfast for y'all in appreciation for your hospitality."

They accepted the gifts and Pat returned to the barn, where he and Raven got a good night's rest. He was dressed and saddling Raven the next morning when the farmer cracked the barn door and and announced that breakfast was nearly ready.

As Pat walked in the kitchen with his saddle bags slung over his right shoulder, the old woman was about to dump some very used coffee grounds in to the coffee pot that was half full of boiling water.

Pat took the cup of used coffee grounds from her and said, "Please, let me do that."

After Pat disposed of the used coffee, he took a pouch from his pocket and poured some of its contents into the pot. It was coffee.

"Young man, you've been brung up right." Then she added, "Ain't that right, Pa?"

# 29

Jud and Deke rode through sundown, spent the rest of the night under the stars and were back in the saddle before sunrise the next morning. They ate hard biscuits for breakfast while sitting astride their mules. By riding into the night and leaving before day the next morning, they had gained some ground on Pat. They arrived at the farmer's cabin just two hours after Pat had left. To the south of them, Hagan, Perkins, and Lawton were drawing closer to Pine Creek.

At the farmer's cabin, Jud and Deke watered their mules at the well and discreetly left a bag of beans and some smoked bacon on the back porch. They knew poverty and hunger when they saw it. When the mules had finished drinking the water that Deke had drawn for them, they were allowed to graze for a few minutes in a pasture behind the old farmer's house. While the mules were grazing, Jud and Deke checked their weapons. When they were sure they were clean and ready to fire, they saddled up, returned the weapons to their saddle scabbards, and continued on their way. They were slowly but surely gaining on Pat. It was not that they were traveling faster than he; they were simply putting in more hours in the saddle than he was.

As they had done the night before, they rode past sundown and into the night. Their thinking was that Pat would stop before nightfall so that he could pitch camp and fix his meal before dark. They were pushing their mules awfully hard, but they figured if they could push on for at least two hours after sundown they would gain a lot of ground on Pat. They were correct in their thinking, but they were in for a surprise when they finally located Pat's camp.

The road on which they were traveling was through a relatively flat area, with only a few curves. They had just slowed their mounts down to a walk to give them a rest when suddenly, both mules stopped in their tracks. With their heads raised, ears pointing forward, they stared straight ahead into the moonlit night. Neither Jud nor Deke could see anything, but the mules had detected something down the road in front of them.

Jud reached over, touched Deke's arm and said softly, "I smell smoke."

"Me too. Do you think it's the chaplain's camp?"

"I don't know, but let's not take any chances!"

They dismounted and eased their Spencer rifles out of their scabbards. After checking to be sure that each gun had a round in the chamber, they began walking forward, leading their mules. Rounding a slight curve in the road, they spotted a fire flickering in the woods off to the right of the road. They tied their mules to a bush beside the road, crept closer to the campfire. Suddenly Jud's arm shot out and grabbed Deke's arm and then he held up four fingers. There were four men in the campsite. They could spot only one horse, and he seemed to sense their presence. Three of the men were huddled together busily sorting through a bedroll and a saddle bag. The men did not notice the horse getting restless, nor did the man next to the tree.

Jud whispered, "That horse is Raven and that's the chaplain next to the tree. It looks like he's tied up."

Deke responded, "You're right. What do you think we ought to do?"

"You ease around to the right about ten steps. Just be sure you have a clear shot and that the chaplain's not in the line of fire. I'll let 'em know we've got 'em covered. If they make a threatening move, don't hesitate to shoot."

Deke mouthed one word, "Yep," and moved about ten

steps to his right.

They were so close they could hear the men talking.

"Hell," one of them said, "He ain't got nothing but a pistol, that hoss, and a little money."

A second man responded, "That hoss and pistol oughta be worth something, but what about him? What are we gonna do with him? We can't let him tag along with us"

The third man answered, "You know damn well what we're gonna do."

From out of the darkness came Jud's voice. "Just set real easy. You ain't gonna do nothin' to the Chaplain!"

One of the men grabbed for Pat's pistol. It was the last thing he ever did. Deke's .52 caliber Spencer saw to that."

The other two jumped up, hands in the air, "Stop shooting! We weren't gonna hurt him." "Oh, I believe you. You ain't gonna harm a hair on his head, 'specially with two Spencers lookin' at you. Now move away from that fire. Deke, cut the Chaplain loose, then pick up their guns and get the chaplain's gun too."

"You all right, Chaplain?"

"I am now, thanks to you two. You don't know how glad I am to see you. Deke, that was some shooting, and in the dark too."

"Thank you, Chaplain."

Jud commented, "He don't say much, but he's a natchel-born shooter. That right, Deke?"

"I reckon it's so, but what are we gonna do about the other two?"

"Whatever the Chaplain says, but first of all I want some information from these two and it better be right."

Jud pointed his Spencer at the two. "Are y'all Rebs or Yanks?"

Together, they answered, "Reb."

After a bit more questioning, Pat, Jud, and Deke concluded they were deserters.

Now they had to decide what to do with them. With Pat and Jud standing guard, Deke went after the mules. When he returned, he helped Pat collect his gear and saddle Raven.

"What are y'all gonna do with us?" queried one of the prisoners.

Both Jud and Deke looked inquisitively toward Pat.

Pat answered, "The first thing we're going to do is let you bury your dead buddy. By the way, take his boots off first."

"But we ain't got no shovels to dig no grave."

"Then you can use your hands, unless you want to use those knives that you carry under your coats. I'm talking about the ones you thought I didn't see when you had me tied up."

Sheepishly, the two reached in their coats, pulled out their knives and started digging.

"After you bury him, we're going to turn you loose, but we'll take your boots and those that belonged to your buddy and leave them about a half a mile down the road."

Pat, Jud and Deke rode off into the night leaving three barefoot deserters behind, one of them dead and buried in a shallow grave. They threw the six boots randomly into the woods on either side of the road.

Deke asked, "You think they can find those boots, Chaplain?"

"If they can smell, they can find 'em with no problem at all."

# 30

On April 16, Easter Sunday, the main body of General James H. Wilson's army smashed through Girard, Alabama and attacked the city of Columbus, Georgia. Captain Wesley and his cavalry troops joined a detachment of Wilson's troops and attacked Columbus from the north on the Georgia side of the Chattahoochee River. This was the last battle of the Civil War. On Wednesday evening after Easter Sunday, John Henry had an unusually large crowd at prayer meeting at the Pine Creek Methodist Church, but they knew nothing of the significant events of the past week. Railroads and telegraph lines south of Macon were in shambles.

John Henry had led the congregation in singing *Amazing Grace* and was beginning the Bible study for the evening, when suddenly the front door of the church burst open. There stood a panting Will Emory, the telegraph operator and station manager for the railroad, waving two telegrams in the air.

"It's over!" he shouted. "It's over! The war's over!"

"Well, come on down front, Brother Emory and tell us what's going on," said John Henry as he laid his Bible down on the pulpit.

"I'm sorry to bother y'all and interrupt everything, but I thought you'd want to know."

"That's all right, Brother Emory, just calm down and talk to us."

"First of all, the telegraph lines have been repaired, but it will be a while before we have any train service."

A voice from the congregation, "Tell us about the war!"

"I'm getting to that. General Lee surrendered on Palm Sunday, April 9. Some other forces have surrendered. However, there are others that are still fighting, but for all practical purposes, the war is over."

"There's one other thing. It's a telegram from a Colonel Randolph. Evidently he is the Commander of the Union Prison where Pat is."

Molly Ann jumped to her feet. "What does it say? Is there any news about Pat?"

"Just give me a minute and I'll read it to you. Here's what it says. 'Patrick Ravenwood, Jud Cofer, and Deke Bracewell released to return to Pine Creek.' It don't say when they were released."

John Henry raised his hands to silence the crowd, "Be quiet, everyone. Let him finish.

Is there more, Brother Emory?"

"Yes, there are two other things the Colonel mentioned, and I'm afraid I must tell you that both of them are bad news. The Colonel says we should be on the lookout for three Union deserters who are likely headed this way. He says they are armed and dangerous. The telegram don't give us any more information about them."

Mayor Davis stood and spoke to the congregation, "Brother John, please forgive me for interrupting, but let me speak to what Brother Emory just mentioned. The fact that the war is over doesn't mean that we no longer have to be concerned about our safety, especially since we know that some deserters are headed in our direction."

The murmuring in the crowd made it hard to hear the Mayor.

John Henry's booming voice rang out above the crowd noise. "Y'all be quiet and let the Mayor finish."

The Mayor continued, "As I was about to say, we cannot relax. There's still a need for caution. Continue to be on your guard. Keep your doors locked. Don't be out at night unnecessarily, and certainly, you should not be out alone. Although

160

I feel a little uncomfortable saying this, keep your firearms handy, but please be careful. As we have done since Deputy Patterson left, we will still have our volunteer marshals on duty."

John Henry took the floor again. "Thank you, Mayor. That's some good advice. However, I'd like to add one other thing to it. If there is a problem or some sort of emergency, come here to the church and start ringing the church bell. Now y'all remember what I'm telling you. If that bell starts ringing at any time other than Sunday morning when it usually rings, then it's a signal to gather at Sam's store. That all right with you, Sam?"

"You know it is, John Henry, any time. If you don't mind, I'd like to add one more comment. You can gather at my store any time of day. If I'm closed, then gather on the front porch, and come prepared for anything."

"'Does anyone else have anything to say?" said John Henry.

"Yes," said Will Emory, "I did not get to finish. I don't know how this will affect us, but it is surely not going to help our relations with the Union. On this past Friday night, which was the evening of Good Friday, President Lincoln was assassinated by a Confederate sympathizer while attending a play at a theater in Washington." At that point, some of the congregation cheered.

Immediately, John Henry was on his feet. "Now y'all hold on just a minute. I have been yore pastor for twenty-five years, and I know and love ever one of y'all, but I'll ain't gonna stand here and say nothing when in God's house you cheer at the news that a murder's been committed. That's right, I'm talking about murder. Now y'all can say whatever you want to in yore own home, out in yore fields, or on the streets of Pine Creek. But there will be no cheering in this here church when another dies a violent death.... No sir! Not while I'm pastor here.

Now, if there is anyone who disagrees with what I have

161

said, I'll be glad to discuss it with you right outside the church right after the benediction."

He paused for a moment and said, "Let us pray."

*Almighty God, come into our hearts and cleanse us. Help us to be thankful people, thankful that this war is over. Give us the will to be compassionate toward the oppressed.*

*If we have been blessed, then let us rejoice with thanksgiving. Let us be instruments of comfort to those who mourn. Let us be a source of strength to those who are weak. Let us be a guiding light for those who are lost, and Let our lives be a reflection of the One who died for us.*

*Amen*

"I appreciate y'all being here tonight. Be sure to be back in church on Sunday morning. Remember we are living in perilous times and our future is uncertain. We're gonna need a lot of healing in this land, but keep in mind, we know the Great Physician."

As he walked down the aisle toward the door of the church, he said, "As you go home tonight, be careful, be on your guard, and be prayerful. Now, God bless you and good night."

No one chose to meet John Henry after the service and discuss his comments about cheering when the news of the assassination of President Lincoln was announced.

John Henry stayed at the church until everyone was safely on their way home.

He was relieved to see that Molly Ann's parents, were going to walk Molly Ann and Johnny home. At least they had neighbors nearby. It was different for Dan and Leona, Pat's parents. They lived out in the country two miles from town and completely isolated.

# 31

Wednesday night passed quietly, but the next night was a night to remember, especially for Dan and Leona and for the people of Pine Creek. Thursday began just as most days began in Pine Creek. There was the usual awakening of the town as families began to face the chores of the day. Stores began to open, and people greeted one another on the street. John Henry was one of the first to enter Sam's general store that morning. It was a ritual with him. He considered the store to be his information center. It kept him up-to-date on the activities of the community and also provided him with a good cup of coffee as he got his morning reports from Sam and others who made the store one of their early morning stops.

John Henry finished his Thursday morning coffee and handed the mug back to Susie, who always washed it for him and had it ready for the next day's visit.

"Thank you, Susie, for another cup the best coffee this side of Macon. I'd love to stay and have another, but I need to be on my way. See y'all in the morning."

Sam spoke from behind the counter, "Where are you off to, Brother John? I know you're going somewhere. I see you have Rambler tied up outside."

"I need to go visit some folks in the Shiloh area. They pay part of my salary, and I want'em to know they're getting their money's worth."

In a moment of levity, Sam said, "Now, don't start that. We all know you and we know you're not gonna cheat anybody."

"Only the devil, Sam, only the devil, I don't know of anybody I'd rather cheat than the devil. You know how I love cheating him out of a new citizen in hell. Every time somebody is converted, I feel like I've cheated him."

John Henry stepped off the sidewalk, put his left foot in the stirrup, and pulled himself astride Rambler. As soon as he was in the saddle, Rambler turned away from the hitching rail and headed toward the Shiloh community. He knew the way as well as John Henry.

Sam watched them leave and called after John Henry, "Preacher, while you're over in Shiloh cheating the Devil, be sure to take your fishing equipment with you."

The old preacher never looked back. He just patted his saddle bag, waved to Sam over his shoulder and kept on riding. In the Shiloh community, he visited the Howell family, ate dinner with the Simpsons and then headed back to Pine Creek around two o'clock. He didn't fish that afternoon. For some unknown reason, he felt compelled to get back to Pine Creek as soon as possible. He had a two-hour ride before him, so he began to push Rambler a little harder than usual. As John Henry was riding toward Pine Creek from the south, three riders in dusty Union uniforms were approaching it from the west. They, too, had a two-hour ride before of them.

The riders from the west, Hagan, Perkins, and Lawton, arrived at Otto's Bar about the same time that John Henry arrived at Sam's general store and dismounted next to Dan Ravenwood's two-horse wagon. Dan's horses were tied to the store's hitching rail. Josh Taylor's horse was also there. Next to Josh's horse was Cliff Johnson's mare. As John Henry swung down from the saddle, he wondered what was going on. Their presence did nothing to ease the foreboding feeling that had been gnawing at him most of the afternoon.

As he walked into the store, he noted that Will Emory was there from the telegraph office. Susie, Leona and Molly Ann were off to one side behind one of the counters.

"Good afternoon gentlemen, you too, ladies," tipping his

hat, "What's going on? Is this a private meeting?"

Sam responded. "Absolutely not, John Henry, we're glad you're here. Dan is here to pick up supplies. The others just drifted in. Frankly, I'm glad to see everybody here. Will Emory just brought us the news that the telegraph service is down again. We were thinking we had better be on our guard, because we're isolated again, and we have no law enforcement except Jeff and Tom and their ax handles."

John Henry poured himself a cup of coffee. "I figured something was going on. My gut's been telling me something was not right all day long."

Will Emory added, "We don't know that anything is going on, John Henry. All we know for sure is the telegraph system is down again. I don't want us to jump to any conclusions and get the people upset over nothing."

John Henry took a sip of his coffee. "Will, when did the telegraph system quit working?"

"Let's see, it's a little after four now. I guess it was about two o'clock. It's just like it was before. The whole system's down."

"Any of you gentlemen speculate on why the system is down?"

"No John, we don't have any idea." Sam responded. "Do you have any ideas?"

"What put the system out last time, Will?"

"Skirmishes with the Yankees, renegade raiding parties, and deserters."

At that, John Henry just looked each of them with raised eyebrows. "And you don't think there's some of that going on again, Will?"

"John Henry, I just don't know. It could be anything. I think we've done about all we can. We have alerted the people to gather here at the store if there's an emergency."

Will paused and then continued. "What do you think we ought to do?"

As John Henry turned to refill his cup, he said, "Publius Flavius Vegitius Renatus."

"What does that mean?" asked Will.

"It's not what. It's who. And the who is Publius Flavius Vegitius Renatus, the Roman writer who said, 'In times of peace, prepare for war.'"

About the same time that John Henry was walking into Sam's store, Hagan, Perkins, and Lawton came stalking into Otto's Bar. It was a quiet afternoon, but that was about to change. As soon as they entered the bar, Otto knew trouble was on the way. He checked to see that his ax handle was handy. Two locals at the end of the bar casually looked the three newcomers over and turned back to their beers. Buddy Jarvis, Otto's part-time helper, was sweeping the floor. At a table in the corner was Virgil Palmer, drunk and sound asleep.

Hagan and the other two stopped just inside the door to allow their eyes to adjust to the dimness of the room. When they got to the bar, Hagan growled, "Hey you, barkeep, how about a little service here."

Otto came to where the three were standing. "What can I get for you?"

"A bottle of your good stuff and three glasses, and make it quick. We ain't got all day," Hagan grouched.

"Coming right up," Otto said as he put the bottle and three glasses before them.

With his hand still on the bottle, Otto said, "That'll be two dollars, gentlemen."

"Two dollars! I ain't paying no two dollars for no bottle of Reb whiskey."

Otto responded, "Suit yourself," as he turned and placed the bottle back on the shelf behind the bar.

"Ah, what the hell," Hagan sneered as he flung two dollars down on the bar.

After they had downed some of the whiskey, Hagan called out, "Hey, barkeep. We'd like a little information. You don't charge for that, do you?"

Otto replied, "No charge, it goes with the territory. What do you want to know?"

"You got any Ravenwoods living around here?"

"Seems to me I've heard the name, but I don't exactly know where they live."

Hagan was in his face, "Now barkeep, you've got a nice little business here, and I'm sure you don't want it messed up which it's gonna be if I don't get some answers in hurry. I've got a message from a Chaplain Ravenwood for his pretty little wife, Molly Ann."

Otto replied, "I don't know exactly where they live. All I know is it's somewhere west of town."

"Scuze me, Yanz", slurred a very inebriated Virgil Palmer. "I just might be able ta hep ya out iffen I had a small toddy to wet my whizzle, iffen you know what I mean."

"Why, that's mighty kind of you, Sir." said Hagan. "Barkeep, give us another glass."

Otto glared at Virgil across the bar. "Virgil, shut up!"

Hagan spoke sharply "I said give us another glass, barkeep!"

Otto put a glass on the bar and continued to glare at Virgil.

"Hagan poured a few drops of whiskey in Virgil's glass. "Take just a little sip of that and see if that's what you want."

Virgil sipped it. Shoved the glass back and said, "More."

Hagan patted him on the back. "You can have all you want when you tell me where the Ravenwoods live."

Again Otto said, "Virgil, shut up."

Hagan pulled his pistol from its holster and laid it on the bar. "You're the one that needs to shut up, Mr. Barkeep."

He poured a little more whiskey in Virgil's glass.

Virgil, licking his lips forced himself to speak clearly, said, "Go back west 'bout a mile."

Hagan interrupted him. "Damn, we came from the west.

You mean we go back that way to the Ravenwood's house?"

Th.. Th.. Thaz right...zen..you turn right at ... the ... nesh... road, zen go maybe one more .. mile. thu .. house ziz on thu right, But Molly ... "

Before he could finish his sentence, Otto knocked him cold with a hard right cross to the chin. Then he backhanded Hagan, who was bringing his pistol up to fire on Otto, but the surprise of Otto's backhand caused him to fire wildly, hitting Otto in the leg rather than his chest as Hagan had intended.

Before he could fire again, Rat Perkins grabbed his arm. "Let's get outta here, Buck, while we've got a chance."

The three of them dashed out to their horses. Just barely in their saddles, they kicked their horses into a dead run headed west. As they rode away, Buddy Jarvis lit out to ring the bell at the Methodist Church.

# 32

John Henry had just poured his second cup of coffee and placed the pot back on the stove when the church bell began to ring. Still holding his coffee cup in his hand, he and the others rushed out to the front porch of Sam's store. As the church bell continued to ring, more people gathered in front of the store.

Josh Taylor stepped into his saddle, "I'm going to the church to see what the problem is."

He was about to ride off when he saw Buddy panting down the street from the church. "We need help at Otto's place. He's been shot."

Josh dismounted, grabbed him by the arm and eased him over to the steps where he could sit down. "Just calm down and tell us what's going on. Who shot Otto? Is the shooter still there?"

"There was three of 'em, all dressed in Yankee uniforms, but they's gone now."

"How bad is Otto hit?"

"He's shot in the leg, and he needs help right now. He's bleeding bad. God! I ain't never seen nobody get shot before."

Josh turned to the crowd and searched out Will Emory's face. "Will, take two men with you and go see about Otto."

"Now just calm down, Buddy, and tell us what happened that got Otto shot."

"Well, things were pretty quiet, just a few of us having a drink like we usually do, when all of sudden these three Yankees come struttin' in just like they owned the place."

"Are you sure they were Yankee soldiers?"

"It's like I said, Mr. Josh. They was wearing Yankee uniforms. One of them was a sergeant and the other two, I just don't know what they was. I think they was privates. I guess all of them was Yankees, though I don't know for certain."

"That's all right, Buddy," Josh continued. "Just tell us what happened and where these three went."

"They got a bottle from Otto and started drinking. After they had two or three drinks apiece, they started asking questions."

John Henry asked, "What kind of questions?"

"They wanted to know where the Ravenwoods live, and they mentioned Molly Ann."

Almost in unison, Dan and Leona asked, "Why did they want to know where we live?"

"I don't know about that. Anyway, nobody would tell them anything. Then they offered to buy anyone a drink who would tell them what they wanted to know. That's when old Virgil got involved."

"My God!" said John Henry, "What did that old sot tell them?"

"He told them where Dan and Leona live and he was about to tell them about Molly Ann. That's when Otto knocked Virgil cold, and in the fracas Otto got shot in the leg."

"So Virgil didn't tell them where Molly Ann lives."

"No, he didn't," Buddy continued, "but I think they're on the way to Dan's house now."

John Henry turned to Dan, "We need to get out to yore house right now!"

As Dan headed for his wagon, John Henry said to the other men. "If you've got a horse, mount up! If you don't have a horse here at the store, ride with Dan in the wagon. Sam, you stay here with the women. Get two or three men to stay with you! Let's ride!"

As the men from Sam's store were galloping out of town, Hagan, Perkins, and Lawton were dismounting in front of the Ravenwood house.

"See if anybody's home." Hagan said as he knelt down to examine his horse's right front foot. "Damn," he said, "He's lost a shoe."

Rat Perkins came back down the steps and joined Hagan at his horse. "Ain't nobody at home. Want us to bust in and see what we can find while you see about yore horse?"

"Don't bother with the house right now. Let's go to the barn and see if by chance there's a horse out there. If this dirt farmer's got a half-way decent one, then I'll swap with him. Otherwise, we'll just have to ride on. I've got a feeling we don't have much time."

The three of them went to the barn behind the house. There was nothing in any of the stalls so they continued on to the back door of the barn.

"Would you look at that! That's a fine looking saddle horse." Hagan exclaimed as he looked out into a small pasture behind the barn.

The horse that Hagan saw was Johnny's horse, Stormy. Since he had never been mistreated and was very trusting, he was no trouble to catch. Hagan had him saddled up and his gear tied on in no time.

"What about yore horse?" Perkins asked Hagan.

"Leave him. He'd just slow us down."

As they were coming out of the barn, they saw the men from Pine Creek charging toward them about a half a mile away.

Hagan mounted Johnny's horse, "Let's get outta here! We're too outnumbered to shoot it out with'em. Perkins, you set fire to that hay in the barn. Maybe they'll stop to fight the fire."

Within minutes smoke was billowing out every opening in the barn. Hagan and the other two escaped just minutes ahead of the approaching posse from Pine Creek. The men in the posse decided the prudent thing to do was to fight the fire rather than continue their pursuit of the three men responsible for shooting Otto. Fortunately most of the barn was saved due to the diligence and quick thinking of the posse. Meanwhile, Hagen, Perkins, and Lawton continued their hard riding until they were certain they were not followed.

With the fire under control, John Henry, Josh Taylor, and Cliff Johnson went back to town. Several men agreed to stay with Dan all night to be sure that the fire didn't blaze up again. They were also concerned for Dan's safety in case Hagan, Perkins, and Lawton returned.

When John Henry, Josh, and Cliff got back to Sam's store, they were greeted with a barrage of questions. "Josh, why don't you tell'em what happened. These old bones of mine ain't what they used to be," John Henry said as he stretched out on the counter.

"I'll be glad to, John. Fortunately the news is not as bad as it could have been, not by a long shot. First of all Leona, the house is all right. Dan's all right. Nobody got hurt. Dan didn't come back with us because he and some of the other men are going to stay at the farm just in case there's some trouble. Those men that Buddy warned us about set fire to the hay in the barn, but we put it out before it did much damage. That's another reason Dan and the others stayed at the farm. They wanted to be sure the fire doesn't blaze up again."

"Thank the Lord nobody was hurt, and we're glad the news is as good as it seems to be, Josh." Susie said as she walked over and gave him a hug.

It was nearly sundown when Will Emory and Buddy Jarvis walked in Sam's store. The expression on their faces told everyone something was terribly wrong. John Henry noticed it immediately.

"You fellers look troubled. What's on yore mind?"

Will and Buddy looked at each other, then Buddy said,

172

"Tell'em Will."

"I hate to be the one to bring y'all bad news, so I'll just go ahead and lay it out for you.

Otto didn't make it. He was still alive when Buddy and me got'im to Doc Bell's office, but he couldn't help'im. He said he'd lost too much blood."

Sam McDaniel took his apron off, wadded it up and threw it on the counter. "If that don't beat all. Finally the war is over and now we have Yankee murderers running loose, Lord only knows where."

"Do we know anything about them ... anything at all?" Leona asked.

Josh responded, "This is what we know, but I think the sketchy information that we have is correct. First, we know that three Union deserters were headed this way. Second, we know that they came from Clonnerville Prison where Pat was a prisoner, and third, we know that they knew Pine Creek is where Pat lives and that he is married to Molly Ann."

"But how did he know Molly Ann's name?" asked Leona.

Suddenly Molly Ann cried out, "The mail! It's the mail! That has to be what it is! I haven't received any mail from Pat, and he probably hasn't received any of my letters. That murderer was reading our mail. I know that's what happened."

John Henry spoke up at this point. "I think you're right, Molly Ann. Based on what happened at Otto's, we know he's a killer and evidently a degenerate, mentally twisted, and morally corrupt demon who may have some sort of fixation on you."

He continued, "Molly Ann, I'm concerned about the safety of you and Johnny. I really believe y'all are in danger so long as those renegades are on the loose."

"John Henry," Sam said, "maybe she and Johnny ought to move in with us."

"I think that would be a good idea, Sam."

John Henry turned back to Molly Ann, "You pay attention to what I say. This is serious. Don't you go anywhere alone, and don't be by yourself anywhere, not even at yore Pa's house.

"Now, I don't want to frighten you unnecessarily, but don't let Johnny be alone either. Do you understand what I saying?"

"Yes, sir, I do. Believe me, I do."

Josh spoke hesitantly. "I hate to give y'all more disturbing news, but when you mentioned Johnny, it reminded me of something else those scoundrels did. When they were at the Ravenwood farm, they not only set fire to the barn, but they stole Johnny's horse."

Molly Ann collapsed into her mother's arms, "I don't know if Johnny can handle this. That horse was his connection with his dad. Oh, God, I wish Pat was here."

At this point, Will Emory spoke. "Josh, both of us are on the town council. I think we need to get with the Mayor and have him call a town meeting at John Henry's church, so we can let the folks know what's going on."

That evening an uneasy calm settled over the town. There was no one on the streets. Doors were locked, shades were drawn, and guns were handy. In the town of Pine Creek, fear had the upper hand.

# 33

The next morning, the citizens of Pine Creek awakened to a seemingly normal day and cautiously settled into their daily routines. Businesses opened, and children walked to school, occasionally accompanied by a parent or grandparent. The telegraph lines were still down. There would be no mail again today because there was no rail service.

Will Emory was at the train station. There was no reason for him to be there, but he was there out of habit and because that's where he was supposed to be. He stepped out on the loading dock and looked at his watch, something he did probably a hundred times every day. It was ten o'clock. He put his watch back into his vest pocket and turned to go back inside the station. As he was about to enter the station warehouse area, he glanced up the street toward the north. What he saw disturbed him. Three riders were coming into town. He quickly stepped back inside the warehouse. Closing the sliding door behind him, he moved quickly over to a nearby window. From there, he cautiously watched as the riders rode past the depot. All three were heavily bearded, unkempt, and dressed in what appeared to be a mixture of Union and Confederate uniforms. They wore black cavalry hats that partially hid their faces. They were armed with readily accessible rifles in saddle scabbards. The leader had a pistol in a military holster on his left hip.

Will continued to watch them as they stopped and dismounted in front of Sam's general store. The tall, gaunt leader of the three entered the store first. The other two followed, taking their rifles with them. Remembering the incident at

Otto's Bar, Will grabbed his musket and headed toward Sam's store. Sam and Susie were in the storage room trying to determine what to order if the trains ever started running again. Molly Ann was putting jars of pickles on a shelf in the main part of the store. She did not hear the three men enter.

The leader, standing in front of the other two, removed his hat, ran his fingers through his disheveled hair and said, "Molly Ann, I come ..."

Without thinking, she replied, "I came, not I come!"

She dropped a jar of pickles, turned around and screamed, "Pat, you're home!"

Then she flung herself across the room into his arms. Jud and Deke just stood there grinning as she smothered a bearded Pat with kisses.

Suddenly, in the door of the storage room, there stood Sam, muzzle loader in hand, cocked and ready. "Mister, you turn her loose right now or you're a dead man."

He had hardly finished speaking when Will Emory burst through the front door with his musket, also cocked and ready. "Don't nobody move!"

Sam spoke again. "I said turn her loose, and I mean right now!"

Pat held his arms out. "I can't turn her loose, Sam! She's got me! Can't a man hug his own wife?"

"Pat? Is that you?"

"If I don't get shot it is."

Sam lowered the hammer on his weapon. Jud and Deke snickered.

Off to the side, a perplexed Will Emory looked at his rifle. "Dang, this thing ain't even loaded. Sure fooled me."

Greatly relieved, Jud and Deke responded, "Us too."

After giving Pat a hug, Susie said, "Sam, would you please go get Johnny from school. Mr. Will, would you please see that Dan and Leona get the word that Pat is home."

"I'll ride out there myself, just as soon as I can saddle

up." As he ran to the stable, Will spread the news of Pat's return. It wasn't long before Sam's store was filled with those who wanted to greet Pat. He was tired, hungry and needed a shave, but he was glad to see his friends. He was about to take a seat on a counter when the crowd parted and in walked Sam with Johnny.

Pat knelt down, opened his arms. "Hello, Son. Come over here and give your daddy a big hug." Johnny just stood there, picking at his fingernails and looking at Pat occasionally.

Finally, he spoke. "Are you really my daddy?"

"I sure am and mighty proud of it."

Johnny didn't know what to say, so he just stood there. He tried to speak but couldn't, then, just above a whisper, he asked, "Are you the one that gave me a horse?"

"I sure am. His name was Stormy, and when you first saw him, I gave you an apple to give to him."

Johnny wanted to say something, but the words just wouldn't come out. The tears began to well up in his eyes. He tried to wipe them away, but they kept coming until they were flowing down his cheeks. He looked at Molly Ann as if he were asking her what he should do. She nodded her head toward Pat ever so slightly. Johnny looked back at Pat who held out his arms once again. Nothing was said, They just looked into each other's eyes.

Suddenly, Johnny sprang across the room into the arms of his kneeling daddy, knocking him flat of his back on the floor. But it didn't matter. Pat got his hug, and all the people in the store cheered. Hardly anyone noticed that Dan and Leona, Pat's parents, had pushed their way through the crowd. They were taken aback by the scene on the floor. Their grandson was rolling around on the floor hugging some bearded man they didn't even recognize.

From the floor, Pat said, "Ma! Pa! It's me, Pat. I'm home!"

At first they were confused, then Johnny yelled, "It's my

177

daddy, and he's home!"

That was all it took. Dan and Leona rushed over, pulled Pat and Johnny to their feet, and the four of them hugged, cried, and laughed. Molly Ann, Sam and Susie could no longer stand it.

They rushed over and joined the hugging. It was the best family reunion ever.

From the back of the room, a familiar, booming voice began singing,

*Praise God from whom all blessings flow!*
*Praise him all creatures here below!*
*Praise him above ye heavenly hosts!*
*Praise Father, Son, and Holy Ghost!*  -Thomas Ken - 1674

John Henry made his way through the crowd and stood to one side while the Ravenwoods and the McDaniels celebrated. He had not been there long when Pat untangled himself from the rest of the family and walked over to John Henry. Not a word was spoken. They just hugged each other for a moment then John Henry stepped back, put his hands on Pat's shoulders and said, "I'm glad you're home, Son."

"Me too, Brother John." Pat paused for a few seconds, then added, "Brother John, I need to talk to you real soon."

John Henry replied, "Son, I see trouble in yore eyes. The sooner we talk, the better it will be. I'll talk with you any time, but first, you need to see to your family."

John Henry gave him another hug, and gently pushed him back toward his family.

As Pat moved away, John Henry turned to the crowd. "Friends we're all glad Pat's home, and this is a great homecoming celebration, but Pat is tired and has been through a lot. He needs to be with his family. Let's let them have a little time together, but before you leave, let me make one announcement. I have some sad news, but you need to have the information that I'm about to give you, so y'all pay attention."

"As y'all know, Otto died after being shot by one of them Yankee deserters that come through here yesterday. He was shot while trying to protect a family in this community. Will Emory and Buddy Jarvis took him to Doc Bell in Dykesboro. However, Doc couldn't save him. He said Otto had lost too much blood. I spoke to Buddy just a little while ago, and he said that evidently Otto knew he was dying, so on the way to Dykesboro, he talked to Buddy about his funeral."

John Henry paused for a moment, then continued, "Otto wasn't a member of any church, and he didn't have no family, but he told Buddy how he wanted his his funeral done. He requested that his funeral be held right here at his bar, and that's what we're gonna do. His service will be tomorrow morning at 10:00 o'clock, and I'll conduct the funeral. Be sure to spread the word about the time and place of the funeral so we'll have a good crowd. I hope to see y'all there. There's one other thing. The Mayor asked me to announce that there will be a town meeting tomorrow evening at the Methodist Church at 7:00 o'clock."

When John Henry had finished, Pat moved over beside Buddy Jarvis who was about to leave. "Buddy, could you wait around for a few minutes. I need to talk with you, but I need to speak to the Johnsons first."

"Sure, Pat, take your time. I'll be right here."

Pat escorted Cliff and Fay back to the storage room where they could talk privately. He seated them on a bench, and he sat on a nail keg in front of them.

He began, "I'm so sorry about Billy. I know this celebration must be tough on you."

Cliff spoke. "Pat, we're just glad to see you and to know that you're safe. So far as this day of celebrating being difficult, it's no more difficult than any other day. There's never a sunrise nor sunset that we don't think about Billy and miss him."

Pat responded, "Only those who have lost a child know

179

the hurt you're experiencing.

I can only hope that you will receive some degree of comfort in the knowledge that Billy's last thoughts were of you. I also want you to know that Billy was not alone in that prison camp. Jud Cofer, Deke Bracewell, and I were all in the same building with him. One of us saw him every day."

Pat told them of his prayers with Billy and what was said at his funeral. When they left that storage room, all three of them felt better for having talked.

Pat looked around for Buddy and found him in front of the store with Jud and Deke.

"I'm sorry I kept you waiting, Buddy, but I see you're in good company. I guess y'all have introduced yourselves."

"We have and we've had an interesting conversation." Buddy responded.

"We sure have, Chaplain," said Jud, "and it looks like the fellow that shot Otto is somebody we know. We believe it was Buck Hagan."

Pat described Hagan to Buddy. He knew that Jud had probably done the same, but he wanted to hear it for himself.

Buddy responded to Pat's description. "That sure sounds like him, Pat. In fact, I heard one of them call the one that shot Otto by name. He called him Buck."

"Thank you for that information Buddy. It looks like we will need to be on our guard at all times until he's caught."

As Buddy left, Pat turned to Jud and Deke, "I could spend a lot of time telling you two how much I appreciate all you've done for me, but I'm exhausted and want to go home."

He hugged their necks and quickly turned away before the tears came. It was an emotional time for the three of them. Together, they had survived Clonnerville Prison.

Together, they had beaten the odds of war and returned home. Jud called after him, "Chaplain, I've got a feeling we ain't through with this Hagan mess. If you need us, we'll be ready."

Pat responded with a wave over his shoulder. He knew

what Jud had said was true, but it wasn't important right now. He returned to the store and hugged his parents and Molly Ann's parents. Then he and Molly Ann walked home, each with an arm around the other's waist. Raven followed with Johnny in the saddle. As soon as they walked in the door, Pat sat down on the couch and promptly went to sleep. Molly Ann and Johnny didn't care. He was home. Later, Sam came by and quietly led Raven back to the barn where he unsaddled him, rubbed him down, and put him in a stall with a generous amount of grain to eat. It was Sam's way of showing Raven his appreciation for bringing Pat home from Clonnerville Prison one hundred sixty miles away.

# 34

The next morning Pat, Molly Ann and their parents attended Otto's funeral which was held at Otto's Bar as he had requested. John Henry conducted the funeral standing behind the bar and using it as a pulpit. Some of the ladies in the church had draped sheets over the bottles of whiskey on shelves behind the bar. Miss Minnie played some hymns on an old piano over in one corner of the room.

John Henry reminded those attending the funeral that it is a special person who's willing to put his own life on the line to protect someone else.

"That is exactly what Otto did. He was willing to sacrifice himself to protect a person in this community."

After the service, a covered dish dinner was spread on the bar.

Pat and Molly Ann got their plates and found a place where they could be by themselves. Both sets of parents and Johnny were seated together not too far away.

Pat began to reminisce, "Do you remember the first time we went to a picnic together?"

"Oh, I remember it very well. I was just dying for you to ask me. It was such a special time for me. I can still see you and your daddy driving up in that wagon, you with that old hat on your head."

Pat put his plate down, reached over and took Molly Ann's hand in his. "That picnic was special to me. When I was in prison, it was my love for you and memories of things like that picnic that kept me going."

"Oh, Pat, darling, you're going to make me cry."

They continued nibbling at their food and talking. When they finally finished eating, they decided to take the long way home, the way they did after picnics at the church before they were married. They left Johnny in the care of Sam and Susie, which was all right with Johnny because he knew there was a good chance he would get to ride Raven.

When they were out of sight, Molly Ann stopped, pulled Pat close, put her arms around his neck and kissed him.

She stepped back, took both his hands in hers. "Pat, we need to talk, or maybe it's you that needs to talk. I know you've been through a lot, and life in that prison wasn't easy for you. I love you dearly, and I know you well enough to know something's bothering you. Would you like to tell me about it?"

"I don't know if I can, Molly."

She persisted, "Well, I know it's not a problem with our love for each other. That was settled a long time ago, and it hasn't changed. So that means that both of us need to face up to whatever is bothering you. Now, if you don't want to talk about it, that's all right. Just remember, when you're ready to talk, I'm ready to listen."

"I know you love me and I love you," he said, "but you can't imagine what that prison did to me."

She replied, "You're right. I can't imagine how it was, but look at it this way, if you know what the problem is, and I have to try to guess what it is, then it's going to make it awfully hard for the two of us to work together. Don't you think?"

He grinned at her, "As I told you once a long time ago, 'Now I'm all confused.'" Then he broke down and told her about everything: his bitterness, his lack of faith, his desire to leave the ministry and his hatred for Buck Hagan.

"He's an animal, a cruel, sadistic beast. A young wounded prisoner died because of his cruelty. He killed Otto. He kept our mail from going through. He even knew your name and

Johnny's name, and somehow he knew how you looked..."

"My God, Molly Ann, did you send me a picture of your-self?"

"Yes, I did. Didn't you get it?"

"No! I never received it, and he's the reason. That's how he knew how you looked. He took it from one of your let-ters."

"While I was in that hell-hole of a prisoner-of-war camp, there were two things that kept me going. One was my love for you and knowing that you loved me. The other was my desire to get out of that place, track him down, and kill him."

He continued. "I'm home now, and I love you dearly, but I hate that man with a passion." Taking her hand in his, Pat said,. "Let's walk. There's something else I want to tell you."

They had walked for a while, holding hands, before Pat said anything. Molly Ann didn't want to push him, but she wanted him to share whatever was troubling him so much.

With a questioning tone in her voice, she said, "You said there was something else that you wanted to share with me?"

Pat responded, "I've made a very difficult decision, and it relates to things that happened in Clonnerville and what those things have done to me."

He continued, "I've decided to leave the ministry. I didn't think I'd ever do that, but I just don't have it any more."

"Have it? What do you mean?" she queried.

"I mean I don't have the desire or the faith to continue in the ministry. I don't know what I'll do, but I can't continue in the ministry."

"I'm not surprised," responded Molly Ann, "not after what you've told me, but there's one thing you need to re-member. I didn't marry a Methodist minister. I married the man I loved, and I still love him."

Pat put his arm around her shoulders and held her close as they continued to walk. "The first thing we need to do is talk to our families. They need to know how I feel. Then I need to talk to John Henry."

Sam had closed his store for Otto's funeral. He had just reopened when Dan and Leona showed up in their two-horse wagon. A little later, Pat and Molly Ann walked in. Pat gathered the two families in the rear part of the store and shared with them his decision to leave the ministry. They were surprised and disappointed, but they assured his of their continued love and support.

That afternoon John Henry and Pat met at the church. Pat began the conversation. "I know this is going to be a disappointment to you, but it's something that I feel I have to do."

"What's that, Son?"

"I've decided to leave the ministry. I want to turn in my ministerial credentials."

"Is that what those papers in yore hand are?"

"Yes, sir, I assumed that I would turn them in to you."

"Have you prayed about your decision?" asked John Henry.

"Brother John, with all due respect, if I thought there was someone to pray to, we wouldn't be having this conversation."

"Tell me what you're talking about."

As he had done with Molly Ann and the rest of their families, Pat shared with John Henry his reasons for leaving the ministry.

John Henry listened patiently, and then he responded. "I am disappointed Pat, but I can understand how circumstances can change the way a person feels. However, in one sense, I think you have made a wise decision. With yore attitude and the burdens you're carrying around on yore back, you don't need to be in the pulpit."

He continued. "The church has some difficult times ahead of it. We have just fought a war over slavery and there are many in our own denomination, some of them in high places, who still approve of owning slaves. On the other hand some

185

northern ministers have come up with the idea that ministers in the South ought to be expelled from the ministry. Frankly, I don't see how they think they can do that since we are two different denominations. I don't know what course the church is going to take in the future, but we will be different from what we were before this terrible war."

"Do you think I'm wrong in quitting, John Henry?"

"That ain't the point. All I'm saying is, if you ain't sure of yore faith then you ought not to be in the pulpit."

"That's how I feel, John Henry. I ought not to be there."

"I know that's how you feel, and I regret that you feel that way, but don't let that be yore final answer. Remember, always be sure yore last answer is yore best answer, and always be open to what God wants you to do."

As they walked toward the door of the church, John Henry said, "Pat, I've talked to you real straight today, and maybe you think I've been a little rough on you, but don't you ever forget you're like a son to me and you always will be."

Pat stopped, started to say something but didn't. Instead, he just grabbed John Henry around the neck and hugged him.

As Pat started to walk away, John Henry called after him. "I'll take care of these papers. In the meantime, you remember that I'll always be ready to listen when you want to talk."

"Thank you, John Henry, I'll remember that."

John Henry patted him on the back. "Take care, Son, and let's go fishing sometime. By the way, don't forget the town meeting tonight. We have some serious business to discuss, and we need to have as many people there as possible."

"I'll be there, Brother John, and I'll remind the rest of the family to be there."

# 35

The town meeting dealt with the subject that was on everyone's mind, the security and safety of the people of Pine Creek. Since Otto's death, it was the subject of nearly every conversation. Fear gripped the town, and rightfully so. Buck Hagan was still alive. No one knew where he and his men had gone. The town was isolated with no contact with any law enforcement agency. The telegraph lines were still down and the trains no longer ran.

In the meeting, a lot of time was taken up by people venting their frustrations. They were afraid, and they saw no answer to their concerns in the immediate future. Mayor Davis knew the people were afraid, so he was very patient with them. When he felt that he had given everyone an opportunity to have their say, he called for order and recognized Josh Taylor.

"Mr. Mayor, I suggest that the town council meet tomorrow morning at ten and consider what needs to be done to make our town safe. I suggest that the decisions of the town council be posted in several prominent places so that our citizens will know what action we plan to take."

"How do y'all feel about this suggestion by Josh Taylor?" There was a roar of approval from the people. "I take that as an approval of what Josh has recommended. The council will meet tomorrow and the results of the meeting will be posted. Brother John Henry, please dismiss us with a prayer."

After the meeting, the Mayor spoke to Josh. "That was a good way to call a halt to this meeting. I was about to think we would be here all night."

"Wasn't my idea."

"If it wasn't yours, then whose was it?"

Josh pointed to John Henry. "He said it was getting past his bedtime."

The council meeting was held at the railroad depot the next day as announced. All three council members were there and as well as a number of Pine Creek citizens who came just to observe the proceedings. The only order of business was Josh's proposal that the council come up with a plan that would make the town of Pine Creek more secure.

There council members agreed that Pine Creek needed a town marshal. However, they did not have the funds available to hire someone to work full-time. After a lengthy discussion, they decided to engage someone on a part-time basis. They also voted to request the Sheriff provide him with some training as he had done previously with the two volunteers.

The two volunteers were present and indicated that they were not interested in the job, so the council was free to consider someone else. It was at that point that Josh Taylor surprised the council with the name of a prospective marshal.

"Gentlemen, I would like for us to consider the name of Pat Ravenwood for the position of part-time town marshal."

The other council members all spoke highly of Pat but they wanted to know why Josh thought he should be considered.

"I'll give you four good reasons. He knows the people in the community. He's very conscientious. He's tough. His time in Clonnerville Prisoner of War Camp proved that, and he knows the man that murdered Otto. His name is Buck Hagen, and he's the man that is responsible for some of the fear among the people of this town. I believe Pat's the man we need, and I think he'll take the job if we vote to offer it to him."

After a brief period of discussion, the town council voted

unanimously to offer the job to Pat. When the council meeting was over, the Mayor and Josh immediately contacted Pat and told him of the council's decision.

Pat responded to their offer with, "I appreciate y'all offering me job, but I don't know a thing about law enforcement."

The mayor spoke to that issue. "We will ask the county sheriff to send a man over here to train you. We did that before when we needed someone to train our volunteer marshals. We're sure he will help us out again."

Pat replied, "I need some time to think this over, and I'll have to talk to my family about it. When do you need an answer?"

"We don't want to pressure you," said the mayor, "but we'd really like to get this matter settled as quick as possible. Why don't we call on you day after tomorrow and see what your answer is?"

"I'll do my best to have an answer for you by then."

Pat accepted the job offer and started to work immediately. The county sheriff complied with the town's request and assigned his Chief Deputy, Jim Bob Patterson, to train Pat. The two of them worked well together, and Pat was on his own after a short period of time.

Life in Pine Creek began to stabilize. Fears subsided, and the people felt comfortable and secure with Pat as their marshal. Even though he was only part-time, they knew he was always on call. He continued to work at Sam's store, but his work as town marshal became more and more demanding as changes occurred in Pine Creek. First, the telegraph system became operational. Then, the trains began to run again. With the trains, came people. Some were just passing through. Others stayed. The trains also brought the daily newspaper from Macon which, in a small way, helped restore Pine Creek's contact with the outside world.

As the town began to grow, so did Pat's responsibilities.

First, there came a cotton gin and a large cotton warehouse. Pat was glad to see the town's new growth, but the cotton warehouse reminded him of his time in Clonnerville Prison. Before long the vast forests of prime pine timber in the area attracted the attention of a lumber merchant from Atlanta who built a sawmill just outside of town. He was also instrumental in establishing a railroad siding for the already existing railroad that ran through Pine Creek. This aided in the shipping of the lumber and cotton that was produced in the area.

At the end of his sixth month as part-time marshal, Pat received another visit from the Mayor. He was accompanied by Josh Taylor.

Pat greeted them jovially. "Good morning, Mr. Mayor, you too, Josh. There must be something serious going on. Is Miss Minnie's cat up a tree again?"

"No, Pat it's nothing like that, but we do have an interesting proposal for you. Actually, this proposal came to us from the county sheriff. He needs a deputy in this part of the county and would like for you to take the job. It would be part time and you would be based here in Pine Creek."

"That's really a surprise. What about my work as town marshal?"

"You would continue as town marshal, but you would be deputized by the county. Actually, you would become a full-time law enforcement officer. We see this as a good thing, Pat. It's good for the town and it's good for you in that you would be working full-time."

The mayor continued, "You've done a good job, and we want you to take the job. The people like you, and Pine Creek is a better town because of you."

"Those are mighty kind words, Mr. Mayor. I suppose you want an answer day after tomorrow just like last time."

"You have a good memory, Pat," said the Mayor. "See you then."

Pat accepted the mayor's offer and became Pine Creek's

first full-time law enforcement officer. He responded exceedingly well to the challenge of his new responsibilities. He soon gained the reputation of being one of the best law enforcement officers in the area.

As Pat began his second year as marshal and deputy sheriff, two events occurred that would affect the life of his son, Johnny. The first was the celebration of his birthday. The celebration actually began at breakfast that morning.

"Good morning, Johnny," Pat said, "and Happy Birthday!"

"Thank you," mumbled a sleepy Johnny.

"Wake up sleepyhead," Molly Ann chimed in." I've cooked pancakes just because it's your birthday. Are you awake enough to eat?"

"Yes, ma'am."

After Johnny had managed to put away several pancakes, Pat got up walked over and got a small package from one of the kitchen cabinets.

He set it down on the table in front of Johnny. "Your mama and I have a present for you. Do you want to open it now or wait until you get home from school this afternoon?"

Johnny answered by enthusiastically tearing into the package. He was now wide awake.

However, his joy turned to puzzlement when he realized that his present was a big red apple.

He was even more puzzled when Pat reached over, took the apple, quartered it and put it back in the box.

"Am I supposed to take this to school for my lunch?" He asked with a little sarcasm.

"You tell him what it's for, Molly Ann. I've got to go to work."

"Well," said Molly Ann, "you may eat it if you'd like, but there's someone out front that might enjoy it more than you."

Johnny grabbed the box with the quartered apple in it and dashed through the front door. He was mesmerized by what he saw. There stood Pat holding the bridle reins of a beautiful Pinto horse, complete with saddle.

"Happy birthday, Son, his name is Chico and he's gonna take Stormy's place."

The next event that affected Johnny's life occurred when a new family moved into town and opened a dry goods store. Their daughter Louise immediately caught Johnny's eye.

The following Sunday morning, after John Henry announced an upcoming church picnic, Johnny went to Pat with a question. "Pa, could I invite Louise to go with me to the church picnic?"

"It's all right with me, if it suits your mama."

"But what do I say when I invite her to go with me?"

"That's a question your mama will have to answer. She's the one who knows all about invitin' girls to picnics."

From the kitchen came a warning, "Patrick Ravenwood, you watch your mouth!"

# 36

The next morning, Pat pinned his badge on his shirt, strapped on his revolver, and walked into town. As was his custom, his first stop was Sam's store, where he got another cup of coffee and began reading the newspaper. He read the headlines and scanned a few other articles but saw nothing really interesting, He turned to the second page and paused. An article in the top left corner caught his attention.

*NEW U. S. MARSHAL APPOINTED TO*
*OCMULGEE DISTRICT*
*Colonel Douglas Randolph, a former United States Marshal and U. S. Army officer, has been appointed United Stated Marshal for the Ocmulgee District. His appointment is effective immediately upon his retirement from the United States Army.*

The article continued with a summary of the Colonel's service record, including his stint as Commandant of Clonnerville Prison. The appointment of Colonel Randolph as U. S. Marshal of the Ocmulgee District would profoundly affect Pat's life.

A few days later, when he was reasonably sure that the Colonel was in his new office in Macon, Pat walked over to the telegraph office.

"Good morning, Mr. Will. I want to send a telegram."

Will Emory handed Pat a pad and pencil for Pat write out his message.

193

*To: Marshal Douglas Randolph*
*Federal Court House, Macon, Georgia*
*Congratulations! Raven and I wish you the best.*
*Patrick Ravenwood, Marshal*
*Pine Creek, Georgia*

The Colonel acknowledged Pat's telegram, and they continued to correspond with one another over the next six months by mail and also by telegram. Most of the telegrams from the Colonel involved routine law enforcement work such as notifying Pat to be on the lookout for someone wanted by the U. S. Marshall's Office. Rarely did the Colonel's telegrams require any response from Pat. That was soon to change.

Pat was in Sam's store drinking a cup of coffee with John Henry and some other men. Suddenly, Will Emory from the telegraph office burst through the door with a telegram for Pat.

"Pat, this telegram sounded very important, so I thought I'd hand deliver it."

"Thank you, Mr. Will, I appreciate it very much."

Pat moved away from the other men and opened the telegram.

*To: Marshal Pat Ravenwood*
*Pine Creek, Georgia*
*Urgent you come my office next available train.*
*Will reimburse travel.*
*Douglas Randolph*
*United States Marshal.*

Pat had thirty minutes before the next train to Macon was due in Pine Creek. He rushed home, quickly told Molly Ann about the telegram.

"When will you be back?"

"I don't know, probably tonight, but I really can't say, because I don't know what this is all about. The Colonel just said it was urgent."

After he had changed clothes, he gave a flustered Molly Ann a kiss and arrived at the depot just as the train pulled in.

Pat rushed up to Will Emory who was waiting for some freight to be unloaded from the baggage car.

"Mr. Will, I need a ticket to Macon."

"A ticket won't be necessary. Come with me. With all the hell-raising that's going on, the railroad will usually let law enforcement officers ride free."

Will approached the conductor and said a few words. As he spoke, the conductor glanced at Pat a couple of times and then nodded in agreement with Will's request. The conductor shook hands with Will, turned, and motioned for Pat to board the train.

Pat had just gotten a seat when Mayor Davis and Josh Taylor boarded.

The Mayor greeted Pat. "Well, look who's here. Where are you headed, Pat? You're not running out on us are you?"

"No, not at all. How about you two, are y'all headed for Macon?"

Josh replied, "Yes, we're on our way to talk to some folks about the possibility of establishing a bank in Pine Creek. Nothing is definite yet. We're just exploring some ideas. What about you? What takes you to Macon?"

"I'm really not sure. I got a telegram this morning from the new United States Marshal for the Ocmulgee District. He asked me to come see him immediately. He was the Commandant of Clonnerville Prison when I was there. I've had some contact with him since then. I have no idea what he wants, but his telegram said it was urgent."

"Hmm, that's sort of strange," mused Mayor Davis. "Just let us know if it's something that involves Pine Creek."

"I sure will, Mayor. You know, I have quite a stake in Pine Creek."

As the train began jerking to a stop at Bailey's Cross-roads, one of the stops between Pine Creek and Macon, Josh peered out the window and said, "Wonder what that's all about." Pat and Mayor Davis looked over Josh's shoulder to see what he was talking about.

When the train came to a complete stop, they got a better view. The scene was sickening. A young boy was tied to a wagon wheel and was being whipped by a burly man wielding a four-foot cane. Four or five men stood by and watched.

The conductor was standing at the entrance to their passenger car shaking his head.

"Hold the train!" Pat said as he stepped past the conductor and off the train.

He muscled his way past the men and snatched the cane out of the man's hand.

"Who the hell are you?" The man asked.

"I'm the marshal in Pine Creek and also a deputy sheriff."

"That badge don't give you no authority to mess wid my bidness!"

Pat pulled off his badge and stuck it in his shirt pocket. "I don't need a badge to deal with the likes of you. I'm all the authority I need. Now, cut'im loose."

"The devil I will. I ain't about to turn no common thief loose."

"What'd he steal?" Pat asked.

"He stole an apple. He thought I didn't see'im, but I seen'im and I ain't turnin' him loose. He stole from me in my store. I'll do anything I want to with him."

"I said cut the boy loose!"

"No two-bit town marshal's gonna tell me what to do!"

Before the merchant could react, Pat struck him two stinging blows across his shoulders with the cane he had taken from the man. "I said cut him loose!"

"If you weren't a lawman, I'd have yore hide." He muttered as he cut the boy free.

"My badge is in my pocket. That means you're dealing with me."

"Where's the apple you said he stole?"

"I tuck it from him and put it back in the basket up there on the porch."

"Whaddya get for an apple?"

"They's two cents each. I don't give 'em away, 'specially to no trash like him."

Pat reached in his pocket, pulled out a nickel and threw it at the man's feet.

"Get me two of 'em, and they better not have any rotten spots."

"You get yore own damn..."

Before he could finish, Pat said firmly, "Get me two apples, NOW!"

"Awright, awright, you don't hafta get so testy over a little ole apple."

Pat walked back toward the train with his right arm across the boy's shoulders. In his left hand he had the two apples. "What's your name, son?"

"Tommy."

"Where do you live, Tommy.?"

"A ways up the railroad, 'bout two miles."

"Let's get you home. Ever ride on a train before?'

"No sir."

Inside the coach, Josh turned to the mayor. "I told you he was tough."

"But you didn't tell me he was that tough."

As they boarded the train, Pat said to the conductor, "Could we let this young man off about two miles up the line?'

"Be glad to, Marshal. Son, you just give me a wave when you're ready to get off."

Tommy nodded and took a seat near a window. When they approached the area where he wanted to get off, he

197

turned and waved to the conductor, who signaled the train to stop.

Pat got out of his seat, gave the boy the two apples, and walked with him to the rear of the coach.

The train had hardly stopped when Tommy jumped off. The conductor was about to signal the train to depart when Tommy turned, tossed Pat one of the apples, and then hurried down a seldom-used dirt road toward an old dilapidated shack.

"Marshal," the conductor said, "do you think he stole an apple from that ole cuss?"

"I never thought to ask him," Pat answered, as he munched on the apple the boy had given him.

# 37

As they exited the train station in Macon, the mayor hired a carriage and offered Pat a ride. At first Pat refused, but the Mayor insisted. "Come on and ride with us, Pat. I think Pine Creek can afford to do something for its favorite marshal."

When Pat reluctantly agreed, the mayor said, "Just tell the driver where you need to go, and we'll drop you off first."

Pat climbed in and said to the driver, "Federal Court-house."

It was only a few blocks to the court house, but Pat was grateful for the ride. He was anxious to see what he Colonel wanted.

"Thanks for the ride. Are y'all taking the five o'clock train back this afternoon?"

"We hope to be on it," Josh said, "if all goes well."

"Good, I'll see you on the train."

Pat entered the court house and asked for directions to the U. S. Marshal's office.

The custodian pointed to the stairway and immediately went back to leaning on his broom. Pat found the office, walked in, and identified himself to a young man seated at a desk in an outer office. The young man motioned for Pat to follow him.

At the end of the hall, he tapped twice on an office door, opened it, stuck his head inside and said, "Sir, Marshal Ravenwood is here."

Marshal Randolph was seated but got up immediately and greeted Pat. "Come in, Pat! Come in! Damn, it's good to see you!"

"It's good to see you too, Sir. I hope you're doing all right."

"I'm doing fairly well for an old warhorse. Tell me. How's the family? Let's see. Is it Molly Ann and Jonathon?"

"That's pretty close Sir. We call him Johnny, and they're both doing fine."

"And how about Raven?"

"A little older and a little grayer, but he's just as strong-willed as ever, Sir."

"You have no idea how much I'd love to see him."

"I'm sure he'd remember you, Sir."

"Good! Good! That's enough of this sentimental stuff. We have some work to do. Would you like a cup of coffee? I was just about to have one."

"I would like one very much, Sir; black would be fine."

"Deputy, could we have two cups of black coffee in here, and while you're at it, see if the gentlemen down the hall would like some. Tell them I'll see them shortly."

The Colonel motioned to Pat, "Come over here. I want to show you something on the map."

As they looked at the map, the Colonel explained, "We've had a series of robberies, shootings and other vicious criminal activities in this area for several months. Every pin on this map marks a place where a criminal act occurred. Now, here's the interesting thing. Most of them were committed by three men working together."

Pat said one word, "Hagan!"

"That's my assessment of the situation also. It has to be Hagan, Perkins, and Lawton. However, I haven't told you the worst part. Three days ago, down in the little community of Antioch, an entire family was slaughtered. A man, his wife and two daughters, fifteen and thirteen were brutally murdered. I need not tell you what they did to all of the women. Neighbors reported seeing three men on horseback in the area."

"Did anybody come up with any kind of description?" asked Pat.

"Very little. All three of them appeared to be about the same size. Two of them were riding ordinary looking horses with no significant markings that anyone could see. However, there was a report that one of the three was riding a blaze-faced horse with four white stocking feet."

Pat turned pale and nearly spilled his coffee.

The Colonel looked at him closely. "Are you all right? You don't look too good. Is anything wrong?"

"Right before I got home, Hagan was in Pine Creek looking for Molly Ann, but he got into a scrap with the owner of a bar and killed him. He and his two henchmen had to leave town in a hurry. He didn't have a chance to find Molly Ann, but they did locate Pa's farm. Fortunately nobody was at home. That's where they got the horse with a blazed face and four white stocking feet. That's Johnny's horse."

Pat took a deep breath and continued. "One of their horses had thrown a shoe so they left him at the farm and stole Johnny's horse. Evidently they had just saddled him when the posse from town showed up. They were able to get away because they set fire to Pa's barn, and the posse stopped to put out the fire. From what you're telling me, it looks like they've been on a rampage ever since."

The Colonel pointed to the map. "I'm more convinced now than ever that Hagan, Perkins, and Lawton are the ones responsible for all these crimes, and that's where you come in."

"What do you mean, Colonel?"

"I'm putting together a four-man squad to track these cutthroats down, and I want you to be a part of that team. Here's what I have in mind. A Deputy U. S. Marshal will be in charge. You will be a Special Deputy U. S. Marshal and will be his second in command. The other two men will also be Special Deputies. They will report to you. Please understand.

A special deputy is not a permanent appointment. You will wear a Marshal's badge for this job only. You and the other men will be working under the supervision of an experienced lawman. We'll talk more about that later. The job is yours if you want it, but I need an immediate answer. These killers must be apprehended as quickly as possible."

"Colonel, I'll do anything to put those three in jail or in the ground!"

"Good, I thought I could count on you. Now I'd like for you to meet the other men you'll be working with. Deputy! Ask the three men down the hall to step in here."

When the men entered the room, Pat was speechless. There stood Jim Bob Patterson, Jud Cofer, and Deke Bracewell. After they had greeted each other, the Colonel explained that Jud and Deke had come in earlier on a train from Dudley. From that point on, it was all business.

"Deputy U. S. Marshal Jim Bob Patterson is my second in command. The three of you will be under his general supervision and will be working this case in the field. Jim Bob is already overloaded with cases, so tracking these killers down is primarily your responsibility."

"Pat, Jud, and Deke, each of you will be sworn in as a Special Deputy U. S. Marshal. Each appointment is temporary and is to be discontinued when the Hagan bunch is apprehended. Pat, you will be the crew leader. Jud and Deke will be under you supervision. Finally, should one of you special deputies wish to do so, you may apply for any permanent position that comes open in the future." He paused, and then added, "Have I made myself clear on everything?"

There was a quartet of "Yes, sirs!"

At that, the colonel called to the young man in the outer office. "Deputy Mitchell, see if the Judge is in his office and available to see us."

"Already done that, Sir. He's expecting you."

"Follow me, gentlemen. We'll get you sworn in right

now. Jim Bob was sworn in when he joined my staff."

The five of them were ushered into the Judge's chambers.

"Good Morning, Judge," the Colonel said.

"Good morning to you, Marshal, and also to you, Deputy Patterson."

Speaking to the colonel, the Judge continued, "And who are these three gentlemen?"

The Colonel responded, "Judge Cox, this is Pat Ravenwood, Jud Cofer, and Deke Bracewell. They are to be sworn in as Special Deputies."

As the Judge was shaking hands with them, Deputy Patterson placed three badges on the judge's desk. Judge Cox swore them in and pinned a badge on each man. As soon as he had shaken hands with them, the colonel led them back to his office. Deputy Mitchell had already anticipated what the Colonel would do next.

On a table in the colonel's office were three Remington 1858 .44 caliber revolvers, each with three replaceable cylinders for quick reloading. There were also three .52 caliber Spencer rifles and three double-barreled shotguns with their factory-made thirty-inch barrels shortened to sixteen inches. All firearms were accompanied with an adequate supply of ammunition.

"There you are, gentlemen. You are probably familiar with these weapons, but nevertheless, I want Deputy Patterson to check you out in their use. You are free to return home after that, but I'm sure Deputy Patterson will get with you shortly and make some plans for the capture of these murderers. You have a difficult job in front of you. Don't come back empty handed. Is that clear?"

"Yes sir!" They responded emphatically.

As they were leaving, Pat lingered behind. "Colonel, I believe I have something that belongs to you." He then unbuckled his gun belt and holster and returned the .44 caliber Remington that the Colonel had given him when he released him from Clonnerville Prison.

As he shook the Colonel's hand, Pat said, "I want to thank you for all you've done for me and for what you've done today."

"Deputy, what I've done is not just for you. It's also for me. As we've talked before, I'll always bear a tremendous burden of guilt for what happened at Clonnerville."

It didn't take long for Jim Bob to check the new marshals out in the use of their firearms. The only gun that was unfamiliar to the three was the sawed-off shotgun with its new metal shells. When Jim Bob was completely satisfied with the way they handled their guns, he led them back to a small meeting room in the District Marshal's office. "We have our work cut out for us, and we need to get started as soon as possible. Here's what I want you to do. Go back home, talk to your families, and tell them what you've been asked to do. Get your affairs in order at home, and let's meet at ten o'clock at the city hall in Dykesboro three days from today. Understand?"

All three men answered affirmatively.

When they had finished their business at the court house, Pat, Jud, and Deke walked over to Cherry Street and headed south toward the train station. They made one stop along the way where Pat bought a small box of apples at a fruit and vegetable stand.

Deke immediately started kidding Pat about his purchase. "You must be some kinda hungry, Chaplain. 'Scuse me, I mean Marshal."

Pat winked at Jud then shoved the box of apples into Deke's mid-section. "Special Deputy Bracewell, as your appointed supervisor, I order you to carry this box of apples to the train station." Jud doubled over in laughter.

When they arrived at the train station, Pat introduced his two companions to the Josh and the Mayor and explained that Jud and Deke would be catching the train for Dudley where they had stabled their mules that morning. As greetings were exchanged, Deke handed Pat the box of apples then he shook hands with Josh and the Mayor.

Looking at the box of apples and then at Pat, the Mayor smirked, "More apples to deal with, I see."

A befuddled Deke remarked to no one in particular, "Whut I want to know is, whut's all this big to-do about apples?"

Mayor Davis replied. "You wouldn't believe it, if I told you."

Deke and Jud left to board their train.

They were hardly out of hearing when Mayor Davis turned to Pat. "Now, what's all this business with the U. S. Marshal's office about?"

Pat responded. "Let's find a bench in a quiet place, and I'll tell you all about it." When they were seated, Pat explained what had transpired at the Marshal Randolph's office.

"Won't that leave us without a peace officer in Pine Creek?" asked the mayor.

Pat replied. "That's something we need to talk about. Although, the work will take me out of town a lot, I'll be based in Pine Creek. So I think we can come up with a plan that will work for me and for the town."

"What do you have in mind?"

"First of all, this job is only temporary. It'll be over when Hagan is caught. Second, I will be paid by the District Marshal's office, so you won't have to pay me while I'm working for the Colonel. Third, since you won't have to pay me, I suggest that you hire a temporary, part-time marshal to work until my job with the U. S. Marshal's office is finished."

"Pat," said the mayor, "I think we can work something out. Believe me, we know how you feel about Hagan and his gang, and we want him out of commission as much as you do. I can't speak for the whole council, but if we can get a good part-time person, then we'll have the law enforcement situation in Pine Creek covered."

When they boarded the train, Pat noted that the conductor was the same one that was on the train when they boarded it at Pine Creek earlier in the day.

"Do you remember where we let that young boy off on your northbound run?"

"Sure do, Marshal."

"If you don't mind, I'd like for you to stop there for just a few seconds."

The conductor replied, "That'll be no problem. I'll let you know when we get close."

Pat had not kept up with the time, but, true to his word, the conductor stopped the train at the dirt road where they let the young boy off on their way to Macon.

Pat grabbed the box of apples, went to the rear of the coach, stepped down to the ground and set the box of apples in the middle of the road. He waved to the folks on the front porch of an old run down shanty, and sprang back onto the train.

"Let's go," He said to the conductor.

# 38

Molly Ann was not pleased with Pat's new job, but she realized that Pat would not rest until Hagan was arrested. For that matter, neither would she. It was particularly disturbing to her when Pat told her about the family that they slaughtered over at Antioch, not more than twenty miles away. That evening Pat walked around in Pine Creek just to make his presence known. He also wanted to make contact with someone that he had in mind for the part-time marshal's job, Buddy Jarvis. He was on his way to visit with Buddy when his spotted his pa's wagon in front of Sam's store. Leona and Dan were in the rear of the store visiting with Sam and Susie when Pat walked in.

They like, Molly Ann, were not pleased when he told them the results of his visit with the Colonel, but they also knew that it was something that Pat had to work out himself. After visiting in the store a few minutes, Pat walked down to Buddy's house on the edge of town. Buddy lived with his elderly parents and had supported them by doing odd jobs and working part-time at Otto's Bar, but since Hagan killed Otto, he had been out of work. Buddy could not work at a full-time job, because he was the sole care-giver for his parents. Sadly, they could not be left alone long enough for Buddy to work full time.

Buddy was sitting on the front porch when Pat arrived at his home. "How you doing, Buddy?"

"Fine, Marshal, come have seat and set a spell."

"Your folks doing all right?"

"I guess so, Marshal, They're doin' about as well as you

could expect for their age."

Buddy was always one who tried to be positive about every situation. Actually, he had to spoon feed his father at every meal, and his mother was so frail and bent over, she could hardly do anything around the house. Yet, Buddy never dwelt on their incapacities.

Once Pat was seated, Buddy said, "What brings you down this way, Marshal?"

"I have something that I need to talk to you about, but I need for you to keep it to yourself for a while."

"You have my word on that, so fire away. What's on your mind?"

Pat told Buddy that he had been appointed a Special Deputy and would have to be out of town frequently. He explained that the appointment was temporary and the town would need a part-time marshal while he was working in his newly-appointed position.

"What does that have to do with me?" queried Buddy.

"I would like to submit your name to the town council for the job. Keep in mind that this is a part-time job and is only temporary."

"But I don't know one thing about marshaling."

"I can teach you that. As you may recall, I didn't know anything about law enforcement when I started. All I need is someone who's level-headed and trainable, and I think you qualify on both counts. When you worked for Otto, you were in some pretty rough situations, and you did a good job of handling some mean characters when they got liquored up."

"Marshal, if you think I can do the job, I'll give it my best. I won't lie to you or the council. I need a job. We're mighty strapped for money right now since Otto got kilt."

"That's fair enough. I'll mention your name to the Mayor tonight and we'll see how it goes from there. I'll let you know what happens as soon as I know something."

Pat left Buddy's house and immediately sought out the

208

Mayor and gave him Buddy's name to be considered for the part-time marshal's job.

"Buddy Jarvis! That's interesting. To my knowledge, he's never had a full-time job."

"You're right, Mayor, and there's a good reason why. Rather than leave his folks at home by themselves, he looks after them himself. Now, if you want a recommendation, you've got mine. I believe Buddy can do the job."

"You really believe in him, don't you!"

"Yes, I do, one hundred percent."

The Mayor responded, "Tell you what I'll do, Pat, I'll ask the council to meet tonight, and I'll present Buddy's name to them."

Pat shook the Mayor's hand. "That's fair enough."

The next morning, Pat saw the mayor at the Post Office. "How did the meeting go?"

"It went just fine. They agreed to hire Buddy, but you have to take the responsibility for giving him some basic guidance. His training is your responsibility."

"That's good news, Mayor. When will you offer him the job?"

"What I'd like for you to do is ride out to his house with me right now. I'll offer him the job. If he accepts I'll go ahead and swear him in, then you two can start working together."

That left Pat with only two days to work with Buddy before he had to be in Dykesboro for the meeting with Jim Bob. Two days was a ridiculously short period of time to give Buddy any training at all. However, if Buddy needed help, he could call on Tom Corley or Jeff Frazier, the two former volunteer deputies. Pat would have spent more than two days with Buddy, but the Colonel had made it quite clear that he wanted Hagan found.

After working with Buddy as much as he could, Pat rode to Dykesboro for his meeting with Jim Bob, Jud, and Deke. The meeting was held in Dykesboro because it was centrally

209

located for all four of them. Not only was it convenient for the four of them to meet there, but the mayor and town council of Dykesboro were gracious enough to make a small room at the city hall available for use as their headquarters.

Jim Bob was the first to arrive and was pinning a map to the wall when the others walked in the room. Jim Bob, like the Colonel, didn't waste any time.

He shook hands with each of them and immediately got down to business. "All right, gentlemen, this is how we're going to operate."

"First of all, I want y'all to be ready to move at a moment's notice. That means you keep your horses, your gear, and your guns ready at all times."

"Second, you three are the ones who will nail these hoodlums to the jailhouse wall. I can't be with you all the time, but I can be reached by telegram if you need me. If you are away from your home base, leave word with the telegraph operator where you will be, and how you can be reached. Stay in touch with me and with each other."

"Third, I have a list of all the criminal acts in the district where we have reason to believe that Hagan's crew was involved. This is not a list of all crimes committed in the area. We are only interested in those where Hagan, Perkins, and Lawton are the chief suspects. At any rate, I want these locations marked on this map with pins so we can see if there is some sort of pattern."

Pat, Jud, and Deke took the list and began pinpointing the locations on the map as Jim Bob requested.

When they had finished, Jim Bob said, "Pat, let's begin with you. Do you see any sort of pattern to the pins we have up there on that map?"

"Not really, but there's got to be something there, something we're missing. All I see right now is a line of pins running North and South with more pins on the side toward the south for maybe ten or twelve miles, but there's not much back toward Pine Creek."

"What about you, Jud," said Jim Bob, "Do you see any kind of pattern?"

"Sorry, but I don"t see nothing except a bunch of pins stuck on a map. I don't see that they tell us much 'cause they do so many different things. One place they rob a bank or a store. Another place they start a brawl in a bar and shoot somebody like they did in Pine Creek. I just don't see the connection."

Pat responded, "Maybe it's not what they're doing but where they do it. Maybe those pins are telling us that they are staying in one area and have a good hiding place they can go back to after they have pulled one of their jobs. Also, it looks like they're trying to avoid Pine Creek."

"That's a good point, Pat. They do seem to just disappear after each job. What about you, Deputy Bracewell. Do you see anything?"

"I'm sorta like Jud. I can't say that I see anything other than a bunch of pins that are shaped kinda like a half moon or maybe one of them fold-up fans like Granny Roland used to have. That thing would fold up and be no bigger than two pencils laid side by side."

"That's it! Pat said. "Their area of operation is fan-shaped! Jim Bob, do you have a ruler or some kind of straight edge? I need a pencil, too."

Jim Bob handed Pat a twelve-inch ruler and a pencil, and stepped back to see what Pat had on his mind.

Using the ruler as a straight edge, Pat drew a line connecting the outermost pins. After finding the mid-point of that line, he drew a line from each pin on the map to that point. When he finished, he stepped back so the others could get a good look at the map.

"I think we're on to something!" Jim Bob said excitedly.

He motioned to Jud and Deke, "Come take a look and see if y'all are familiar with that area where the lines meet. Y'all

211

grew up in that area."

Jude and Deke moved up to the map and peered closely at the intersecting lines.

"Dang!" said Jud, "It runs right through Woods Lake over there in Gum Swamp!"

"Dadgumed if it don't!" Deke exclaimed. "There's Little River, and that there big shady area is Gum Swamp, jest like Jud said. Now, that there little open area right in the middle of the swamp is Woods Lake, and they's a fish camp there."

Jim Bob grabbed his hat and headed for the door, "Gentlemen, I think that's the lead we've been looking for. Y'all mount up! You've got some hard riding ahead of you. If you need me, I'll be in Hawkinsville. Telegraph me there."

Immediately, Pat thought of Molly Ann and Buddy. They needed to know what was going on. Grabbing a pencil and a piece of paper, he quickly scribbled down their names, addresses, and a brief message.

Pat handed the message to the Dykesboro marshal. "Send this by telegram as soon as possible. I have the names and addresses written down for you."

Pat then put some money on the table, "That ought to pay for the telegrams. If it's not enough, I'll settle up with you when we get back."

The marshal shoved the money back. "There's no charge. We'll take care of it."

# 39

As Pat, Jud, and Deke rode out of Dykesboro on their way to Gum Swamp, Jim Bob left for Hawkinsville. At the same time, Hagan, Perkins, and Lawton, were riding away from Gum Swamp. After robbing the Sugar Creek bank, they had spent the night at the old fish camp deep in the swamp on shore of Woods Lake. When they had divided up their take from the bank, they made the decision to split up and go their separate ways.

Hagan was the one that brought up the idea. "I've been thinking. We've been together long enough. Our takes have been pretty good, but by now every lawman in the area is looking for three fellers working together. So, I think it's time that you two went your way and I went mine."

Lawton spoke first. "I agree, What about you Rat? You got any ideas?"

Rat responded, "That's a good idea. We've stirred up some hornets' nests lately, so it's prob'ly time to take it easy for a while. Who goes which way, Buck?"

"Why don't y'all head kinda northeasterly and I'll head in a southerly direction."

Rat and Lawton agreed with his plan.

Meanwhile, the Dykesboro town marshal headed for the telegraph office to send Pat's note to Molly Ann and Buddy. As he entered the office, he collided with the telegraph operator who had a telegram clutched tightly in his hand.

"What's the hurry, Pete? Have you gone to work for the Pony Express?"

"I'm sorry, Marshal, but I need to get this to Marshal Jim

Bob Patterson immediately."

"He just rode out of town, but I'll be sure to give it to him when he gets back."

"That'll be fine Marshal, but I think you ought to read it, since it's about a bank robbery."

The town marshal took the telegram from the operator and read the message.

*To: Deputy Marshal Jim Bob Patterson*
*Dykesboro, Georgia*
*Sugar Creek Bank robbed yesterday. Teller wounded.*
*Hagan gang suspected.*
*Douglas Randolph*
*District Marshal*

The course of history is often altered by unforeseen circumstances. This was the case in the hunt for Hagan, Perkins, and Lawton. Due to an unforeseen chain of events, three special deputies were riding toward an empty hideout in Gum Swamp, and Jim Bob Patterson was riding toward Hawkinsville. What would have happened if the telegram from Sugar Creek had arrived at the U. S. Marshal's office earlier? No one will ever know. History is not allowed to speculate. It can only record what has happened.

It was late afternoon when Pat, Jud, and Deke arrived at the trail leading to the fish camp on Woods Lake in Gum Swamp. As much as they wanted to go in after the Hagan gang, they yielded to better judgment and decided to keep the trailhead under surveillance through the night and go in at first light the next morning.

"Deke," said Pat, "scout around and find us a camp site. Make sure it's off to the side so that we aren't visible to someone coming out of the swamp."

"Jud, you come with me. We'll leave the horses here and scout out the area around the entrance. I want to see what sort

214

of traffic has been going in and out of this place."

Both men were wearing their side arms. Jud was carrying his Spencer repeater. Pat was carrying his double-barreled shotgun. Both the rifle and the shotgun could be used quicker than their side arms, which were carried in military style holsters with a flap over the grip of the pistol.

When they were near the entrance, Pat said to Jud, "You're a better tracker than I am, tell me what you see while I keep an eye on the trail."

Jud immediately began to examine the tracks at the entrance. Beginning with a wide circle around the area, he gradually closed in on a spot right in the middle of the trail.

"Chaplain, there's something mighty funny about them tracks."

"What do you mean?"

"This is the way I see it. Look at them tracks right there. They tell me that three horses come in here from yore right. It looks like they all come in at the same time, but I can also make out tracks of the same three horses comin' back out later."

"Are you sure of that?"

"Yeah, I'm sure, but what's got me buffaloed is, it looks like they split up after they come out. One rider went toward the south, and them other two kinda went north."

"Jud, if what you're sayin' is right, then they aren't in there. They must've decided to split up and leave."

"That's the way I see it, Chaplain"

"You're probably right, but I don't want to risk going in until daylight. We'll take turns standing guard out here tonight to make sure nobody goes in or out. First thing in the morning we'll hit the camp."

"You take the first watch. Deke can have the second, and I'll take the third."

They woke up early the next morning and had a breakfast of coffee, hardtack, and beef jerky. After they broke camp, saddled up, and secured all their gear behind their saddles, they cautiously crept along the trail to the Woods Lake fish camp. At Pat's direction, they were on foot, leading their horses. Each man was carrying his sawed-off shotgun. Pat had taken the point. Jud and Deke were about ten yards behind.

They had gone about a half a mile into the swamp when Pat signaled them to stop. He stood still, listened for a moment, and then signaled the other two to move up beside him.

As they approached him he whispered, "I smell smoke."

They continued slowly for another fifty yards to a rather sharp bend in the trail to the left. At that point Pat handed the reins of Raven to Deke and slowly moved forward to get a better view of what was around the bend. He was out of sight for about five minutes. Jud and Deke were beginning to get anxious when Pat walked back around the bend in the trail. With all stealth abandoned, he motioned for them to join him. They followed the trail to its end on the south shore of Woods Lake. Ahead of them was an abandoned campfire with ashes smoldering just enough to give off a faint odor of smoke.

"Let's look around and see what we can find," Pat said. "but be on your guard!"

Deke was the first one to come up with something, "Will you look at this. Some lady's done lost her pocketbook."

"Or had it taken from her," replied Pat.

While Jude and Deke continued to search around the perimeter of the camp, Pat was examining the ashes of the campfire with a stick. Among the ashes, he found charred papers with the name Sugar Creek Bank just barely visible.

"It looks like they robbed a bank we didn't know about." Pat said.

Deke Responded, "What bank is that?"

"The Sugar Creek Bank. It's about twenty miles southwest of here."

"Wonder why it wasn't reported," Deke pondered.

"Maybe it just happened," Jud answered as he poked around in some high grass on the edge of the lake.

All of a sudden, there was a big thrashing sound right near where Jud was standing.

He jumped about three feet in the air and cried out, "Great Gawdamighty whatta gator!"

He didn't stop running until he had put Pat between himself and the giant gator. The hilarity of the moment briefly overshadowed the seriousness of the hunt for the Hagan bunch.

Once some degree of order was established at the the camp, Pat said. "Fellers, we're wasting our time here. Let's ride back to our camp and take another look at those tracks that Jud found at the trailhead."

When they were finally out of the swamp, Jud dismounted and was examining the tracks that he had found the day before.

Deke just couldn't resist saying something. "Are you shore them ain't gator tracks, Jud?"

"One of these days, Deke, you're gonna say too much. When you do, I'm gonna pull you off that mule that's smarter'n you, and I'm gonna whup up on you big time. So just keep yore dang mouth shut for a change."

"Yes sir, Mister Jud, I'll behave. As high as you can jump, I'll bet you could jump right up here on this mule with me."

"All right, you two," said Pat, "cut it out. We have work to do. Y'all will have plenty of time to fuss and fight when this is all over and I am not around. At least, I hope I'm not around."

"Jud, I want you and Deke to follow the tracks that head north, and I'll follow the one rider that took off toward the southwest. Remember to stay in touch with Jim Bob in Hawkinsville, and try not to kill each other. Let's move out."

# 40

Jud and Deke finally declared a truce and began to concentrate on the tracks they were following. The day-old tracks were difficult to follow, but it soon became evident that the two riders they were following were headed toward Little River. Beyond the river lay the little town of Chester, the place that both Jud and Deke called home. However, once they forded Little River, they were unable to distinguish the tracks they had been following from the many other tracks on the road. After searching up and down the river bank with no success, they had to face up to reality. They had lost the trail.

Deke rode up beside Jud and asked, "What do we do now?"

"I think we ought to ride on into Chester. If those two have been there, somebody will know about it. If we don't come up with something, we'll telegraph Jim Bob and ask for some more instructions."

Meanwhile in Chester, two drunks were in old man Adams' livery stable sleeping off a night of drinking. When they finally became conscious enough to realize they were hungry, they checked their pocket and discovered that each of them had barely enough money for breakfast. After that, they'd be flat broke. It took a while longer for them to remember that they'd lost most of their money in a poker game the night before at The Buckeye Bar. After a breakfast of biscuits, ham, eggs, and several cups of coffee apiece at Velma's Cafe, they went back to Adams' livery stable, saddled up, and began making their way east toward Dexter. As they were leaving, Jud and Deke were riding hard toward toward Chester. When they arrived at the Buckeye Bar on the outer edge of Chester, they stopped to inquire if two strangers had been in the night before.

Junior, who tended bar there, was sweeping up when they walked in. "Well, look what the cat drug in. I thought you two must have been shot by some Yank or a jealous husband since I ain't seen you in a while."

Shaking hands with them, Junior continued, "How y'all doing? It shore is good to see both of you. Whatcha doin' now?"

Jud replied, "We're doing fine, Junior, but we are in kind of a hurry. We're both Special Deputies for the U. S. Marshal's office in Macon and we're looking for two fellers that are on the run. They's a part of a gang of three and all of 'em is wanted for murder and robbery."

"What did they look like?"

"We ain't got no positive identification but we think they's about our size," responded Deke, "and they might've been wearing Yankee uniforms. One might be called Rat and the other Jake. If they's who we think they is, one is Rat Perkins and and the other is Jake Lawton, but they's a chance one of 'em goes by the name of Buck Hagan."

"Dang! Don't know about names, but they was two fellers in here'til real late last night playing poker with old man Sands. They was drinking a lot and weren't no good at poker. He weren't drinking and was playin' a hot hand. They left here drunker and lighter than when they come in. They could be the one y'all's lookin' for."

"They staying some place in town?" asked Jud.

"My guess would be ole man Adams' livery stable. He'll let drifters sleep there now and agin."

As they were leaving Deke said to Jud, "Let's stop by Velma's Cafe and see if she can help us. She knows everthang that goes on 'round here."

"Won't hurt to ask."

Velma greeted them as they came in the door. "Well, look who's here. Two big shot lawmen done come home to roost. Mercy! I'm glad to see y'all."

"We won't be here long, Velma," responded Jud. "We're lookin' for two Yankee deserters that's wanted for murder over in Pine Creek. Don't guess you've seen any strangers around town this morning, have you.? They'd prob'ly be wearing Yankee uniforms."

"Lordy mercy! They was in here not more'n an hour ago, hung over worse'n a fat man's belly. They put away a pile of vittles and lit outta here toward Dexter."

Both Jud and Deke dashed out the door to their mules. They were mounted and riding hard toward Dexter before Velma could say another word.

Rat and Jake did not suspect that anyone was on their trail. Both of them were fighting a hangover as well as the bright glare of the morning sun. There was also the challenge of keeping a heavy breakfast down while sitting astride horses that were rocking them back and forth like a boat in choppy water. Jud and Deke had no such hindrances. They were pushing their mounts hard. The mules that the Colonel had given them might not be pretty but they had staying power, and they could cover some ground. Ahead of them Rat and Jake were entering Dexter.

Rat said to Jake, "We need some money."

"Now where do you think we're gonna get some money?"

"Where do folks usually get money?"

"A bank, I guess," answered Jake.

"You guessed right, and there's a bank right up the street on the right, and we're gonna make a withdrawal."

"How do you plan to handle this here withdrawal? We don't know one thing about that bank. They could be a guard in there for all we know."

Rat replied, "See that water trough in front of that store next to the bank? We're gonna stop there and let our horses drink some water and rest a spell. While they're restin' up we're gonna check our gear and tighten the cinches. We'll check their feet to be sure we ain't got no loose shoes, but all the time we're gonna be keeping one eye on the bank."

After taking another look at the bank, Rat continued with his instructions. "When it looks like there ain't nobody in there, I'll walk in like I'm a customer and git us some cash. Now listen real careful, just time I walk in the door, you untie the horses and bring them up in front of the bank. Have both of them ready to ride. When I come out, we'll head east."

Rat walked nonchalantly toward the bank, giving the appearance of just another drifter passing through town. He casually opened the door to the bank and went inside. As soon as he closed the bank door behind him, Jake untied the horses and led them to a spot in front of the bank. He was totally unaware that two men riding mules has just entered Dexter on the same street.

Jud and Deke slowly made their way into town and continued east on the town's main street. They studied the people and the horses, giving particular attention to any hitching rail where two horses were tied side by side. They were about two blocks from the bank when they spotted two horses in front of the bank. Only one of the horses had a rider, and that rider appeared to be waiting for someone.

Just as Jud was about to comment on the scene before them, gunfire erupted from inside the bank. Then a man ran out of the bank and sprang into the saddle of the horse the other man was holding. They immediately had their horses running at full speed as they headed east out of Dexter.

"Dang, that looked like Rat Perkins and Jake Lawton!" Deke exclaimed!

"Whoever it was just robbed the bank! Let's git after'em!"

The two lawmen kicked their mules into a run in pursuit of the robbers. The mules, sensing the excitement of the chase, began to close the distance between them and the robbers. About a mile outside of town, Rat and Lawton, realizing that they were being chased, abruptly left the road, jumped off their horses, and took cover in the foundation of an old burned-out tobacco barn. From there, they began firing at the two marshals. Jud and Deke took cover and began to return their fire. Both of them had Spencer repeaters, but they shot sparingly in order to conserve ammunition.

The shootout was pretty much a stalemate until Jud decided to move to his left about twenty yards so that he and Deke would have Rat and Jake in a crossfire.

"Deke," Jud yelled, "cover me." He then signaled with his hands what his intentions were. Deke signaled that he understood. When he had made sure that the magazine on his Spencer was full, he began to fire at the slightest movement behind the old barn foundation.

With Jud's new vantage point, he was able to get a quick look at the two robbers behind the foundation wall.

Jud yelled back to Deke, "You're right! It's Rat and Jake!"

"Thought so," replied Deke as he squeezed of another shot.

Even though Jud could not get a clear shot, he could raise havoc by firing into the rocks causing them to shatter sending pieces of shrapnel-like rock chips in every direction.

"Give it up, Rat. Put your hands in the air and come on out!" Jud yelled.

"Not a chance, Reb. If you want us, come get us! We ain't surrendering for no hanging." Rat emphasized his reply with two more shots over the wall.

Jud responded with more rock-shattering shots.

The next thing that happened will always be a mystery, but desperate men will do desperate things. For some unknown reason, Rat and Jake sprang over the barn's foundation like two madmen and charged Jud and Deke. It was the last stupid thing they ever did. Jud dropped Rat with a shot to the chest. Deke brought Jake's life of murder and mayhem to dramatic end with a shot between the eyes.

After the shootout, Jud and Deke mounted their mules and caught the robber's horses that had been spooked by all the gunfire. When they managed to calm the skittish animals down, they discovered the bank's money in a bag tied to the saddle of one of the horses. Jud took the bag and tied it to the saddle of his mule. Then, they draped Rat's body over the saddle of one of the horses and Jake's body over the other.

On their way back to Dexter, Jud commented on Deke's shooting, "Dang, that wuz some good shootin' back there. You nailed ole Jake right twixt the eyes."

Deke responded with a grin, "Prob'ly wouldn't work on a gator though."

"I'll swear, Deke, don't you ever forget nothing?"

The marshals created quite a stir in Dexter when they rode into town leading two horses, each with a body draped over the saddle. They dismounted in front of the bank, tied all the animals to a hitching rail, and walked into the bank with the stolen money.

Jud and Deke waited until the money was counted. As it turned out, they had recovered every cent of the stolen funds. The bank president gave them a receipt for the return of the money and thanked them profusely. He then suggested that it might be a good idea if they moved the bodies from in front of the bank.

"I'm sure you boys can understand how it might be bad for business to have two dead bodies right out in front of the bank."

"I understand, Mr. Carlton, and I'm sure you know that robbery is bad for business too," responded Jud.

Jud and Deke left immediately and sent a telegram to Jim

Bob advising him of the death of Rat Perkins and Jake Lawton in a shootout following the bank robbery in Dexter. While they were enjoying a meal at the Dexter Café, a telegram arrived from Jim Bob. They were to meet him at the marshal's office in Dykesboro at ten o'clock the next day. He also requested that they come prepared to make a report on the robbery and the shootout since the Colonel would want definite proof that the men they killed were a part of the Hagan gang.

The next day when Jud and Deke arrived in Dykesboro, Jim Bob asked if they had positive proof of the identity of the Dexter bank robbers.

Pointing toward the street, "The proof is out there Marshal," Jud said.

"Fine, bring it inside."

"With all due respect, Deputy, we can't do that."

"Why not?"

"Sir, you wanted proof, so we brung their bodies back here with us. That's them hanging over their horses out there at the hitching rail"

Jim Bob threw up his hands. "All right! All right! I'll take that as the proof the Colonel wants."

Jim Bob continued, "I want a written report from each of you on the shoot-out. Jud, give me a report on the man you killed. Deke, you give me a report on the one you killed. I must have both reports in writing. Am I clear on that?"

Both answered, "Yes, sir."

They went to a vacant office and began to scribble away. Jud finished first and handed his report to Jim Bob.

"Thank you. Jud. Is Deke nearly through with his?"

"Can't say, but he's working on it. I'll go see if I can speed him up, but it won't do no good. He can be downright stubborn if he's a mind to."

Down the hall, Deke, who was limited in his writing skills, mumbled to himself as he laboriously scribbled his report. "We brung them killer's bodies back after we shot'em dead; 'at oughta be enough. Ain't no sense in all this here paperwork. It's a waste of time, but if Jim Bob wants it writ down so's he can read about it, 'at's what he's gonna git."

When Deke finally finished his report, he got up from the table where he was seated and stomped down the hall and into Jim Bob's office. There, he unceremoniously laid his report on Jim Bob's desk.

*To Marshal Jim Bob.*
*Jake Lawton shot at me and mist.*
*I shot at him and kilt him.*
*Depidy Marshal*
*Deke Bracewell*

# 41

At the same time that Jud and Deke left their camp at the entrance to Gum Swamp in pursuit of two riders, Pat and Raven headed in the opposite direction is pursuit of the single rider.

As Pat rode away, he smiled as he remembered their bickering. "It's a good thing they're good friends." he thought.

The unknown is always troubling, and Pat was apprehensive as he began his search.

Neither he nor the other two marshals were absolutely certain that the riders they were pursuing were Hagan, Perkins, and Lawton. If it was the Hagan gang, then who was the single rider? Was it Hagan or one of the others? Pat decided that he would assume that it was Hagan and be prepared for anything.

Raven was quick to set his own pace. That was fine with Pat. It would enable him to focus on the difficult task of following the tracks of the lone rider in the midst of numerous other tracks on the road, but after about an hour of riding and searching, Pat became frustrated and had to admit that he had lost the trail. He was about to give up when he came to a fork in the road. According to his map, the road to the left led to Bay Springs, and the one to the right led to Eastman. In the fork was a small store. Pat guided Raven over to the store, swung down from the saddle and walked inside.

The elderly storekeeper greeted him. "Good afternoon young feller, kin I hep ya?"

"I hope so, I'm Deputy Marshal Pat Ravenwood, and I'm trailing a fellow about my size and probably wearing a Yankee uniform. I'm not sure, but he could be riding a blaze faced horse with four white stocking feet."

"What's he wanted fer, Marshal?"

"Murder and robbery."

"Well, you can add another robbery to that list. The feller you're looking fer was in here yestiddy. I seen him when he rode up, and the horse he was riding had a blazed face and four white feet, just like you said."

The old storekeeper continued. "He come in here, tuck everthang he was of a mind to and didn't pay me one cent. No sir, not one red cent. He just tuck it and left."

"Which way did he go when he left?"

"I can't rightly say which way he headed. He said fer me to lay flat on the floor and stay there, else he'd shoot me. I was skeered, so I done what he tole me to do."

Pat thanked the old storekeeper, walked outside, untied Raven and pulled up into the saddle. There was no doubt about it. The person he had been following was Hagan, and he was on Johnny's horse. But which way did he go when he left the old man's store? Did he take the road to Bay Springs or the one to Eastman? For Pat to follow either one, could be a total waste of valuable time. Finally, he decided that he would ride to Pine Creek and telegraph Jim Bob for more instructions.

Pat pushed Raven hard and arrived in Pine Creek an hour before the telegraph office closed. He wrote out a message to Jim Bob reporting that he had lost Hagan's trail. After giving the message to Will Emory, the telegraph operator, he went home to see Molly Ann and Johnny.

About thirty minutes after the telegraph office closed, Will Emory knocked on the door of Pat's house. Pat answered Will's knock.

"Pat, this telegram sounds important so I thought I'd bring it by on my way home."

"Thank you, Mr. Will. I appreciate that."

"Think nothing of it. Have a nice evening."

"You too, Mr. Will."

The telegram was from Jim Bob asking him to be at the town marshal's office in Dykesboro by ten o'clock the next day.

When he arrived in Dykesboro, he found Jim Bob seated at a table, his head in his hands.

Pat greeted him with, "Got a headache, Jim Bob?"

"Yeah, I've got one and it's called Deke." Jim Bob handed Pat Deke's report of the shooting of Jake Lawton.

Pat read the report and handed it back to Jim Bob. "He's not much at writing, but you'll have to admit the man can shoot."

"I guess you're right, Pat. Call'em back in here. We have work to do."

# 42

"Gentlemen, you've done a good job, but we're not finished." Jim Bob said to the three special deputies seated at the table with him.

"Jud and Deke, you are to be commended for nailing Hagan's two cronies."

"Pat, I know you're disappointed at not catching Hagan, but look at it this way. We've made progress. We're closer to catching him than when we started, but we're not through, and we're not quitting. In fact, that's why I called you here this morning."

"What do you have in mind?" Pat asked.

Before Jim Bob could answer, Deke spoke up. "You want all three of us to go after him?"

"No, I don't. We have Federal Court beginning tomorrow in Macon. Since this is the first court session since the war ended, the Colonel wants as as many marshals as possible at the courthouse. You and Jud are to be with me at the courthouse in Macon. Pat, that leaves you to follow up on the Hagan search."

"Any idea where I should start looking for him?"

"Yes," Jim Bob replied. "We'll start looking for him on the map like we did when we located that hideout in Gum Swamp."

"I'm not sure I follow you." Pat commented.

"Do you think you can find the spot on the map where Hagan was last seen?"

"I'm almost certain I can get you within a half a mile of it."

Pat looked closely at the map and found where the Bay Springs road forked off the Eastmn road. "That's it right there."

"Then that's where we'll start." Jim Bob said as he pointed to the spot Pat had identified.

Jim Bob explained, "I want you to send a telegram to the town marshals and sheriffs in the towns where Hagan might have gone after he was seen by the storekeeper that you talked to. Make a list of the towns that I call out."

When they had completed the list, Jim Bob said to Jud and Deke, "While Pat and I deal with this Hagan situation, you take your mules to the livery stable down the street and leave them there. You're going with me to Macon this afternoon so we can be at the court house in the morning before court starts at nine."

Jim Bob then turned to Pat. "I'm going to write out what I want you to put in the telegram to the marshals and sheriffs on that list. Send it over your name and have them reply to you at Pine Creek. Be sure it gets off this afternoon. With any luck, you could have some responses tomorrow."

Jim Bob continued, "Follow up on any leads that you determine are valid. Just keep me informed."

The Dykesboro telegraph operator advised Pat that two of the towns on the list had no telegraph service, but the message was sent to those that did. It was the best they could do. Pat left the telegraph office and headed home. Raven had been ridden hard lately, so Pat let him set his own pace. They arrived back in Pine Creek a few minutes before sundown. Sam's store was still open, so he stopped by to speak to Sam and Susie.

A pleasant surprise greeted Pat when he opened the door. Molly Ann was there!

"Oh Pat you're home!" she cried as she gave him a big hug.

"Yep, I come home to ..."

"Patrick Ravenwood, don't you ever forget anything? You're as bad as your Pa. I don't know what I'm going to do with you."

"You could give me another hug. After all, I've been gone since this morning."

She rolled her eyes and elbowed him in the ribs. "The reason I was so surprised is that when you left this morning, I didn't know when you would be back. With this new job you have, I never know how long you'll be gone."

"I know, Honey and I'm sorry it's that way. Maybe I won't be involved in the Hagan case much longer. Jud and Deke brought in his two henchmen this morning, and we've a pretty good idea where Hagan is. I may know more in the morning when the telegraph office opens."

Sam and Susie had remained silent up to this point, but Sam was concerned. "Do you think you'll be going after him alone?"

"It looks that way."

Susie asked, "Won't Jud and Deke be with you?"

"No, I'll be going alone because they have to be on duty at the courthouse in Macon."

"But why do they have to be there? Why can't they go with you?" cried Molly Ann.

"It's the first session of Federal Court since the war ended, and the Colonel wants plenty of security at the courthouse. Jim Bob has to be there too."

Molly Ann continued. "Can't you wait until court is over? Why do you have to go after this killer alone?"

"Because that's what I've been asked to do, and because I don't want him to kill again."

As Molly Ann began to cry, Pat took her in his arms, held her close and said, "I'm coming back, Molly Ann. Believe me, I will be back."

"I hope so," she sobbed. "What would I do without you?" She continued to cry. "What would Johnny do without you?"

"I'm not gonna give either of you a chance to find out."

# 43

Pat was at the telegraph office when it opened. "Good morning Mr. Will. Do you have any messages for me?"

"Not yet, Pat, but I'll let you know when I do get something."

"I'd appreciate it if you would. I'll be over at Sam's store if you have something for me."

"If something comes in, I'll bring it right over. You can buy me a cup of Sam's coffee while I'm there."

"It would be my pleasure Mr. Will." Pat said, as he headed out for Sam's store.

He was on his second cup of coffee when Will Emory walked in.

"Pat, I'll swap you three telegrams for a cup of that coffee."

Will handed Pat the telegrams and turned to get his coffee. "Good morning, Susie, how are you today?"

"Fine," She said as she handed him a steaming cup of coffee.

Pat read the three telegrams. They contained no helpful information, so he decided to take a walk through town. He was on his way back to the telegraph office when he saw Will Emory running toward him, waving a telegram above his head.

"This sounds urgent, Pat." Will said as he tried to catch his breath.

Pat thanked him and began reading the telegram.

*To: Deputy U. S. Marshal, Pine Creek*
*Suspect you seek involved in shootout nearby.*
*Escaped, but may be wounded.*
*Sheriff Gray, McRae, Georgia, Telfair County.*

The information in the telegram was extremely sketchy, but Pat felt it should be checked out as soon as possible.

Pat handed the telegram back to Will. "Please send a reply to this message, Tell him I'm on my way."

As Will headed back to the telegraph office, Pat called to him. "When is the next southbound train due in here?"

Will checked his watch. "There's a freight that's due here in thirty minutes."

"Do you think it would have a box car or cattle car so I could take my horse with me to McRae?"

"If it doesn't, we'll hitch one up."

Pat thanked Will and quickly headed home to tell Molly Ann where he was going.

As he burst through the front door, he met Molly Ann who had just walked into the sitting room from the kitchen. "I know. You don't have to say it. You've got to leave. I saw the way you were hurrying down the street."

She smiled weakly and continued, "I knew you weren't just rushing home to dinner. Now, give me a hug and a kiss, and you take care of yourself."

He held her close and repeated what he told her the day before, "I'm coming back." Then, he packed his bag, checked his guns and walked out to saddle Raven. When he was saddled up, he put his Spencer rifle in the left scabbard and his shotgun in the one on the right.

Once he was satisfied that everything was secure he turned, held Molly Ann close one more time, then swung into the saddle, and rode to the train station. He got there five minutes ahead of the south-bound freight. Will had the engineer position one of the boxcars next to the depot's loading platform so Raven could be loaded.

After Will had spoken with the conductor, he motioned for Pat to lead Raven up to the platform and into the boxcar.

"I told the conductor that you would be getting off at McRae."

As he shook hands with Pat he added, "You take good care of yourself and come back home real soon. You hear me, Pat?"

At first, Raven was not too happy with his train ride, but he quickly adjusted to it. After he had settled down, he spent the rest of the trip watching the countryside through the car's open door. Although it was only thirty miles from Pine Creek to McRae, it would probably take more than an hour to cover that distance due to the stops the train would have to make.

When they arrived at McRae, the boxcar in which Pat and Raven were riding was not positioned next to a loading dock. This presented no problem Pat or Raven. Pat nimbly jumped down to the ground. Raven took note, did the same, and was right proud of himself for doing so. Pat asked a bystander where he might find the sheriff, and within a few minutes he was tying Raven up at the hitching rail in front of the sheriff's office.

Standing in front of the office was a tall man who was obviously the county sheriff. He looked to be about fifty years old, and his demeanor indicated that one had better not be foolish enough to mess with'im.

"You must be the Deputy Marshal from Pine Creek."

"That's right. I'm Pat Ravenwood."

"Been expecting you. I'm Sheriff Harley Gray. How's ole Jim Bob doing?"

"Tough as ever." replied Pat.

"That's Jim Bob for you. Come on in, Marshal. We've got a shooting to talk about.

On second thought, it's dinner time. Have you et?"

When Pat said he hadn't, the Sheriff said, "Why don't we

walk down to the City Café and get some dinner and a piece of pie. We can talk there. Better put your rifle and that Jim Bob special in the office."

Apparently the sheriff was a regular at the City Café. By the time they were seated, the daily special, a cup of coffee and a piece of apple pie were placed on the table before him.

"He'll have the same, Lucile," said the sheriff.

"Let's talk while we eat because when you hear what I have to tell you, you'll want to get on the road pretty soon."

"Last night, probably around midnight, old man Clayton Harwell's fourteen-year-old grandson, Freddie, come riding into town looking for Doc Edwards. Freddie lives with his grandpa and grandma. His pa was killed in the war, and his ma had died with the fever before that. So there is just the three of them. Freddie rode in and said his grandpa had been shot and needed a doctor. Doc Edwards went out there and patched ole Clayton up. He had a pretty bad leg wound, but Doc said he'll over it."

"Did Mr. Harwell try to defend himself? Was the other fellow hurt?"

"I'm getting to that. Evidently, this fellow showed up at the Harwell's house demanding some supplies. When Harwell refused, he tried to force his way in. I don't know all the details, because I haven't been out there. I don't have a deputy right now, so I can't leave town. It appears that in the fracas ole Clayton took a bullet in the leg, but he got off a shot at the intruder. He thinks he hit him. At least that's what he told Doc Edwards."

"Did Mr. Harwell give a description to the doctor?"

"He sure did. That's the reason I answered your telegram as quick as I did. That fellow matches the description of the fellow you are after, word for word."

"Sheriff, it sounds like I ought to get on out there, Where exactly is the Harwell place?"

"Go out River Road about four miles toward Abbeville.

235

Their house sits about a hundred yards off the road on the left. There's a big oak tree in the front yard and a big pine tree down where their lane runs into River Road. You can't miss it."

Sheriff, you've been a big help. Who do I pay for my dinner?"

"Don't worry about it. This is on me. Lucile! Put all this on my ticket."

"As they walked back to the sheriff's office, Pat commented, "Sheriff, I don't want to meddle or speak out of turn, but I believe Lucile's sweet on you."

"She ought to be. We've been married thirty-two years."

Opening the door to his office he said, "Let's step inside and get your rifle and shotgun. By the way, I like that Remington you're wearing on your hip."

"I like it too. So far I've never had to use it. That Walker Colt you're wearing is a good gun too. An old preacher friend of mine wears one when he's out riding his circuit."

"Are you talking about John Henry Troup? Lord have mercy! Is that old coot still living? He's the one that married me and Lucile. Tell him I asked if he still lies about his fishing."

"I'll tell him I saw you and also what you said about his fishing. He performed our wedding too."

Pat continued, "Wish we could talk longer Sheriff, but we've got a killer on the loose."

He then put the shot gun and rifle in their scabbards, swung into the saddle, and gave Raven a gentle nudge in the ribs. Raven got the message and set a pace that would get them to the Harwell farm in no time.

When Pat rode up in front of the Harwell home, he noticed the barrel of a muzzle loading rifle pointing at him through one of the front windows. He dared not make any sudden moves. Neither did he dismount from Raven. He slowly raised his right hand in the air.

236

With his left hand, he slowly pointed to the marshal's badge pinned to his shirt and called out, "Hello Mr. Harwell.".

"Who are you and whadda you want?" A woman's voice inquired from inside the house.

"My name is Pat Ravenwood, and I'm a Deputy United Stated Marshal on the trail of the man who shot Mr. Harwell last night."

"How do we know you're telling the truth?"

"I was sent here by Sheriff Gray. He told me about Mr. Harwell getting shot. He also told me that you sent your grandson, Freddie, to get Doc Edwards in the middle of the night last night."

"All right, Deputy you can step down, but after you step down, unbuckle that pistol you're wearing and hang it over yore saddle horn. You do that, and we'll talk."

Pat did as the voice requested and slowly moved away from Raven.

The door slowly opened, and out stepped an elderly lady who was holding a rifle aimed at Pat's midsection.

"Are you Mrs. Harwell?"

"Yes, I'm Mrs. Harwell, but I can shoot as good as Mr. Harwell."

Pat smiled, "Ma'am, I don't doubt that one bit."

If you would feel safer, I'll just stand right here. I need to ask Mr. Harwell a few questions. Can he hear me from where I'm standing?"

From inside a voice replied. "I can hear you. Go ahead and ask your questions."

Pat very carefully led Mr. Harwell through a series of questions about the shooting. The description of the intruder that Harwell gave was sketchy, but there was no doubt in Pat's mind. that it was Hagan. When Pat asked if he could describe the intruder's horse, Mr. Harwell said he couldn't. Suddenly, a very excited young boy, presumably Freddie, appeared in the doorway.

"I seen his horse. He was real purdy. He had a white blaze on his face and four white stocking feet."

"What's your name, son? Are you Freddie?" Pat asked.

"Yes sir, name's Freddie Harwell. My ma's dead and Pa is too. He was kilt in the war."

"Where were you when your grandpa got shot?"

"I was hiding in the other room, but I peeped out the window after the shooting. That's when I seen his horse."

"What can you tell me about the man that shot your grandpa?"

"He was about as tall as you are and real rough looking. It looked to me like he had on some kind of uniform, or what was left of one. I think he musta been a soldier at one time or other, prob'ly a Yankee."

"Thank you Freddie, you've been a big help."

"Oh, I almost forgot, Marshal, when I seen him leaving the house after the shooting, he was kinda doubled over like he was hurt, and he had a bad time getting in the saddle."

"Do you know which way he headed when he left here?"

"Sure do. He tuck out on River Road toward Abbeville."

By this time Mrs. Harwell had put the rifle away and was sitting in a rocking chair listening to Pat question Freddie.

Pat felt that he had gotten all the information he needed from the Harwells, so he shook hands with Freddie and Mrs. Harwell. As he was shaking hands with Mrs. Harwell, he asked if he could go in and speak to Mr. Harwell. She readily agreed.

When he had shaken hands with the old fellow, Pat decided to ask one more question.

"Mr. Harwell," he said with a smile, "would she have really shot me?"

"Just be thankful you didn't have to find out, Son."

As he rode away from the Harwell's farm, Pat was troubled. Since his time in Clonnerville Prison, he had been driven by one burning desire, kill Buck Hagan. Now that he was hot on Hagan's trail, he knew that he could encounter him at any time. Even though it appeared that Hagan was wounded, he was as lethal as a coiled rattle snake and could kill with absolutely no regrets. As for himself, Pat had never fired a gun at another human being in his whole life. He was beginning to wonder if he could pull the trigger when the time came. Only time would tell.

# 44

Pat had been in the saddle for about two hours with nothing to indicate that he was drawing nearer to Hagan. The search was a very slow and tedious process and was not nearly at the pace Raven would have chosen. It was impossible to distinguish one hoofprint from another on the sandy road, so Pat had to resort to the time-consuming chore of checking everything, every path, every stream, any place where Hagan might have left the main road. Uncertainty made him wonder if this would be another futile search. He was about to return to McRae and send a telegram to Jim Bob telling him that he had lost the trail again, when suddenly, Raven stopped, raised his head, cocked his ears forward, and snorted. He had detected something up ahead. Pat leaned forward and spoke softly to Raven. At the same time he slowly and quietly pulled his shotgun from its scabbard. He brought it up across his body and cocked both barrels. In his left hand he held Raven's bridle reins and the fore-end of the shotgun. His right hand held the grip, but his trigger finger was forward of the trigger guard. He did not quite understand Raven's behavior, but the big gelding had detected something ahead.

Foot by foot, Raven slowly moved forward. Finally, when they topped a little rise in the road, Pat saw what had captured Raven's attention. Off to the left, and down a hill, was a house. Beside the house was a barn with a pen. In the pen were two horses and a young boy. Pat eased the hammers down on his shotgun and inserted it back into its scabbard. He reached back and pulled a telescope from his saddlebag and focused in on the scene before him. One of the horses was a bay that had traveled too many miles and pulled too many plows. The young boy appeared to be grooming the second horse. Pat could hardly believe what he was seeing! The horse the boy was grooming had a blaze on its face and four white stocking feet. It was Stormy. But Hagan was nowhere in sight. Was he hiding somewhere in the barn or in the house?

Pat drew Raven back a few steps, then circled down through the woods so that he could come up to the barn and not be seen by anyone in the house. Leaving Raven near the back of the barn, Pat carefully approached the pen where he had seen the boy and the two horses.

He peered around the corner and spoke softly to the boy. "Don't be afraid, son. I'm a Deputy United States Marshal. My name is Pat Ravenwood."

The boy didn't speak. He just stopped his grooming, turned and looked at Pat then resumed his grooming.

"Hope I didn't scare you," Pat said.

"You didn't scare me none. I seen you up yonder on top of the hill when you was looking us over with yore spyglass."

"You've got a pretty good-looking horse there."

"Ain't my horse."

"Who does he belong to?"

"Don't know who he belongs to."

Nodding his head toward the house, "Feller inside rode him in here last night."

"Do you know that fellow's name?"

"Can't say as I do, but he's hurt real bad."

"What do you mean? Tell me about it"

"He's gut-shot."

"What part of the house is he in?"

"He's in the back room on a cot."

"Are your folks here?"

"Ain't got nobody but Grandpa and Granny. Pa got kilt in

241

the war, and Ma run off with somebody first chance she got."

"What's your name, son?"

"Name's Daniel Wells. I was named after my pa. I go by Danny."

"All right, Danny, the man in the house is a killer. He's wanted by the law, and I have been sent to bring him in. To do that, I gonna need some help from you. First of all, I've been ridin' my horse mighty hard, so I want you to put'im in the barn and give'im some hay if you have any. Then, I want you to walk up to the house with me. When we get there, I want you to get your grandpa and grandma out of the house real quiet like. Get them out in the yard where I can talk to them. Understand?"

"Yes, sir."

While Pat watched the house, Danny put Raven in the barn and fed him as Pat had requested. When he came back, he and Pat walked up to the front of the house. Danny went inside and returned shortly with his grandparents. Pat introduced himself.

"Good afternoon, Mr. and Mrs. Wells, my name is Pat Ravenwood. I'm a Deputy United States Marshal."

The old man responded, "Name's Wells, John Wells. This here's Miz Wells."

Pat continued. "I have been trailing a killer, and I think the man inside your house is the one I'm looking for."Did he give you a name when you took him in last night?"

Wells replied, "We couldn't get anything much out of him. Fact is, it took all the three of us could do to get him inside."

"His name is Hagan, and he's about my size and could be wearing some army clothing."

"Can't say how tall he is, Marshal. He was all bent over when we took him inside, but he was wearing some kinda uniform."

"Does he have a gun with him now?"

242

"No, we took it and his boots when we was trying to get him comfortable. I'm telling you, Marshal, he ain't gonna last long."

"It may be as you say. He got shot trying to force his way into a home back toward McRae. Harwell was the name of the fellow that got shot."

The old man looked startled, "Marshal! You don't mean ole Clayton Harwell, do you?"

"Yes. Do you know him?"

"I shore do. Him and me growed up together. Was Clayton hurt bad?"

"Yes, he was shot in the leg, but the doctor says he's going to be all right."

"Do you mean to tell me that I've got a man under my roof that shot Clayton?"

"Probably so, but I'd like to be sure. I'm going in there, but I want y'all out of the house before I go in. I don't know what might happen."

# 45

Pat walked up the steps and onto the porch. With both barrels of his shotgun cocked and ready, he took a quick look into the house and saw that the door to the back room was closed. Standing to one side of the door, he slowly pushed the door open with the barrel of the shotgun. There was a bloody figure on a cot. It was Hagan. His clothing, the crude bandages and the cot were soaked with blood. He was gasping for breath. It was obvious that he was in severe pain and could not last much longer. He was able to speak only in short breathless phrases.

"Thought you ... might be ... after me."

"Hagan, I swore in Clonnerville Prison that I'd get you. I never thought it would be like this. Keep you hands where I can see'em."

"I ... ain't... got... no gun. If I did ... I'd use it ... on myself. Put me ... out of ... my misery."

"I can't do that. If you weren't hurt, I'd shoot you in a heartbeat, but I'm not shooting a man who's already down."

"You ... are a better ... man ... than ... me...Will you ... forgive me?"

Pat let the hammers down on the shotgun, turned and was about to walk out of the room when Hagan called to him, "Chaplain."

As Pat turned, Hagan slowly reached into his shirt pocket and pulled out a picture. It was the picture of Molly Ann that he had taken from Pat's mail at Clonnerville Prison.

He held it out to Pat and said, "Forgive ... me."

Pat shifted the shotgun to the crook of his left arm,

reached down, took the picture in his right hand and looked at it carefully. When he had read what was written on the other side, he slipped it into his vest pocket and took Hagan's right hand in his. He gave it a gentle squeeze and nodded his head ever so slightly. Neither man spoke a word, but there was peace in Pat's soul for the first time since Clonnerville Prison.

Pat turned, walked back into the other room, and asked, "Where's his gun?"

Young Danny retrieved it from a storage cabinet and handed it to Pat.

"I think it's loaded," he said.

Pat took the pistol, checked to be sure it was loaded, and walked back into the room where Hagan lay. He was still breathing laboriously when Pat placed the pistol in his trembling hand.

"It's fully loaded," Pat said as he turned and walked out of the room, quietly closing the door behind him.

Danny and his grandparents were puzzled as Pat motioned for them to follow him out to the front porch. When the four of them were out of the house, Pat reached back and closed the front door.

"Mr. Hagan needs to be alone for a minute."

He had barely finished speaking when a gunshot reverberated from the back room.

Pat went back into the house and into the room where Hagan lay. He carefully picked up the gun from the floor where it had fallen after being fired and placed it on a small table next to the bed. With both hands he gently pulled the sheet up over Hagan's face. There was no need to check for a heartbeat. Hagan was dead. Pat's official report would state that Hagan ended his own life after being critically wounded in an attempted robbery.

Pat collected any personal items that would verify to Colonel Randolph and Jim Bob that the deceased was Buck

Hagan. Then, he and Mr. Wells wrapped Hagan's body in a sheet and transported it to an isolated area on the Wells farm. There they buried it in grave marked by two stones, one at the head and the other at the foot. Not a word was spoken by Pat or Mr. Wells. They simply turned and walked away.

When they got back to the house, Pat took Hagan's gun, unloaded it, and put it in his saddle bag with the other personal items that he had removed from Hagan's pockets. He also got a signed statement from Mr. Wells verifying that the items were taken from the body of the deceased.

"Do you happen to have another sheet of paper?" He asked.

They managed to find another sheet and handed it to Pat. He thanked them, sat down at a table and began to write.

*To whom it may concern:*
*One gelding with a blazed face and four white stocking feet is the property of young Mr. Daniel Wells.*
*This horse was given to him by Special Deputy U. S. Marshal Patrick Ravenwood of Pine Creek, Georgia.*

Pat paused for a moment then signed the document, dated it and handed it to Danny. "That's a mighty fine horse you've got there, Danny. Take good care of him. By the way, his name is Stormy and the saddle and bridle go with him."

# 46

Pat got back to McRae in time to catch the northbound freight back to Pine Creek. It was about ten o'clock when he got home. Molly Ann was overjoyed.

"Oh darling, I'm so------"

Before she could finish, Pat interrupted her. "Molly Ann, it's over! I'm home to stay. However, I will have to go to Macon and turn in my badge and guns... but it's over!"

He added, "And before you ask, no, I didn't kill him. Now, if you'll just calm down I'll tell you all about it." So Pat told her the whole Hagan story, but it took him a while because of her many questions.

The next morning Pat sent a telegram to Jim Bob and the Colonel reporting that Hagan was dead. He also let them know that he would be in Macon at the district marshal's office the following day. Will Emory, the operator, was so excited that Pat was back home safely he could hardly tap out the message. From the telegraph office, Pat went to see his parents and Molly Ann's parents to let them know that the manhunt for Buck Hagan was over. That evening, after writing his report, he checked his saddle bags to be sure that he had everything to confirm Hagan's death.

Pat was at the depot early the next morning and boarded the train for Macon. However, he did not ride in one of the passenger cars. He rode in a freight car because he had Raven with him. When they got off the train in Macon, Pat climbed into the saddle and headed north on Cherry Street. He and Raven took a right on Third Avenue and arrived at the Federal Courthouse in less than fifteen minutes. Pat dismounted, tied Raven to a hitching post, untied his saddle bags and threw them over his shoulder. He then removed his rifle and shotgun from their scabbards. With them in the crook of his arm, he made his way up to the Colonel's office.

Deputy Marshal Mitchell greeted him in the outer office. "Good morning, Deputy. Go right in. The Colonel and Jim Bob are expecting you."

Pat walked in and both the Colonel and Jim Bob warmly greeted him.

The Colonel said, "Pat it's good to see you. Jim Bob, help him get rid of all that weaponry so he can have a seat."

"Deputy Mitchell! Let's have some coffee in here!"

"Coming right up, Sir."

After the coffee was brought in and all the pleasantries were concluded, they quickly got down to business. That's how the Colonel operated.

Pat told them how Hagan was apprehended and said, "It's all here in my written report, Sir, and I also have evidence verifying that the man I apprehended was Hagan." Pat pulled Hagan's gun and several other items from his saddlebag and placed them on the Colonel's desk.

The Colonel carefully examined all the evidence which included a barely legible order from the Colonel assigning Hagan to the grave detail in General Wilson's Cavalry Corps.

"I believe this is more than adequate verification of Hagan's apprehension and his demise. Do you agree, Jim Bob?"

"Absolutely, Sir, the Hagan affair is over."

"Pat," The Colonel said, "You've done an excellent job. What plans do you have for yourself now?"

"Sir, right now, I'm not absolutely certain. I'll have to do some thinking about that. My purpose here today was to turn in my badge and guns along with my report on Hagan."

The Colonel responded. "I was afraid that's what you would say. I don't suppose you would consider working as a deputy marshal full time, would you?"

"No sir, I appreciate everything you've done for me, but I don't think I'm cut out for law enforcement."

"I see. Well, as much as I hate to do it, I accept your resignation. Jim Bob will take care of your guns. Are they clean and in good shape?"

"Yes, sir, they've never been fired."

The Colonel stood up as if to say the meeting was over, but before he could say anything, Pat spoke up. "Sir, I don't want to impose on you, but I would like for you to grant me one favor."

"Now you've got my curiosity up. What sort of favor do you want?"

"Walk down to the street with me. I want to show you something."

As Colonel Randolph, Jim Bob and Pat walked down the stairs, Jim Bob looked at Pat and raised his eyebrows. Pat returned the look with a smile and a wink. When they exited the courthouse onto third Avenue, the Colonel turned to Pat and was about to ask a question.

Suddenly he exclaimed! "My God! It's Raven!"

"Yes, sir, it's Raven, and I'd like to return him to you. Since I am no longer a deputy marshal and no longer work for you, I will not take no for an answer, besides it's impolite to refuse a gift."

After the Colonel and Raven had finished their mutually affectionate reunion, the Colonel turned to Jim Bob and said, "Deputy, would you take my horse around to the stable and see that he is well cared for. And you, Mister Ravenwood, are to accompany me back up to my office where I have a gift for you."

Pat had no idea what the colonel was leading up to.

When they walked in his office the Colonel said, "Have a seat. I know you have a train to catch, but this won't take but a minute."

The Colonel walked over to a cabinet and pulled out a Bible, the same one that he had given Pat in Clonnerville Prison.

"Pat, you traded this Bible for a gun when you left Clonnerville. Now, based on our talk today, I've gotten the idea that you are ready to trade your guns for a Bible. You have turned them in, and we've accepted them. The trade will be complete when you accept this Bible. Remember, as you said, it's impolite to refuse a gift."

He handed Pat the Bible and quickly returned to his desk. "Now get out of here before Jim Bob sees us getting sentimental."

With slightly moistened eyes he added, "Pat, thank you for Raven."

"Thank you for the Bible, Colonel."

Pat got home from Macon just in time for supper. As they were finishing off their meal with a piece of sweet potato pie, Pat told Molly Ann and Johnny about his visit with Colonel Randolph. They were surprised that he had given Raven back to the Colonel, but they agreed that it was the right thing to do.

The next morning, they all walked to town to visit with Sam and Susie at Sam's store. As it turned out, Dan and Leona were also there, so Pat brought both families up-to-date on everything that had transpired in Macon. He had barely finished when Johnny announced that he was going across the street for a few minutes.

When Pat saw that he was headed toward the new dry goods store, he was puzzled.

"What's Johnny up to?"

Molly Ann replied, "He wants to invite the daughter of the new store keeper to a picnic."

"Well, let's pray he doesn't say 'I come' like I did."

"Patrick Ravenwood! You're so bad," then she added, "but I love you anyway."

Pat replied, "I love you, too."

When Sam and Susie had finished their snickering, Pat told told them that he was going to see John Henry since he hadn't seen him in a while.

John Henry was sitting out on the front porch when Pat arrived. "Well bless my soul, if it ain't Pat Ravenwood. Come on in and have a seat. Seems like I ain't seen you in Lord knows how long. Whatcha got on your mind?"

"Brother John, I want to talk to you about getting my ministerial credentials reinstated."

"Is that a fact? Why don't we go inside where it's more comfortable and talk about it. While we are there, maybe we could get a glass of Marthee's lemonade?"

When they got inside, John Henry called out, "Marthee, Pat's here. Would you please bring us some of yore cool lemonade?"

John Henry put his glasses on and began to putter around in a cabinet. "Here they are, my boy. You wanted to get your ministerial credentials back; well, here they are."

As he handed Pat the sheaf of papers, Pat said, "But I thought we'd have to contact the conference office to get me reinstated."

"Patrick, I've been in this here preaching business for nigh onto fifty years. In that time I have learned that the Lord works in strange and mysterious ways. Fact is, the Lord don't want you to go to all the trouble of meeting with the conference office to get yore credentials back.

"Why not, Brother John?"

"Because I never sent'em in. Marthee! Where's that lemonade?"

Pat was speechless. John Henry just sat there enjoying one of his holy pride moments.

"I don't know what to say, John Henry."

"No need to say anything, Boy. Go ahead and drink that lemonade. Marthee wouldn't want it to go to waste. The Lord

251

don't want a good preacher to go waste either. Now, drink up and go home and work on a sermon. I want you to preach Sunday night."

"John Henry, how can I ever thank you?"

With a twinkle in his eye, John Henry replied, "Preach, Boy! Preach!

Pat caught up with Molly Ann just as she was coming out of her parent's store.

"Ma'am, may I walk you home?"

They had not gone very far when Pat stopped, took Molly Ann in his arms, and asked,

"Would you like to go to church with me Sunday night?"

"Of course I'll go with you. Why did you ask such a silly question?"

"Because I'm preaching."

Under John Henry's supervision, Pat resumed his work on the Pine Creek Circuit.

It was no accident that in the months to come, Pat assumed most of the preaching responsibilities in all three churches. That was by design, John Henry's design. He knew that his health was failing, and he was determined to leave the Pine Creek Circuit in good hands, Pat Ravenwood's hands.

# EPILOGUE

The second Sunday in June was an important day in the life of the Pine Creek Circuit. The members from all three churches gathered at the Pine Creek Church to honor John Henry upon his retirement and to welcome Pat as their new pastor.

John Henry's retirement was a bittersweet event. He had been a pastor for over fifty years. Of those fifty years, he had spent the last twenty-five as pastor of the Pine Creek Circuit.

Although the churches would honor him in a number of ways, John Henry considered the assignment of Pat to the Pine Creek Circuit to be the high point of his twenty-five year ministry there.

After the congregation sang a hymn, Josh Taylor, Sunday School Superintendent and Chairman of the Pine Creek Church Board of Stewards, spoke to the congregation. "Good morning to all of you, and welcome to this great Sunday worship service here at Pine Creek Methodist Church. We are pleased to have our sister churches, Shiloh and Friendship, with us today on this very special occasion."

Josh continued, "The first thing I want to do is recognize one who has served as pastor of our church for twenty-five years, Rev. John Henry Troup. Brother John, would you please step down from the pulpit and stand here next to me. I also want to recognize the power behind the man behind the pulpit, John Henry's wife of sixty years, Martha. Miss Martha, would you come stand beside John Henry."

"Now you know something's up, don't you! First of all, Miss Martha, our gift for you is a brand new rolling pin. I know it doesn't look like much of a gift, but it is important because it's to be used in your kitchen, which is to be re-modeled by the men of the Pine Creek Circuit."

Josh then turned to John Henry. "Don't feel hurt, John Henry, we have a little something for you. Right here in this box, I have a can full of night crawlers, because you're always opening up a can of worms. Since you always know what to do with a can of worms, we have something else for you. We have a brand new fishing pole. It's something new on the market. It comes apart and fits into a nice little case so folks won't know you're going fishing."

"There's one more thing, and it's for both of you. We have this nice, brand new paint brush. It's important because it's one of several that the men will be using when they paint your house. All right, Brother John, It's your turn to say a few words to the congregation."

Before John Henry could speak, Martha quipped, "He said a FEW words, John." No one could remember ever hearing her speak out in church before.

With glistening eyes, John Henry began to speak. "I've been your pastor for twenty-five years. We have laughed together, and we have cried together. I've married your young people, and I have baptized many of you here at this altar. I have mourned with you as we have buried your loved ones. Over the years, I have tried my best to preach God's word to you as He would have me preach it. I want you to know that I love ever one of you and I appreciate what you have done here today. God bless you. Now, let's do the most important thing we can do today. Let's worship the Lord, because: 'This is the day the Lord hath made. Let us rejoice and be glad in it!' Amen!"

Before John Henry could sit down, the congregation was on its feet cheering. Josh Taylor made no effort to get them quiet. It was John Henry's moment. It was their moment too, a time when love was shared, a time to remember, and a time of thanksgiving.

When the congregation finally settled down, Josh moved back to the pulpit and officially welcomed Pat as their new pastor. Pat, who had been seated with his family, walked up to the pulpit, shook hands with Josh, and gave John Henry a big smile.

"To John Henry, thank you for everything. To you, the people of Pine Creek, thank you for a great place to call home. To you, the members of the Pine Creek, Shiloh and Friendship Churches, thank you for your willingness to accept me as your pastor. To my parents, Dan and Leona, to Sam and Susie, to Molly Ann, and Johnny, thank you for your love, your patience and your prayers. To two of the best friends anyone could have, Jud Cofer and Deke Bracewell, thank you, gentlemen, for always being there when I needed you."

"Before I read the scripture, let me say one more thing about John Henry. You know he's a fisherman. I am not, but I know how the fish must feel when John Henry is fishing. He caught me once, but I slipped away from him. Then, by the grace of God, John Henry caught me again. I will never forget that. Because of what he did for me, John Henry will always have a special place in my heart and in this pulpit."

Pat's sermon was short that Sunday. He remembered that in one of his early sessions with John Henry, he was told to summarize each sermon in one sentence so people would remember it. That's what he did that Sunday, and the people remembered what he said.

As Pat settled into his ministry on the Pine Creek Circuit, he often thought about his conversation with John Henry in which he told him that he was going to leave the ministry.

John Henry had said, "Always make sure your last answer is your best answer and always be open to what God wants you to do." They had parted that day with thoughts of going fishing sometime.

A strong bond existed between the two of them, and they

255

were good for each other. Pat fondly remembered how John Henry fished him into the church, into the ministry, and back into the ministry after he had turned in his credentials. They visited together often, and Pat called on him to preach quite frequently. Every time John Henry preached Pat was amazed. The old man hadn't lost his touch.

Molly Ann was equally fond of John Henry and his preaching. One afternoon, as Pat was relaxing on their front porch, Molly Ann came out and sat down beside him. She wasn't there long before she brought up the subject of John Henry's preaching.

"Honey, when was the last time you invited John Henry to preach?"

"It's been several Sundays. Why do you ask?"

"He was in Papa's store today, and I kind of got the feeling that he wants to preach again. I'm not sure, but he sounded like he was saying he wanted to preach one last time. You know, he's a really good preacher, but he is beginning to get a little feeble."

"Well, I sure don't want him to feel neglected. I owe that old fellow too much for him to feel like he's forgotten. How long before you'll have supper ready?"

"It'll be long enough for you to walk over to John Henry's house and ask him to preach."

"For a highly respected wife of a preacher, you are one sneaky, conniving, woman. I'll be back in a little while. Does he know I'm coming?"

"Not exactly."

John Henry was sitting in a rocking chair on his front porch when Pat arrived. Martha was sitting in the swing nearby. Pat spoke to both of them as he opened the gate and walked into their yard. Marthee, as John Henry called her, was busy darning socks. She just nodded, smiled and went back to her sock mending.

"Come on in Pat, my boy. I've been kind of expecting

256

you. Marthee, do you think you could find us some of that cool lemonade back there in the kitchen?"

Pat thought to himself, "I'll bet you've been kind of expecting me."

"John Henry, how are you doing? Been doing any fishing lately?"

"Thought I might saddle up old Rambler and go out to Walden Creek tomorrow afternoon. Maybe we have one more fishing trip left in us. Wanna go with me?"

"Brother John, I would love to do that, but I have to be in the Shiloh community tomorrow."

He chuckled, "You do have to earn your keep don't you, Son!"

"I do, indeed. You left me some mighty big shoes to fill." Pat continued, "Speaking of earning one's keep, would it be worth another one of Molly Ann's sweet potato pies for you to preach at Pine Creek a week from this Sunday?"

"Why, you know I'd do it. I'd preach a two-week revival for one of her pies. Rambler and me'll work on a sermon while we're fishing tomorrow. You know, that ole hoss listens real good. Marthee! Where's that lemonade?"

Pat spent part of the next day visiting members of the Shiloh church. He was back in Pine Creek by mid-afternoon. Blackie, Raven's replacement, had hardly broken a sweat on Pat's visit to the Shiloh community. In fact, he was still full of energy and a mite frisky when they arrived back home. Rather than unsaddle Blackie, Pat tied his reins to the picket fence in front of their house, walked up on the front porch, stuck his head in the door and called to Molly Ann.

"Honey, while I've got Blackie saddled, I'm going to ride out and see Ma and Pa and maybe go down to the creek see how many fish John Henry has caught."

She came hurrying into the living room and gave him a quick peck on the cheek. "Tell your folks I said 'Hello.' Don't be late for supper." Then she scurried back to the kitchen without another word.

Pat's parents were in their front yard sitting in the shade of an oak tree when he rode up.

He dismounted and got a hug from both of them. "Have y'all seen John Henry? He said he was coming out here to fish in Walden Creek."

Dan replied, "He was by here about three hours ago, but we haven't seen him since then."

"Do you think you ought to go see about him?" Leona asked Pat.

"Maybe we should do that." Pat said as he turned and climbed back into the saddle.

"Pa, if you'll put your foot in the stirrup, I'll pull you up behind me. Blackie can tote double with no problems at all. That'll get us to the creek a little faster."

As they drew near to the creek, Dan peered over Pat's shoulder. "That's kinda strange. Old Rambler's over there grazing. He must have pulled loose."

He added, "I don't like the looks of this at all."

"I don't either," replied Pat.

They found John Henry by the creek, leaning back against a cypress tree. His tackle box and new fishing pole were at his side. On his lap lay his Bible. It was opened to the twenty-first chapter of John. He had underlined the words of Jesus in the sixth verse, "Cast your net on the right side of the boat."

On top of the Bible, was a note pad on which he had scribbled what he wanted the people to remember from the sermon that he was preparing. John Henry had summed it up in one sentence.

*I have cast my net on the other side.*

## THE END